Here's What Critics Are Saying About Angie Fox

"With its sharp, witty writing and unique characters, Angie Fox's contemporary paranormal debut is fabulously fun."
—*Chicago Tribune*

"This rollicking paranormal comedy will appeal to fans of Dakota Cassidy, MaryJanice Davidson, and Tate Hallaway."
—*Booklist*

"A new talent just hit the urban fantasy genre, and she has a genuine gift for creating dangerously hilarious drama."
—*RT Book Reviews*

"Filled with humor, fans will enjoy Angie Fox's lighthearted frolic."
—*Midwest Book Review*

"This book is a pleasure to read. It is fun, humorous, and reminiscent of Charlaine Harris or Kim Harrison's books."
—*Sacramento Book Review*

The Skeleton
in the
Closet

ANGIE FOX

The Skeleton in the Closet
Copyright 2015 by Angie Fox

This edition published by arrangement with Moose Island Publishing.

Moose Island Books
First Edition

ISBN-13: 978-1-939661-29-6

More Books from Angie Fox

The Southern Ghost Hunter series
Southern Spirits
The Skeleton in the Closet
The Haunted Heist

The Accidental Demon Slayer series
The Accidental Demon Slayer
The Dangerous Book for Demon Slayers
A Tale of Two Demon Slayers
The Last of the Demon Slayers
My Big Fat Demon Slayer Wedding
Beverly Hills Demon Slayer
Night of the Living Demon Slayer

The Monster MASH series
Immortally Yours
Immortally Embraced
Immortally Ever After

Want an email when the next book comes out?
Sign up for Angie's new release alerts at
www.angiefox.com.

Chapter One

I CLOSED MY eyes, breathing the clean fall air still tinged with the warmth of the fading summer. And I nearly ran smack-dab into the large Civil War reproduction cannon sponsored by the Sugarland Heritage Society. In my defense, it hadn't been there yesterday.

The lawn outside the library—heck, the entire town square— had been transformed.

With good reason.

Today was the first day of the annual Cannonball in the Wall Festival.

As far as parties went, Cannonball in the Wall Day was right up there with Christmas, Easter, and the biscuits-and-gravy breakfast at Lulabelle Mason's house.

This year would be even better. A History channel documentary crew had rolled into town to film the celebration, and it seemed every man, woman, and child from four counties had descended on us like bees to honey butter.

"Melody?" I called, spotting a blonde with a ponytail through the crowd. I strained to get a better look. "Melody!" I waved.

The woman turned and I realized it wasn't my sister. This perky blonde was an actress I'd seen on television. I didn't know whether to be impressed or frustrated.

I'd told Melody I'd meet her near the library, but that was before we realized what a spectacle this year's event was going to be. It might take some doing to pick her out of the larger-than-usual crowd.

I ran a hand along the gun barrel of the old cannon, over the layers of caked-on paint, warm from the sun. During the war, Tennessee was one of the most divided states in the nation, and our boys had gone off to fight on both sides. That left the town vulnerable when the Yankee army came through in 1863. The local militia fought to keep everyone safe, but our homes and businesses were on fire all around them. We thought it was over when the Yankees got their cannon up and shot straight into the town square. Wouldn't you know it, that ball did not explode. It lodged deep in the wall of the Sugarland Library for everyone to see. That small victory gave our ancestors the extra bit of spit and vinegar they needed to drive the invaders out and save our town.

The preacher at the time declared it a miracle. While I wasn't so sure faulty explosives qualified as the hand of God, the entire town had assembled to celebrate every year since. We'd come together—people of all different backgrounds and walks of life—and we'd saved the place we loved. The Cannonball in the Wall Festival reminded us to be grateful for that.

A smile tickled my lips and I couldn't help but gaze at the rusting iron cannonball still embedded in the white limestone near the foundation of the historic library.

Soon everyone would know our story.

"Five dollars for a picture with the cannonball," barked a scratchy voice to my right.

I turned to find Ovis Dupre's thin, bent frame nearly on top of me. The old man didn't understand the concept of personal space. Instead, he drew even closer with his vintage Polaroid.

"No, thank you," I said, doing my best to duck around him while taking care to be kind. He meant well. Besides, I couldn't afford to alienate any of my neighbors after a recent event had left my reputation a little questionable.

But Ovis was eighty if he was a day. And he did not get subtleties at all.

He lowered the camera to reveal the bushiest pair of silver eyebrows south of the Mason-Dixon Line. They stood out starkly against his mahogany skin. "Pretty girl like you deserves a picture," he said quickly. "Five dollars."

Ahem. Problem was, he'd trapped me between the cannon and the crowd, and I didn't have five dollars to spare. Not after the incident involving my ex-fiancé. I'd managed to avoid selling my house —barely—after my ex-almost-mother-in-law had forced me to pay for the wedding she'd orchestrated, the one that didn't happen. But I'd had to empty my savings and sell most of my furniture. I scarcely had enough left for the things that really mattered, such as food.

Ovis cocked his head. "All proceeds go for historic preservation," he added, as if the cannonball needed my five dollars more than I did. "Did you know my great-great-granddaddy stood in almost this exact spot when he helped save Sugarland?"

He was good. If I'd had the five dollars, I would have produced it right then. But I didn't.

The entire town knew my predicament, but they didn't realize I was so strapped that I'd been forced to eat Royal beef ramen noodles for breakfast this morning. And for dinner last night. I'd kept those sorts of details to myself, along with the fact that I couldn't have preserved my own slice of Sugarland history, the historic home my grandmother had left to me, without the help of Frankie, the gangster ghost I'd grounded in my grandmother's heirloom rosebush, and Ellis Wydell, an unexpectedly sweet man who was tall, gorgeous, and very much alive.

To tell you the truth, I still didn't know what to do about either one of them.

"I've got it," said a familiar voice.

"Ellis?" I turned and saw my recent partner in all things spooky. He wore a Sugarland Deputy Sheriff's uniform and a smile that showed off the dimple in his chin.

I shot Ellis a bright smile as he slipped a five into a box marked "Historic Preservation."

Ovis captured my grin with a sharp *click*.

"Thanks for that," I said to the deputy sheriff.

He shrugged a broad shoulder. "I saw a damsel in distress."

Ovis watched us for a moment too long as he pulled the Polaroid photo from the camera. Ellis stiffened, and I fought the guilty flush that crept up my cheeks. We'd have to be careful how friendly we appeared together. Hardly anyone knew how close we'd grown after our recent adventure, and if any man in this town was off-limits, it was Ellis Wydell.

He was the brother of my ex-fiancé, the middle son of the woman who would give her eyeteeth to ruin my life. And even though I was highly intrigued by the black sheep son of the Wydell family, events like today had a way of reminding me of my place.

I turned to the elderly photographer. "I saw some people earlier with commemorative picture holders. If it's not too much of a bother…"

Ovis appeared pleased that I'd noticed. "I was just about to get you one." He weaved through the crowd toward a nearby table while I took a second to admire the scenery right in front of me. I'd almost forgotten how tall Ellis was, and how well his uniform fit over those work-sculpted muscles. He still had a slight scar under his eye from when he'd saved me from a killer. If anything, it made him even sexier.

"I see you're working today."

He gave a sharp nod. "Crowd control." He glanced over his shoulder at the reenactors lounging on the lawn. "Plus the Yankees have been drinking since ten o'clock this morning."

Oh my. "I suppose you can't blame them." Everyone who was anyone wanted to play a town hero in the reenactment. But the militia parts went to the older families in town, the ones with ancestors who fought. Anyone whose family had settled here less than one hundred and fifty years ago had to play the part of an invader. On television, no less.

"Poor Yankees," Ellis mused. "It must be tough to lose every year."

Yes, well, they should have thought about that before they shot at our library. "Your mother has to be loving this."

He shook his head. "She's convinced the family story is Hollywood material."

"More power to her," I said, meaning every word.

My ex-almost-mother-in-law might be slightly evil, but this time she was using her power and sizable fortune for good. She'd formed a film production company dedicated to promoting the history of Sugarland, and her family's legacy, of course. So far, she'd managed to attract today's documentary crew and also finance an independent movie about the skirmish that forever entrenched the cannonball in the wall. Filming would start next week.

That kind of national recognition would do the town good. Plus, the more she focused on her family's fame and glory, the less time she had to meddle in my affairs.

Ovis handed me the picture, complete in its commemorative cardboard Cannonball in the Wall Day frame. I was stunned to see how happy I looked.

"For you," I said, handing the picture to Ellis. He *had* bought it. Plus, I sort of wanted him to have a picture of me.

He took it gallantly, but I saw how the tips of his ears reddened.

I was glad to see I wasn't the only one who might need to work on reining things in.

Bloodcurdling screams sounded from across the square, and from behind city hall, I heard shouts: "The Yankees are coming!"

Ellis checked his watch. "Twenty minutes early. Somebody needs to get them under control."

"Hop to it, lawman."

He shot me a wink and left to go check out the action while I wondered for the hundredth time whether I'd been blessed or cursed.

I also wondered if anyone besides Ovis had noticed me talking to the good-looking sheriff.

Melody made me jump when she drew up behind me and whispered in my ear, "Boo."

My hand went to my chest. "Can't you just say hello like everyone else?"

"So you're saying that scared you?" she asked, her blue eyes twinkling. "Impossible. Not after—"

"Never mind," I said quickly. "I'm just glad you found me." Melody and Ellis were two of the very limited number of people who knew about my ghost-hunting skills, and I intended to keep it that way. "Besides, I'm finished with that business." I wanted to forget about haunted houses, hidden passageways, and buried secrets. "The ghosts of Sugarland have caused me too much trouble."

Melody gazed down on me, thanks to her impossibly high platform sandals, and handed me a piping hot bag of kettle corn. "If you're serious about keeping out of hot water, you should stay away from Ellis."

"I know," I said, plucking a piece off the top. Nobody would understand the way Ellis and I had bonded over our adventure. They'd only see me chasing after the older brother of my ex-fiancé. "But he's like kettle corn. You can't have just one little taste."

Melody tsked. "You just like him because he saved your life."

"Yes, well, I saved his too," I pointed out. "Besides, you know it's more than that."

He was funny and brave. Kind. He was a darned good police officer, even though his family would never forgive him for joining the force instead of the high-powered Wydell legal empire. I admired a man who wasn't afraid to follow through with what he felt in his heart. I frowned. That kind of thinking could get me all tangled up if I let it.

Melody glanced out over the crowd. "We'd better get moving. The grandstand is filling up."

Portable metal benches took up the entire east side of the square. They were sponsored by the two leading families in these parts: the Wydells and the Jacksons. The Wydells ruled the roost in Sugarland. The Jacksons owned most of the land surrounding the town. Both families were careful to sit as far as possible from each other on account of a feud that had been going on since Lieutenant Colonel Lester Jackson may or may not have forgotten to salute Colonel Thaddeus Wydell during the War of 1812.

Melody took my hand and dragged me along. "Come on. My boss said he'd save us some seats."

"No kidding?" Montgomery Silas was not only our library historical expert, but he was also the man who literally wrote the book on the Battle of Sugarland, the one that was being made into the movie.

Melody waved to Montgomery as we made our way over.

"We are in high cotton," I said as he waved back. The eccentric scholar wore an ill-conceived pair of muttonchops and had a personal style that relied heavily on tweed and bow ties, but he was the closest thing to a celebrity we had around these parts. At least until filming started.

I couldn't wait.

We were just about to enter the grandstand when Darla Grace, Sugarland Heritage Society Volunteer of the Year— every year—closed a hand over my sister's arm. Darla stood five feet nothing, not counting her stacked auburn hair done up with daisies for the celebration. It looked nice, and I could tell she felt pretty.

She gave my sister a conspiratorial grin. "Thank you so much for all your help in the library this morning. I don't think I could have handled that fiasco without you."

Melody let out a small laugh. "It was nothing."

"I really appreciate it," she continued. "I mean, who in their right mind would think it's a good idea to add Myra Jackson's false eye into the jewelry display? Even if it is a family heirloom." Darla Grace shuddered.

My sister chuckled. "You just need to learn how to say no."

"No," I said under my breath as Virginia Wydell sat down in the front row, right next to Montgomery. "Those were supposed to be our seats. He just let her take them."

"Oh." Melody cringed. "Well, the Wydell Family Foundation is funding the movie. He probably didn't think he had a choice. Don't worry. We don't have to sit anywhere near them."

"We won't," I said. Not while I was still breathing. "But we'd better find a spot. And soon."

Melody and I started toward the stands with Darla in tow when one of the young college volunteers rushed us. Panic widened her ice blue eyes and her bangs tangled in the sweat on her brow. "Disaster. Anarchy. I need you and Darla right now. The Jacksons are demanding we expand the exhibit."

"Don't you dare," I told them both. "I'm sure you've already done a wonderful job." They deserved more than political bickering in return. "Let's go, or we're going to miss the whole Yankee charge." I'd witnessed every reenactment since I was three years old, and I wasn't about to be left out this year.

"Expanding the exhibit is the only way to keep the peace," the student pleaded. She held up her phone. "I have a text from Montgomery. He says to work it out."

Darla groaned. "We don't want to offend the Jacksons or the Wydells, not at this hour."

Melody shot an apologetic glance to Darla. "I shouldn't have put out the Wydells' vintage corsets and lingerie. That might have tipped the scales."

"It did." Their panicked coworker looked ready to swoon. "The Jacksons retaliated with two muskets and a fainting couch." She drew a deep breath before rushing on. "Rumor has it Virginia Wydell just sent her eldest son to go dig into the family taxidermy collection."

"Perfect," I said. I had the solution. "This is a fine time to teach our fellow citizens the meaning of the word *no*."

Both Melody's and Darla Grace's heads whipped around to cast equally horrified stares at me. "No!" they sobbed in unison.

Hmm…perhaps this was why I tended to get into trouble, while they did not.

Melody touched her forehead, gathering her wits. "Don't worry. We'll sort everything out. As long as the heirlooms don't keep coming." She dropped her hand. "Verity, I have to handle this. You might as well go ahead and enjoy the reenactment."

"Not in a million years," I told her. I couldn't have fun while Melody and Darla were in such a spot. Besides, I didn't want to be anywhere near Virginia Wydell without my sister there for moral support. "If you simply cannot leave this undone, then you can count on me to help." Besides, it would be neat to see all the old relics and knickknacks.

Darla's brows pinched together. "We'd love that, but you can't. We had to sign papers. Approved personnel only."

Melody cast me a helpless look. "I'm afraid the rules are pretty strict."

"Okay, then." I felt for them, I truly did. "Just think," I said, trying to make it better, "after tomorrow's brunch it will be all over."

Both of them winced.

"Thanks for the deadline reminder," Darla groused.

Shoot. I hadn't quite thought of it that way.

"Go," Melody urged. "Find a seat."

That could be hard. The crowd had thinned around the grandstand, which meant most of them were in it. I watched as Melody and Darla made their way toward the library, trailed by the volunteer. I wished I could have done more.

Well, at least I could watch history being made. Again. I joined the last of the audience filing into the long benches and began working my way up, hoping to find a single seat...anywhere. I was craning my neck, distracted, when the last man on earth I wanted to see climbed up behind me and blocked my escape.

"You look gorgeous today, Verity." He had that slight, sweet, humble-if-you-didn't-know-him Southern drawl that made me want to punch him in the face.

I straightened and turned, already knowing what I'd find. "Beau."

Beau Wydell appeared quite harmless on the surface. Tall, with Matthew McConaughey good looks and a self-effacing charm that had bedazzled plenty of women over the years. He'd sure fooled me.

My ex-fiancé tilted his chin down and treated me to a shy smile, as if he didn't have a care in the world. And why should he? He was the one who'd cheated on me, lied to me, and then made me look the fool when he tried to force me to show up at our wedding. That was the day after he hit on my little sister, by the way. She'd gone to get another bottle of wine for our suite and he'd trapped her in a corner to paw at her. I didn't dare mention that here. No one knew.

So far, Melody had stayed clean of this and I intended to keep it that way.

I'd told him the wedding was off. He'd waited at the altar anyhow, in front of the whole town. He'd made it appear as if I'd stood him up, and I became persona non grata to just about everyone who ever mattered to me.

"Please leave," I said, knowing I'd have to face him sooner or later, my heart racing all the same.

He shrugged. "The way I see it, you're standing in my family section."

I was? I almost dropped my popcorn. "Then I should leave," I said, trying to figure out a way to make it around him. We had folks on the seats above watching us, along with several packed rows underneath straining to hear.

Lord have mercy.

"It's all right if you sit by me, darlin'," he said, drawing closer.

"I'd rather set my teeth on fire." Before today, I hadn't seen or spoken to Beau since he'd invited me to join him at our reception. The whole town was there, he'd said, enjoying our five-course sit-down dinner. Dancing to the ten-piece band his mother had insisted we hire. Consoling him. Assuring him he was better off.

He'd sent me photos of the cake.

I'd snapped. That he would play the victim, that he would humiliate me like that after what he'd done... I'd like to plead temporary insanity, only I knew exactly what I was doing when I drove straight to the Hamilton Hotel, marched right into my almost-reception, and plastered Beau's face straight into our almost-wedding cake. Only I hadn't counted on everyone taking pictures. And videos. Not to mention the way I'd slipped on frosting and fallen on my rear.

I needed to escape. Now. Maybe I could shimmy under the seat and drop down to the ground below. Would I even fit? My luck, I'd get stuck. Then we'd have more embarrassing pictures of me for Beau's Facebook page.

His mouth tipped into a slow smile. "Are you going to make another scene?" he asked smugly, as if he'd read my mind. "Can't say that I don't enjoy your moxie."

His words hit me like a bucket of cold water. My outburst at the reception had consequences. Beau's mother had sued me for the entire cost of the production she'd orchestrated. I'd had to sell everything I owned. I'd darn near lost my family home. Half the town still thought I was crazy.

No. I would not let Beau Wydell humiliate me again.

A cry erupted from the crowd around us. "Sit down," the woman behind me hissed. "The Yankees are coming. For real this time!"

I sat, next to Beau Wydell, and tried not to cringe as our shoulders touched.

He took it as an invitation and leaned his lips toward my ear. "I'm kind of glad we got stuck like this, darlin'. We should talk."

"Don't call me darling," I said, keeping my voice down and my eyes on the town square. "We have nothing to say."

The camera crew from the History channel sprang into action. I focused on the drama of the advancing army, on our outnumbered, outgunned small-town militia as they were pushed back, on Miss Emily Proctor's dance classes, ages five through sixteen, as they danced in front of the limestone buildings of our town square, dressed as red and orange flames.

"I'm sorry about what my mother did to you."

He actually sounded sincere, and I felt my cheeks redden. I glanced up at him. "What about what you did?"

He huffed out a breath. "You know I didn't mean that, sugar." His fingers inched toward mine on the bench. "I'd had a couple of beers. Your sister looks a lot like you. I made a mistake." He shrugged. "It happens to a lot of guys."

"No, it doesn't." I folded my fingers in my lap. "And you didn't have to embarrass me later."

"Hey," he said. "Look at me. I was hurt." He appeared so sincere a girl would be tempted to believe him. If you didn't know him. "I didn't hear that my mom sent you the bill until after I got back from our honeymoon."

And then he'd done nothing to stop her when she unleashed her team of lawyers.

The Yankees were now overrunning the square. Our men were trapped, flanked, through no fault of their own. I knew exactly how they felt.

"Excuse me!" a woman protested on Beau's left side as someone knocked into her popcorn, scattering pieces.

"Sorry," a familiar voice called back. "Pardon me," Ellis said as he shoved past his brother. I hoped it wasn't an accident that he stepped on Beau's foot.

I scooted over as far as I could to make room.

"What the hell?" Beau protested as Ellis squeezed in between us.

I'd never been so glad to see him. "Shouldn't our sheriff be protecting the town?" I asked. It was too late to save me.

Then again, having him here did make me feel stronger.

"It's all going well," he said pragmatically. "The whole place is on fire. There's hand-to-hand fighting in the streets. They'll be talking about this for years." He angled for some space and elbowed his brother in the process.

Beau elbowed back. "You're an idiot, Ellis."

Everyone watched as the Yankees pointed a cannon and fired on the Sugarland Library. Well, most everyone. Virginia Wydell sat six rows down, her platinum hair pulled back into a girlish ponytail, her pearl earrings large, and her eyes hard as she glared back at us.

Fun day.

My ex leaned over his brother as if he weren't there. "I miss your back rubs," Beau murmured to me.

Ellis stiffened. "You realize she dumped you, right?"

"Oh, look," I said, "one of the Yankees just lost his uniform pants. He really should have worn a belt." Or laid off the hooch. "I wonder if that will make it into the documentary."

Both men ignored me. They were too busy glaring at each other. Of course, Beau had no idea about Ellis and me. If I wanted to be perfectly honest, even I didn't even quite understand what was going on between us. It had begun innocently enough.

But now, seeing the two brothers together, I was starting to realize I might have started something I didn't quite know how to finish.

Ellis and I hadn't gotten to the back-rub stage. We were barely at the dating part. We'd fought for our lives together and had gotten close. Too close, maybe. Then we'd enjoyed one very nice, very quiet dinner a few miles out of town. He'd brought me daisies, and I'd baked cookies and pretended it was no big deal. He'd said they were delicious.

It had been wonderful.

Until now.

Beau groaned. "Can you move out of the way, Ellis?"

"No," Ellis said simply.

Oh, brother.

I'd never been so glad to see the Sugarland militia push the Yankees back and save our town.

We watched the two colonels, a Wydell and a Jackson, shake hands, as they did once a year. The patriarchs of the two families put aside their differences to lead the militia, a moment of cooperation before they went back to hating each other. Everyone in the grandstand stood and cheered. The cameras rolled.

Beau leaned past his brother to get to me. "I don't care if my family thinks you're bad for me. Let me take you out tonight."

"No," Ellis and I barked out.

Virginia Wydell looked ready to climb over six rows to get to us.

Suddenly shimmying underneath the grandstands wasn't looking like such a bad option.

Ellis cleared his throat. "I love you, brother, but sometimes you don't have the sense God gave an ant. What you had with Verity is over. You need to give up."

Beau shook his head, rueful. "You have no idea. You never kissed a girl like her."

Maybe I could just whack my head on the metal bleachers and hope to forget I'd met either one of them.

"I've got to go," I said, sliding past the brothers, ignoring it when Beau ran a hand up my leg. Ew. I was done—with this, with him, with the whole blessed day. I had no more celebrating left in me. I was heading home. By myself, mind you.

And if I had a wish left in heaven, nobody would follow me. Then again, if wishes were fishes, I wouldn't be eating ramen for dinner tonight.

Chapter Two

I HEADED STRAIGHT home to the antebellum house my grandmother had left me. It stood on the outskirts of town, on what had once been a working orchard. Over the years, my family had sold the land around the house, piece by piece, so that the rows upon rows of peach trees and even the grand front drive had given way to tidy bungalows lining the long road to the main house. Today, the surrounding front yards and porches sat vacant. No doubt the festival kept my neighbors occupied.

When I spotted the white columns of my house, I felt that fist in my chest ease just a little. This place was safe. Mine.

Sure, my home had seen better days. The paint on the front steps had chipped in places, and the roof over the veranda drooped like an elegant, aging Southern belle. But the freshly washed dollhouse windows sparkled, and the lilac bushes lining the front walk smelled like heaven. I ran my fingers along the leaves and blooms, my sandals clacking against the brick path.

No place had ever felt more like home, especially when a furry little skunk dashed out from under the white-painted porch.

"Lucy!" I greeted her.

She waddled, her body churning as she ran. I met her halfway, kneeling to let her nuzzle my palm as I stroked her soft head and white-striped back. I tried to pick her up, but she was too excited. She turned in circles before flipping over into a backward somersault and popping back up.

"Good girl!" I crooned, not because it was a particularly smooth trick, but because she'd done her best. A while back, I'd tried to teach her to roll over like a puppy dog, but it turned out she didn't have that kind of coordination and this was what she'd taken from the lesson. She seemed so proud every time she did it. Plus, I had to admit it was rather darling. "You want to go inside with me?"

Lucy loved hanging out under the porch, but this time, she came eagerly into my arms. Even skunks needed girl time. "How about we find you a treat?"

She wriggled and grunted happily. Lucy understood the word *treat*. She was actually due for a Vita-Skunk supplement, and when I sprinkled the added nutrition onto a bit of chopped banana, it became the Holy Grail of skunk happiness.

I cuddled Lucy close as we slipped past the cheery yellow front door, but two steps inside the house, a violent chill seized me. Lucy let out a squeak as we walked straight through it and into my sunny, warm foyer.

"Heavens to Betsy, little girl, what was that?" I brought a hand up to still my galloping heart while Lucy sniffed the air.

I'd never felt anything like it.

Dust motes glimmered in the light pouring in the windows. The hardwood floors gleamed. Nothing seemed amiss.

I held her close. "I don't see anything." We glanced left into the empty front room, and right into the equally bare dining room. I'd sold every stick of furniture in the place to pay off my debt to Beau's mother, and the house felt cavernous without its customary antique decor. At least that made it easy to see that Lucy and I were alone.

The skunk buried her face in the crook of my arm, her cold nose coming to rest on the inside of my elbow. "Come on, baby," I cooed. "You'll feel better after you've eaten something." We continued down the hall, only to run smack-dab into a cold spot more raw than the first. "Oh, no. That is *it*." I held Lucy close, trying to shelter her as best as I could. "Will someone tell me what is going on?"

I saw nothing. No shadows. No wayward spirits. Of course, that didn't mean there wasn't an ornery ghost skulking about. My back stiffened. "Frankie," I warned. I had only one place of refuge and this was it. He'd better not be up to anything.

My home had been blessedly ghost-free—quite a feat in the South—until last month when I'd accidentally trapped the spirit of a 1920s gangster on my property. Frankie "The German" wasn't exactly easy to live with, but it was my fault he couldn't leave. I'd tied him to my land when I'd emptied his funeral urn out onto my rosebushes. At the time, I'd believed my ex-fiancé had given me a dirty old vase long overdue for a rinse with the hose. And perhaps a fresh flower. But as it turns out, there's a reason why ashes are customarily scattered to the wind, or at least spread out a bit. When I poured the entirety of Frankie's remains in one spot and then hosed him into the ground, the poor gangster had become quite stuck.

I stroked Lucy's head. "Frankie, I know you're around here somewhere." I scanned the high walls, covered in white flowered paper, up to the original Greek revival–style moldings. "I'm not in the mood for games."

He shimmered into view next to the gilded light poking from the wall, overlooking the dark square on the wallpaper where my grandfather's portrait once hung.

Lucy wriggled deeper into my embrace. She wasn't particularly fond of ghosts.

Frankie appeared in black and white, his image transparent enough that I could see through him if I really tried. He wore a 1920s-style pin-striped suit coat with matching cuffed trousers and a fat tie. His shoulders stood level to my line of sight, which would have made him unusually tall for a man of his time, if he weren't padding his height by floating a foot off the ground.

He used his ill-gained height to full advantage as he glared down at me with those sharp features that made him look every bit like the killer he was. "You think I'm playing a game?" he asked, twirling a white Panama hat in his fingers. He cocked his chin. "'Cause I'd give anything for a laugh, princess."

My gaze traveled to the neat, round bullet hole in the center of his forehead. He noticed and, in one smooth movement, slid the hat over his wound with a cocky flick of the wrist. "I didn't get to go to no Cannonball party," he huffed. "I got to tramp around making cold spots all day."

That could actually prove useful come summertime, since I couldn't afford to run the air-conditioning. Still, I'd upset him and I could see why. "I'm sorry. If I knew how to unground you, I would." Right now, the only way he could leave my property was if I took his urn with me. A stubborn spot of him lingered, one that hadn't quite rinsed away. No doubt our situation was unusual. "It's not exactly something we can Ask Jeeves."

The ghost drew closer, blocking my way. "What about that idea you found on Google last night?"

Lordy. I never should have let the ghost watch me do an online search. "Not everything you read on the Internet is true."

He watched me expectantly. "It looked legit to me. The thing had graphs and numbers, and you could see how he separated the dirt from the ash."

I stepped around him and headed for the back parlor. "It was a fifth-grade science project, and I got the distinct impression the kid was winging it." That kind of trick might be good for a school assignment, but this was Frankie's afterlife we were talking about. I could tell by the slight chill in the air that the ghost hovered right behind me.

"Hey," he snapped, "we don't know until we try it."

True. Enough strange things had happened around here lately. Perhaps this was one more that would work out in an entirely unexpected way.

I turned to face him. "All right," I said, ignoring the victorious grin that flashed across his features. It wouldn't hurt to at least attempt an ungrounding. "But we'll need to borrow supplies." I didn't have much of anything in the house. "Once my neighbors return home from the festivities, I'll start making some calls. Just...try to keep your expectations realistic."

Frankie punched the air with his fist. "You know what the first thing I'm going to do once I get out of here?"

"Um—" I wasn't quite sure what he did before.

"Nothing." The ghost swept his hands to the sides, as giddy as I'd ever seen him. "I'm going to wander around and go wherever I want and do nothing."

All right, then. Everyone needed a goal. "Good for you."

The corner of his mouth turned up. "Or maybe I'll rob one of those newfangled armored cars."

"Frankie..." Forget it. He was happy. No sense reminding him that he couldn't touch money, much less spend it.

He was still chuckling to himself as he faded away.

At least we had a plan.

I kissed Lucy on her soft little head. "Thank you for being so patient." I eased her onto the kitchen floor and set about fixing the most delicious banana skunk treat ever.

We always split the fruit—she didn't eat much—and it was an indulgence for me, too, since I wasn't going to buy fresh produce for myself. I only stretched my budget to keep Lucy healthy.

I watched her tail swish as she chewed. In spite of everything, I really was lucky. I had a house, a pet who loved me, friends.

Even if my ghost buddy was eager to escape.

That evening, I set about calling my neighbors and gathering the supplies for a fifth-grade science project. We needed measuring cups, an aquarium net, and Tupperware. I was heartened by the way my neighbor Stuart even offered to deliver his grandson's old kiddie pool to my backyard. I'd told him I needed to give Lucy a good scrub-down, which made me appreciate the gesture even more.

Some folks—believe it or not—had a bias against skunks. As if Lucy had ever done anything to them.

Never mind.

We'd start Frankie's ungrounding tomorrow, which should make the ghost happy.

He hadn't made an appearance all evening, which was nice in a way. I treated myself to a granola bar for dinner, then took a long, leisurely soak in the tub.

The house lay silent. Warm.

Just as it would be if Frankie were truly gone.

My cell phone rang as I slipped out of the tub. It was Melody. I reached for a bath towel and answered. Maybe she'd made quick work of the new donations and had gotten back to the festival.

"How's it going?" I asked, struggling to balance the phone while wrapping the towel around myself.

"Did you enjoy the reenactment?"

I let out the water in the tub. "It was like nothing I've ever seen before." I'd give her the details later. "Are you about through all of the donations?"

"We were. Until your crazy almost-mother-in-law sent over Leland Wydell's entire Civil War collection."

I wiped the moisture from my cell phone and brought it back up to my ear. "Leland Wydell the first?" That was Ellis's great-grandfather.

"The man was obsessed. He collected uniforms, letters, even furniture from dozens of different families in the county and especially liked to buy the estates of war heroes. These aren't even strictly Wydell family heirlooms anymore."

Actually, I liked that. "This way, there will be more families represented."

"True," Melody said, "but we're going to be here all night. In fact, that's why I called. I was hoping you could help me out tomorrow. I'm not going to have time to set up tables or direct the caterers. Can you meet me at six and handle those details while I finish going through the artifacts?"

"Six in the morning?" I asked.

"Lots of people get up earlier than that," she said drily.

Yes, but I wasn't usually one of them. "Of course," I said. How hard could it be?

Good thing I had no idea.

The next morning, I pulled into the back parking lot of the library at 5:59 a.m. Melody was just getting out of her car, balancing a tray of three coffees. I helped her with them while she reached into the passenger seat for her satchel. She wore a stylish pink suit and had tucked her hair into a French twist.

"If you went for a run this morning, I'm going to officially declare you a superwoman."

"I wish," she said, taking a coffee while I did the same. "I was here until almost two this morning. I could barely see straight." We headed for the back door of the building. "Even then, Darla Grace wouldn't quit. Not that I'm one to do anything halfway, but let's just say that when this woman volunteers, she *volunteers*. I left her sorting through an antique secretary."

I took a sip of the drink. It was hot, delicious. "That does sound kind of fun." I loved looking through antiques.

Melody swung the door open. "True. But Darla Grace really does need to learn when enough is enough," she said. "She left me a message at three this morning, saying I had to get back down here. She'd found something urgent." Melody took a fortifying sip of coffee. "Luckily, I didn't get the voice mail until I woke up," she added under her breath. "What could be so important in a bunch of old letters?"

"Maybe you'll have to expand the exhibit again," I said, half joking. I loved history as much as the next person, but preserving it should be a labor of love, not this battle between the families. Every light in the library blazed. "You're going to have to preserve this month's electric bill for posterity," I said, trying to get her to smile a little. "It'll be epic."

I was glad to see Melody's mouth tug into a grin as we walked down a back hallway and up the stairs to the main level.

"It'll be fine," she said. "I just worry about Darla sometimes. She needs to learn to take it easy and treat herself better. Maybe I could teach her some of my yoga stretches."

"And hope she survives." Melody was as bendy as an acrobat.

I pushed open the doorway to the main reading room and let my sister enter first. "Darla," she called, "we're here."

Velvet-covered tables spanned the edges of the historic high-ceilinged room, which was packed with artfully displayed Civil War muskets, family albums, and letters sent home by long-dead war heroes. Headless mannequins stood in full military uniform. The room appeared even larger now that they'd taken out all the heavy wood tables. The catering company would replace them with sleek serving stations for the banquet.

My footsteps echoed in the cavernous space. "I can't believe none of this is under glass."

"It was all in someone's attic last month," Melody said.

"Try yesterday." I snorted. One of the display cards proudly declared its contents as part of "How the Jacksons Saved Sugarland."

"The Wydells are on the other side," Melody said, sipping her coffee.

"Of course." We wouldn't want their artifacts to mingle.

"Maybe Darla finally went home," Melody said. "Although if that was the case, I wish she would have locked up." She ventured past me. "I'm going to head into the donations room and see how far she got."

"I'll be here to greet the rental company," I told her. "You want the banquet tables set up the same as last year?"

"Yes," she said, before a pained look crossed her features. "I'm sorry. I wasn't even here last year, but you were."

I'd attended as Beau's fiancée. The newspaper had taken our picture. He'd proudly told stories about his family leading the defense. I told about my ancestor who grabbed his rifle and ran from our house on the outskirts, straight into town and, as silly as it sounds, I'd felt like I was part of something. This year...

"No worries," I told her. "That was a lifetime ago." I was better off now.

Even still, I found myself drawn to the Wydell exhibit.

Melody gave me a small, one-armed hug, then headed toward the storage office-turned-staging room while I browsed.

I studied the old photographs, skipped the documents, and thanked heaven that I didn't have to fit into any of those tiny corsets. I stopped at a table display of Wydell family taxidermy, the subject being stuffed squirrels. I couldn't see what was so historical about squirrels, no matter how strange their poses. Three of these poor animals were preserved forever paddling a hand-carved dugout canoe. Another squirrel sat sewing. Two more rode a tandem bicycle. I averted my eyes, not sure what to think, and a shoe poking out from under the draped velvet caught my attention.

It didn't appear antique, just a modern white flat. But if it did belong in the display and Virginia Wydell stopped by and saw it on the floor, poor Melody would have a scene on her hands. I walked over to where it was and bent to draw it out from under the draped velvet. Only it was attached to a foot.

I yanked my hand back, taking the table curtain with me. Stuffed squirrels went flying, but my attention was drawn to something else entirely.

Darla Grace lay curled on the floor under the table, as if she'd tired herself out completely and slept where she fell. She wore the same flowered dress from yesterday.

My stomach felt hollow. "Darla." I nudged her, hoping to wake her up gently. "Darla Grace..."

She felt cold.

Her eyes were open.

And when I moved more to the left, I saw a rusty bayonet lodged in her back, the wound around it wet with blood.

I screamed.

Chapter Three

MELODY WAS ON me in a second. "What happened?"

I stepped back quickly to let her see. "I just found her. Like this."

Melody gasped. "I think she's dead."

There was no "thinking" about it. The woman had a bayonet lodged in her back. I gathered my courage and crouched low near Darla's head. Her glassy, lifeless eyes stared into nothing. A wilting daisy had fallen from her hair and onto the cold marble floor. "Call the police."

Melody dialed her cell phone, her voice trembling as she told dispatch what we'd found.

"Close her eyes," she said, ending the call.

"I wish I could." But I wasn't about to touch the body. It occurred to me to say a prayer, but my rattled brain couldn't think of one.

I stood, shaking. Poor Darla Grace.

I didn't want to look at the body anymore, but it seemed almost disrespectful to shield myself when Darla had suffered.

My sister shivered next to me. She'd wrapped her arms around her chest, as if that would protect her from the tragedy in front of us. She wiped away a tear. "I should have answered her call last night. I didn't know." Her voice caught. "She was always calling about details that didn't matter. I never thought she needed help."

None of us could have imagined it.

"If you'd shown up, you might have been here when…this happened." I couldn't even say it.

She nodded. "Maybe I could have done something."

Or maybe my sister would be lying dead next to Darla Grace.

Darla had died in a place where my sister often volunteered to work late, where Melody would have been if she hadn't had the sense to go home.

I struggled to understand what had happened. It was the only thing I could do. "Darla left you that voice mail at three o'clock this morning, saying she'd found something urgent. Did she say what it could be?"

Melody chewed her lip. "No. She just wanted me to come down right away."

I scanned the display tables. Everything seemed to be in order, save for the smattering of dead squirrels.

Steeling myself, I gingerly bent down to take another look at the poor, deceased library volunteer, her fingernails bitten to the quick, her eyes wide with shock. Then I saw the outline of something in Darla's dress pocket. "What's that?"

Melody took a deep breath and joined me. "Probably her little pink notepad. The library kept a comprehensive list of donations as they came in, but Darla liked to have her own backup."

"She recorded everything?"

Melody nodded. "Down to the last antique button."

We shared a glance as we heard the wail of police sirens approaching.

Melody and I quickly stood as Police Detective Pete Marshall strolled in, joined by Ellis, who wore his police uniform. Ellis appeared grim, with a hand braced on his gun belt, while the aging Marshall seemed almost excited at the prospect of a murder. I'd read about his recent promotion in the paper. No doubt this would be his first big case.

Marshall had been one of the first to arrive after I'd solved a decades-old murder last month. With Ellis too personally involved, Marshall had led the investigation, and clearly, his star was on the rise. His ruddy cheeks flushed, and he moved with more spunk than typical for a man in his early sixties. Although to be fair, I usually encountered the chief (and only) detective in town at the diner, enjoying his after-work serving of peach cobbler à la mode. I always said hi. Ever since I'd become a persona non grata in town, he rarely said it back.

"Verity Long," Marshall said, in a noncommittal tone that felt like an accusation all the same, "you going to visit every one of my crime scenes?"

Because there were so many in Sugarland.

"I didn't choose this, Detective," I said, moving aside so he could see the body. "We came in this morning and found Darla Grace just as you see her."

He and Ellis approached the scene with caution.

"Was the door locked?" Ellis asked, studying the placement of the body.

"No," Melody stated. "Darla was supposed to lock up behind me. When the back was open this morning, I assumed she was still here."

"The front was left open as well," I added, "since you didn't need us to let you in."

Marshall gave Melody a quick once-over. "Was there anyone else here with you two?"

"Not since about nine o'clock last night. We sent the rest of the volunteers home," she said. "Darla Grace was the only one willing to stick it out longer."

"Even longer than you?" the detective challenged.

Melody stiffened, and I couldn't help but get a little angry when I saw the hurt and the guilt flash across her features. "She couldn't stop until everything was perfect."

"I'll call the medical examiner," Ellis said, stepping away.

Marshall gave a quick nod to Ellis. "Also grab the camera from the car." The detective reached into his back pocket and slipped on a pair of latex gloves. "When did you last see her?"

"At about two in the morning, when I left." My sister's breath hitched as he began a cursory examination of the knife stuck in Darla's back. "I should have insisted that Darla go home too."

Marshall drew back, resting his forearms on his knees. "Was your sister, Verity, with you this whole time?" He said it casually, but I knew what he meant. *Did I have an alibi?*

I'd shot a man to defend myself, so therefore, at least in his mind, I must be capable of cold-blooded murder. "They wouldn't even let me inside the library last night," I told him. "I was only helping out this morning because Melody needed me. And," I made sure to point out, "I had no reason to hurt poor Darla Grace."

He stood. "We've had two dead bodies in twenty years, and you've been on the scene for both." He held out his hands. "I'm just trying to cover all my bases."

"I was on the scene both times, too," Melody said hotly. "We may have been quite involved last time, but Verity and I had nothing to do with this."

"Except find the body," he countered, before losing steam. "I have to ask, okay?" He slipped off his gloves and gave her a pat on the shoulder. "Look at it this way, sugar. I know a sweet girl like you could never do something like this." His eyes settled on me and his tone cooled. "Ain't your fault the rest of the world's full of crazies."

Meaning me? The man had the manners of a gnat.

Ellis returned with a camera slung over his shoulder. He placed his phone in his back pocket. "What'd I miss?" he asked, seeing the detective stone-faced and me a bit put out.

Marshall kept his attention focused on Melody and me. "We need to ask you both some questions," he said. "Separately. After that, we'll start processing the scene," he added to himself.

Ellis nodded to his partner. "You talk to Melody up front. I'll take Verity over by the circulation desk."

"Good," I gritted out. I was still feeling shaky, and Marshall would be the last person who could help with that. I walked with Ellis to the very back of the room, making it all the way to the research help desk before I let loose some of my frustration. "He doesn't like me," I whispered.

"Relax. Marshall doesn't like anybody," Ellis said, easing close, trying to get me to settle down. "You might also want to stop glaring at him."

I hadn't even realized I was doing it. "If I did, he deserves it. He might as well have accused me." I sneaked a glance past Ellis's formidable frame, watching the older officer give a fatherly talk to Melody.

"Look at me," Ellis urged, his expression intent. "I've got this. Now, first questions first: What happened?"

When he focused on me like that, I wanted to tell him every single secret I had ever kept, like the fact that I had fantasized about him in his cop uniform one Christmas when I was dating his brother, but that didn't have anything to do with this investigation. I had to stick to the facts at hand. I had nothing criminal to hide.

He drew out a small notebook as I began. "Last night, Melody called and asked me to help set up the brunch." I blew out a shuddering breath. So much had changed since then. "They were overloaded yesterday and got behind. Melody and Darla kept getting new donations for the display. In fact, when Melody had to work on it yesterday afternoon, I ended up in the bleachers alone, where Beau found me."

He appeared almost relieved at that, a crack in the cool veneer he wore as an officer of the law. "I was wondering how you ended up in the grandstand with my brother." He huffed, almost to himself. His tone was wry, but he bent stiffly over his notebook, as if he were afraid of my answer.

"It wasn't my choice. Beau trapped me," I said, needing him to get that fact perfectly straight.

He gave a sharp nod and his broad shoulders relaxed just a bit. "Noted," he said.

He couldn't actually think I'd wanted to be there with Beau. Still, when it came right down to it, Ellis dealt in facts, and the fact of the matter was I'd come within a hairbreadth of marrying his brother.

His striking hazel eyes met mine and held. "When was the last time you saw Darla?"

"Right before the reenactment yesterday."

"What time did you and Melody arrive at the library this morning?"

"We met in the parking lot a minute or two before six and walked in the back together."

He raised his brows. "Did you have any other contact with Darla after you saw her yesterday?"

"No. I hardly knew her. Besides, Lucy and I ate too much dessert and were in bed early. I should never have let her talk me into a second banana."

The corners of his mouth turned up as he wrote that down. No doubt his mind was going back to the same place mine just had—to the night when Lucy had snuggled up beside him in his bed.

Everybody does better with a skunk to love. Even sexy guys in uniform.

Or out of uniform, as he had been.

He lowered his voice. "Did you touch anything?" he asked, his tone intensifying.

"No," I said. I'd wanted to. "Wait. Yes, I touched the tablecloth because I saw Darla Grace's shoe poking out from under it. I thought the shoe might be a display piece that dropped."

His stoic expression was back. I didn't know if that was good or bad. "What else did you touch?"

"Nothing," I stated. "But there's one more thing." He'd walked in and seen me, hadn't he? Oh my. I leaned close enough to catch the spicy scent of his aftershave. For courage. "Melody mentioned a pink notebook where Darla kept a list of donations. We think it may be in her pocket. I stooped down for a closer look, but I didn't touch anything."

His lips twisted. "Good. Because I saw you bending over the body when we walked in, and I was going to need an explanation."

"So you thought the worst? I'd never fiddle with a crime scene!"

"I believe you," he assured me. At my surprise, he added, "You forget. I know you." His voice warmed. "You don't just attract trouble. You have it on speed dial."

"It's part of my charm," I said, glad to have him on my side. "But don't worry. I wouldn't do anything to make your job harder than it already is."

"Thanks, Verity," he said, glancing over my shoulder at Marshall. "We'll figure this out."

The older detective approached, wearing a stony expression. He carried something in a clear plastic baggie. Melody trailed a short distance behind.

"Did you find the pink notebook?" I asked.

Marshall seemed way too pleased at that. "What do you know about it?"

"Melody told me," I said, shooting my sister a glance. I assumed she'd mentioned it to him.

The older officer cast an indulgent, self-satisfied smirk my way. "I think you know something you're not letting on."

Marshall dangled the bag in front of me and jiggled it a little. It held a set of car keys, a library key on a white plastic fob, and a folded-up program from the reenactment yesterday. He didn't have the notebook.

"Pete," Ellis said, stepping in between us, "let's focus on the task at hand."

"I always do." He snorted, his attention running coolly over Ellis before turning it back to us. "You can go for now." To me, he added, "Don't leave town."

I caught Ellis's eye and nodded a quick good-bye. He had his hands full on this one. Not for the first time, I was glad to have him on my side.

Melody and I walked out the back, glad to avoid the body.

We made it through the rear corridor and down the stairs. "He's acting like just because you found the body, you killed her in cold blood," Melody whispered under her breath.

"Well, you know me. Public enemy number one."

She gripped her purse strap tighter. "I was there, too. I could be a murderer too," she said, as if it were a competition.

"Don't say that too loud," I cautioned as we reached the back door.

"I just feel so bad for Darla," Melody said. "She was a good person."

We walked out and saw Montgomery Silas pulling into the lot. The historical director appeared frazzled as he jerked his car to a stop and exited the vehicle.

If he was worried about today's brunch, we were about to make things a whole lot worse. "I have something to tell you," Melody began, approaching his car.

He rushed over to her. "Melody! I'm so glad to see you safe. What a terrible tragedy." He'd missed a button on his shirt and his jacket was askew, as if he'd hurried to put them both on and arrive here as soon as possible.

"How did you hear about it?" I asked, joining them.

He straightened his jacket and eyed the building behind us. "My downstairs neighbor knocked on my door after her mother heard it go over the police scanner."

"Of course." This was Sugarland, after all.

"They didn't say who they found...inside," he added, cringing.

In all fairness, there was no good way for him to ask the question.

Melody touched his arm. "It was Darla Grace."

He drew a sharp breath before he nodded, somber. "Did they say when or how?"

"It must have been sometime after I went home last night. I left her alone," my sister said, her voice laced with guilt. My heart ached for her. She shouldn't blame herself.

"It's not your fault," he said, shell-shocked. He stared at the back entrance of the library without really seeing it. Absently, he drew a bow tie out of his pocket and began winding it around his neck. "We can rally. We've lost part of the morning, but I'm going to go talk to the police." He tied the bow tie into place and began smoothing his collar over it. "I wonder if we can still go on with the event."

"You've got to be kidding," I said. "Darla is dead." Right in the middle of his display.

He looked to Melody for confirmation. "I'm sorry. I'm not thinking." He ran a hand over his face. "I don't know how to act. I'm better with facts than I am with people." He gave a small, scattered laugh. "This is why we have Sheila." Sheila Ward served as our library director. Unfortunately, she was out of town for a family emergency, and that left Montgomery in charge.

"I'll make some calls to cancel the event," Melody said. "Maybe later, we can think of some special way to honor Darla."

"Of course," he said, straightening. He retucked his shirt into his pants. He'd forgotten his belt. "You don't need to take this on. I'll do it. I'll make those calls. I'll talk to the police and then handle everything from here. You two girls get some rest," he said. "Take care of yourselves."

Poor Montgomery. I wondered who would take care of him as he strode unsteadily into the library.

We watched him go. "Is he going to be okay?" I asked.

Melody nodded. "He's an odd duck, but he's a stand-up guy. He'll handle the police and the History channel. And Virginia Wydell."

I didn't envy his job in the slightest.

My sister and I parted with a big hug. "You're welcome to hang out at my place," I told her. She didn't have to be alone right now.

Melody pulled away. "If it's all the same to you, I'd like to go home and take a nap."

"Of course." Whatever she needed.

We parted ways after making promises to talk soon.

My car started with a wheezing chug, but it did start. I jammed it into gear and steered past the crowd gathering out in front of the library, mainly the older folks in town who manned their police scanners as though they were on the force. They'd called in the weekday morning McDonald's crowd, who were sipping coffee in take-out cups. A reporter for the *Shady Oaks Extended Living Center Gazette* lingered on the front steps. Frankly, I wouldn't be surprised if the day tour bus from the senior center pulled up.

As for me, I was glad to make my escape.

I'd dealt with murder before, but never up close. And never anyone I knew. Darla had given her all to this event, and then some. She deserved justice, appreciation...a period of mourning, which was tough to have in the middle of a crowd.

I returned home to find everything the same as I'd left it, only it felt like so much had changed. I opened the door and welcomed the sight of Lucy tottering out to greet me, her little body wriggling with each step. I picked her up and buried my nose in the soft white stripe on her head. "Life is precious, sweetie."

She grunted in agreement as I stroked her head. The white fur made a little diamond shape right between her eyes and slicked to a darling white stripe down her nose. I swore the cute fairy had blessed her. She snuggled in tight, and I just held her for a minute. Pets always know what you need to make you feel better.

Yet my mind kept going back to what I'd seen after I lifted that table skirt at the library, the blood and the knife. Darla's lifeless eyes.

She'd died for…something.

We just didn't know what.

I let out a slow breath and carried Lucy down the hall. "The sad thing is, if Darla made an important discovery last night, it's probably gone now." Lucy snorted in what I assumed was agreement. "The killer would have taken it, and her notebook as well, to cover his tracks." I stopped. "I don't know what to do." I supposed there was nothing I *could* do. Ellis and Marshall were the professionals.

I sighed and resumed my trip toward the kitchen, thinking an ice-cold glass of water might help me think, when the skunk squirmed and scrambled to escape my embrace. I eased her onto the floor and soon saw the reason for her sudden change of mood.

Frankie lounged on my kitchen island. Brooding.

"It's about time you stopped gallivanting," he said, sliding down. "You've got promises to keep."

"What?" I asked, momentarily startled.

He approached me with a confident swagger and clear expectations. "You said you'd unground me today."

Oh, Lordy. Today was not the best day. "I said I'd try."

"Well, then. Let's get to it. Your neighbors have been dropping off supplies all morning." He turned and walked through my back wall and out onto the porch.

It would only encourage him if I followed. I did it anyway, curious to see what my neighbors had brought.

And heavens to Betsy, had the good people of Orchard Street heeded my calls. I stopped short when I saw the glorious mound of highly unscientific supplies stacked on my back porch.

The gangster passed straight into the pile and stopped knee-deep. He held out his arms. "Ta-da."

We had two aquariums—someone must have misunderstood. Two aquarium nets. I'd requested those. Enough Tupperware to enter a cooking contest, a shovel, spare measuring cups, and even a plastic baby pool shaped like a turtle.

For research purposes, of course.

Never mind that any self-respecting researcher would have taken one look at my equipment and hightailed it the other way.

Frankie let out a low whistle. "I ain't never been a science guy, but I gotta tell you, this is a beautiful sight."

"It is something." I tried to be stern, but couldn't help the smile that crept up on me. This would all be quite useful for our experiment. Despite everything that had happened lately, I had great neighbors.

Naturally, Frankie thought my lopsided grin was all about him. "I knew you'd see it my way," he gloated.

I rolled my eyes and reluctantly picked up the shovel. We'd see soon enough whether I could truly unearth Mr. Obnoxious.

According to the report, our first step was to gather the dirt into a plastic container.

"There's no guarantee this will work," I warned. Although I had to admit I might almost, sort of, maybe miss him a smidge if it did.

Which didn't make any sense at all.

I carried the shovel down off the porch and left it near the flower beds. Then I made a second trip for the kiddie pool and the aquarium nets. We'd leave the Tupperware and measuring cups for now. We didn't have any Frankie to measure or store yet.

The morning had grown warm. We hadn't had a day under eighty degrees yet this fall, which was good because I could still wear my sundresses. I'd held three back from the estate sale and wore them on a regular rotation. The purple one I favored today would hopefully keep me cool as I worked.

"Be careful," Frankie warned, before I'd even positioned the pool by the rosebushes at the back of the house.

"Of what?" I slid the toy up against the bricks that bordered the flower beds. "Splashes the turtle is plastic. He's not going to hurt anything."

"Easy now." Frankie reached for Splashes, as if he could somehow direct his placement by sheer will. "You think this is jake?"

I had no idea what he was talking about. "Frankie," I said, losing patience as a trickle of sweat already ran down my back, "this is the most un-jake thing you'll ever see."

His expression grew stony. "You don't even know what 'jake' means."

"True. But I'm standing here in my backyard, wearing one of my last nice dresses, ready to shovel my flower bed into a kiddie pool for you, so why don't you at least pretend to be grateful?"

He muttered something I was sure I didn't want to hear as I turned and got to work.

Of course, the gangster's relative silence didn't last for long. As soon as my spade hit the dirt under my largest,

most beautiful rosebush, he made a noise like I'd lopped off
one of his toes. "Argh! Wait! Back up a few inches."

I scooped up a healthy portion of dirt. "No. This is
where I dumped you."

He flailed his hands as I hefted my shovelful of dirt into
the baby pool. "You're off target."

"No, I'm not." I went back for another round.

My shovel hit the ground and Frankie gasped like I'd
swung it at the *Mona Lisa*. "You weren't paying attention
like I was."

Oh my word. He was such a backseat...excavator.
"Fine." I moved a few inches back, even though I knew I
was right. "Here?"

"Maybe," he said, skirting around me. "I think so. Can
you see a difference in the dirt?"

It was regular black potting soil. "You mean does some
of it look like you?"

Frankie's hands flew to his throat. "Are you actually
making a joke? Is this funny to you?"

I scooped up another shovelful of dirt in the location
where I'd originally wanted to start. "Nothing is funny
about this. Believe me."

"Then dig right here," he said, pointing to a totally
different spot two inches over from the one he'd shown me
before.

"Keep this up and I'll show you another place I can put
this shovel," I groused.

Still, I scooped exactly where he said and then
transferred the dirt to the growing pile in the kiddie pool
behind me.

"You missed a spot," Frankie said.

"No, I didn't," I said automatically. I turned around to
look. "Where?"

He pointed. "See that little clump on the brick? There
could be parts of me in there."

I captured it with my bare hands and transferred it to the pile. I really did care.

Until he opened his mouth again.

"You need to dig deeper," he instructed. "You hosed me in good."

I squinted at him through the glare of the sun. He wasn't even sweating. "I'm aware."

Frankie and I kept at it until I was exhausted from shoveling a large, deep hole, and he was satisfied we'd scooped up every speck of dirt that could have possibly touched one of his ashes.

Although I was pretty sure he didn't have any more knowledge than I did as to where they could all be.

"This good?" I asked, wiping the sweat from my brow. It smeared with the dirt from my hand, no doubt creating a lovely brown streak down my face. Two of my rosebushes were exposed down to the roots, I smelled like an ox, and I had serious doubts about my ability to lose the crick in my back and stand straight ever again.

Frankie touched his fingers together. "You may continue with the experiment."

"Gee, thanks," I said, going for the hose.

Our elementary expert called for the dirt to be mixed thoroughly with water, the theory being that once the soil was soaked, the heavy earth would separate and fall to the bottom of the pool while the light ashes would float.

Then we'd scoop up the ashes with thin mesh aquarium nets and somehow produce a Frankie.

To be dried in Tupperware and eventually returned to his urn.

I adjusted my nozzle to a heavy spray and began hosing down the soil in the pool.

Frankie hovered nearby. "You are good at this part," he mused. "All that hosing ashes into the dirt practice really paid off."

Maybe I wouldn't miss him when he was gone. "You realize I'm trying to help you."

I heard the crackle of tires on my rock driveway a few seconds before Ellis's squad car rumbled into view. He parked in back, next to my ancient avocado-green Cadillac, and I could tell he was trying not to stare as he closed his door and approached us. He'd definitely seen me look better.

He still wore his uniform and had most likely come straight from the library. "Doing some gardening?" he quipped.

"More like penance," I told him, keeping my hose aimed at the swirling, muddy mass in the pool. "We think this might be the key to releasing Frankie's spirit."

"Are you sure you're not wearing him?" he joked, brushing a spot of dirt off my shoulder.

I smiled at that. "Don't even get him started."

Ellis cocked his head. "Do you have a second?" he asked, growing serious. "I need your help."

I cut the hose and Frankie groaned. "You were about to overflow anyway," I told the gangster. I turned to Ellis. "Let's talk in private," I said, motioning him over toward the porch. "This dirt needs time to settle."

Ellis joined me and we took the back steps together. "We looked for Darla's pink notebook," he said. "It's gone."

I'd figured that when I saw Marshall's evidence bag. "I don't know what she could have found that would drive a person to murder."

"That's the million-dollar question," he said, rubbing the back of his neck. He suddenly looked very tired. He was polite enough not to mention the stack of Tupperware on my porch as I brushed the dirt from my dress and led him into the kitchen.

I closed the door, wishing I could offer him a seat and some sweet tea, but I couldn't afford a kitchen set. "Let's sit on the couch," I said, showing him into my back parlor. I now had two pieces of furniture in the room, thanks to an adventure my sister had sent me on last week. Melody's friend had paid me in used furniture after I solved a ghostly mystery in her resale shop. I didn't mind. I loved my new-to-me purple couch. So did Lucy, although right now she was trying to hide under one of the pillows. Her stealth act didn't quite work with her tail sticking out.

"Hi, Lucy," he said, giving her a loving stroke on her flank. She flinched and disappeared completely behind the big pillow. "We had some good times," he said. "Am I that easy to forget?"

"It's not you," I assured him, touched that he cared what my skunk thought of him. "Frankie's getting her stirred up. Lucy doesn't care much for the supernatural, and she's still getting used to his moods."

He nodded. "About last night, the coroner thinks Darla died between three and five in the morning."

My heart sank. "Shortly after she called Melody."

"We'll know more after the autopsy tomorrow morning. Whoever did it also stole the security camera outside. We don't have any witnesses." He paused. "Or at least none that we can talk to."

A flutter began in my stomach. I knew where this was going.

Ellis leaned an arm over the back of the couch. "I need your help, Verity."

Oh my. "This isn't a habit I want to encourage," I said, even if I could talk Frankie into helping me. It took a lot of his strength to show me the other side. "I'm not a professional ghost hunter."

"You're good at it," he pressed.

"I almost got us killed last time." He'd hired me to clear out some ghosts in a property he was renovating. It hadn't exactly gone smoothly. "I've never talked to such a new ghost." I didn't even know if Darla could be found. "And aren't you the one who agreed I shouldn't be doing this?"

He shook his head. "You're right," he conceded. "At some point, this has to stop. But not tonight. We need to know what happened in that library. You don't have to talk to Darla. I'll take any witness you can find. The building has got to be haunted," he said. "I've heard stories since I was a kid."

"Well, of course." Sugarland Library had served as a field hospital during the Civil War. No doubt a few well-loved, long-deceased patrons chose to hang around as well. But that didn't mean I could go in there and start chatting up the local ghost population. "The library has crime-scene tape all over it. I'm not even allowed in there."

Ellis fixed his gaze on me. "It also has a twenty-four-hour police presence, and I'm on the force." Right on cue, his radio squawked. The detective's voice took over the line, yelling at somebody. He flipped it off and stood. "Marshall is serious about protecting his crime scene. But I'm on guard duty this evening."

"Of course you are." I knew exactly where this was going.

"Come by after ten," he said, as if it were no big thing. "I'll let you in." Ellis might be a sexy, sweet paragon of justice, but even he had to see how ridiculous this sounded. "This is important," he stressed.

Of course it was. A woman had died, and the police had no idea who killed her. "I know you want to follow up on every lead you can, but how are you even going to introduce any evidence I uncover?"

"Leave that to me." He hesitated briefly before he said more. "Marshall is a solid officer, but he's never led a murder investigation. He's in over his head."

"And you're going to help," I stated.

"We are," he corrected. "Come on, Verity. It's a chance to use your powers for good."

He had a point. "Why can't things just get back to normal?" I asked out loud. Everything had been so simple before.

"I have a feeling it's going to get weirder before it gets better," he said, heading for the door. "Speaking of such, you may want to leave early. My brother is planning to drop by tonight with a ham pizza and a DVD of *The Notebook*."

I about choked, and not just because I didn't like ham on my pizza. You'd think Beau would have realized that by now.

"I did nothing to encourage him," I said quickly.

Ellis hunkered down to pet Lucy, who had evidently decided he was a good catch and followed him to the door. She rubbed her face into his palm as he scratched her on the head. "I wouldn't be surprised if he stopped by the gas station for roses and massage oil."

I cringed. "You know there's no way on this earth…"

"He says you give a hell of a back rub," Ellis added as my skunk gave him the kind of loving she usually reserved for fresh bananas.

I had no idea what Beau thought he'd accomplish by showing up unannounced, but he wouldn't make it past my door. I wasn't about to let his grand fool attempt at reconciliation mess up my budding romance with his older brother.

"Ellis, I'd rather sit in a locked room with fifty of Lucy's wild cousins than get back together with Beau." He had to believe that. "You know how stubborn your brother can be. He's not going to drop this until he can't ignore the fact that I've moved on." Then the horror of it hit me. "He might not stop until he knows about whatever is going on between you and me."

Ellis's jaw ticked. "Is there something going on between you and me?" he asked, teasing, but not.

A small laugh bubbled from me. Something going on? I hardly dared to hope. He was the most interesting man I'd met in a long time. And did I mention gorgeous?

I wished I could have been the seductress in that moment, said something to draw him in and let him know how I felt. But I was still trying to figure it out myself. It was bad enough to be the crazy girl in town, the fool who ruined her own wedding day. Did I really need to be known as the girl who started seriously dating her ex-fiancé's brother?

Then again, it wasn't fair to let Beau keep ruining my chance at happiness.

I hesitated before reaching out and touching the handsome officer on the arm. "You have a murder to investigate. I'll talk to Frankie about tonight."

His posture relaxed and he shifted, his hands buried in his pockets. He glanced past me, as if he was looking at something else. "Where is Frankie?"

"Probably still outside, overseeing our experiment. I'll find him." And hope he was in a good mood.

Ellis gave a sharp nod. "Thanks." He started to leave, but then stopped suddenly to give me a quick, almost guilty kiss on the cheek. "I'll see you soon."

I watched him go, wishing I could say something to make things right, but unable to imagine what that could be. As his squad car bounced down the gravel driveway, I sighed and closed the door.

"You two are precious," a voice crooned behind me.

"We are something," I said, turning to find Frankie hovering next to my kitchen island. I wasn't even mad at him for spying. Just the opposite. I needed him to reinstate my ghost-seeing skills, but I didn't want to ask directly. Allowing me into the world of ghosts took a lot of energy, and Frankie wasn't what you'd call a giver. "Did you hear what's going on?"

He shrugged a shoulder. "The gist. You want to use my powers while you moon over some cop. You want me to show you the other side, when there ain't nothing in it for us."

He must not have heard right. "We'd be helping a murder investigation."

He rolled his eyes. "Pfft."

I was wrong. He'd heard right. He just didn't care.

"It'd get you out of the house," I told him.

"So will a kiddie pool and a few aquarium nets." Frankie glided straight through the kitchen island. "The library ain't what I had in mind."

"Look, a woman was killed," I said, appealing to his sense of right and wrong. "You know what that's like." He'd refused to tell me much about his death or who murdered him, but I knew it weighed on him. This was his chance to help someone else avoid that kind of pain.

He took off his hat. "There's no money in it," he said, looking up as if invoking the heavens. "You never go after the money." He shoved his hat back on his head. "It's the first rule when striking a deal. If you're gonna rake me over the coals, we need to benefit."

I didn't want to be some mobster protégé. "You are not my life coach."

"Your what?" Frankie gave a funny squint. "Don't matter," he said, shaking it off. "Tell you what. We'll start off small. Ask for a few hundred bucks, buy yourself a decent place for your skunk to hide. Maybe buy her some blueberries."

Blueberries were too expensive. Bananas worked fine. And leave it to Frankie to show consideration for the one creature who couldn't care less for him.

"I'm doing okay. Lucy too." Well, maybe not Lucy. She'd wedged herself back under the covers pretty good.

"She don't like me," the ghost said. I could tell he was bothered by it. "Why don't she like me? I didn't do nothin'."

"I know." They say animals are good judges of character, but in Frankie's case…well, it could be that. But it could also be because ghosts scared wildlife like Lucy. "Look, I don't need to ask for money. My graphic design business should take off any day now. I have a lot of work samples out to local merchants." They were bound to forget about my public shaming and hire me eventually. In the meantime, I'd do what was right. But Frankie had to know; he needed to understand. "My *real* business is art. I'm not a ghost hunter."

"We agree on that," he said, hovering near my skunk. She grunted and buried herself deeper under the covers. Frankie sighed. "We can't keep doing this."

True. It cost him every time I borrowed his powers, and it wasn't doing anything for my home life, either.

"We won't," I told him. "For all we know, you might be free tomorrow." Although I highly doubted it. "You need to do something while the dirt separates outside."

He shoved his hands into his pockets, making lumps. "What if that doesn't work?"

It was the first time he'd expressed any doubt. I tamped down a twinge of sympathy. I knew he wouldn't want that from me. "If our first try doesn't free you, then we'll try again. And while we work on that, I'll take you out. We'll go someplace fun."

"One with dames," Frankie said. "Blondes with nice stems."

"Deal," I promised, wondering where that might be. Perhaps he'd enjoy a trip to the farmers' market to look at flowers. But I wouldn't dwell on that right now. I had enough worries about what we'd find in the library.

Chapter Four

WE PREPARED TO leave early so I could be out of my house before Romeo Beau showed up. I'd bathed and changed into my dress with the blue hydrangeas and the white trim. This one was terribly out of season. I'd have to run by the thrift store soon for something more fall-like. But I'd cleaned and pressed it nice, and it would have to do for this evening.

I secured the front door of the house and stood in the kitchen, giving my bag a final check.

"What am I missing?" I had a flashlight, my phone, a granola bar, and Frankie's urn.

I rubbed my thumb on one of the square-cut green stones circling the flare at the top of the urn. It had started to come loose after our last adventure, so I used superglue to stick it back on. It seemed tight enough now.

"You didn't have to tape the top shut," Frankie groused, leaning over me to look into the bag.

"Oh, yes, I did. We don't want to lose any more of your ashes." There wasn't much of Frankie left. Most of him was under the rosebushes, and now hopefully in the kiddie pool. Still, if we didn't keep at least a little bit of Frankie in that urn, he wouldn't be able to leave the house. He'd be stuck in my rosebushes for eternity. "Urns have lids for a reason."

If anything, it could use even more masking tape at the top. Burial displays aren't designed to be toted around all over town. Frankie's especially. I hated to admit it, even to myself, but his final resting place didn't appear to be put together very well. The copper felt thin. A healthy dent already gouged the lower half. I owed it to him to keep it as clean and presentable as possible.

"You're making it look stupid," he said, hesitant, as if he were reluctant to admit he cared about such things.

I nestled his urn gently in my bag. "You know it's a work of art." At least to him, it was. His friend Suds had spent a lot of time decorating it. I ran a finger over the crude hand-painted scene that marred the dull metal exterior. Sure, it would never make the front cover of *Artist Weekly*, but it had been illustrated with care and affection, and that made it special.

He appeared a bit horror-struck at my soft side. "You want to meet up with them ghosts, or you want to flap your gums?" he huffed, passing through my kitchen wall and abandoning me for the back porch.

So much for sentiment.

I locked the back door good and tight. I didn't usually. But I didn't want to return and find that Beau had made himself at home. I squared my shoulders as I descended the porch steps and wound around to the side drive.

Frankie had settled into the passenger seat of my 1978 avocado-green Cadillac. My grandmother had bought it new and maintained it well before handing it down to me. She'd loved that car, and so did I. Good thing it was worthless or I would have had to sell it.

The engine cranked up with a wheezing rumble that didn't sound all that healthy, but the car had started, so I considered it a victory.

Frankie eyed me, his hat pulled low over his forehead. "Good thing we're not trying to sneak up on anybody."

"Do you have a car?" I asked sweetly as I turned the oversize manual steering wheel.

He shrugged a shoulder. "No."

"Exactly," I said, hitting the gas.

He rolled his eyes as we bumped down the long, snaking drive from my house. It was barely past six o'clock and I wondered how we should occupy ourselves while we waited for Ellis to sneak us into the library. We didn't need to be shopping or eating. Both cost money.

So I decided to drop in on an old friend.

We bypassed the main part of town and headed for the neighborhood just south of it. Thick, mature trees lined the road. The neat bungalow-style houses along Magnolia Street had stood since the early 1900s. I loved the wide variety of styles and personal touches as well as the inviting porches. No two were alike.

Lauralee and Tom lived in a yellow house that reminded me of a picture on the cover of a child's storybook. It wasn't just the white brick porch and bright blue shutters, or the blanket of ivy that kept the front yard in an eternal state of green. Birdhouses, painted by the children, hung from mature black oaks. Colorful pots of camellias lined the walk, and large Thunder Cloud sage bushes burst in a riot of deep purple flowers on either side of the front steps.

I smelled honeysuckle and lilac in the breeze and tried not to let the cushioned Adirondack rocking chairs tempt me as I knocked gently on her front door.

It flew open, but I didn't see anyone right away.

With a thick screech, Tommy Junior fled from behind the open door and was tackled from the side by his skinny little brother George. They rolled on the floor wrestling while three-year-old Ambrose tossed Legos into the mix. Hiram was nowhere to be seen, which could be good…or bad.

Frankie appeared shell-shocked. "What is this place?"

"Heaven," I told him. No wonder he wanted to get out.

I left him staring and found Lauralee in the kitchen, her dark hair tied back in a messy ponytail as she took fresh rolls out of the oven. Five-year-old Hiram sat on the floor driving Hot Wheels over an obstacle course made from wooden kitchen spoons.

Lauralee had three standing mixers going on the counters and pots bubbling on all six stove burners. "I know you have four boys," I said. That alone should keep her busy for the next twenty years. "But this is overkill."

"Ha!" she said, stirring each pot in turn. "The terror squad doesn't get to touch any of this. You're looking at the official caterer for the Wydell Studios production of *The Battle of Sugarland*."

As soon as she finished, she came over and wrapped me in a warm hug. "I heard about this morning. How are you doing?"

"As good as I can," I told her, taking in the controlled chaos surrounding her. "I figured you'd use the kitchen at the diner."

"I wish! But I don't own the diner or that kitchen." She checked on several loaves of bread baking in the oven. "And I don't have to tell you what a big opportunity this is."

"Can I help?" I asked. I wasn't much of a cook, but I took orders well.

"No. I've got this down to a science." She turned to me. "You eat yet?" she added innocently, knowing I probably hadn't. "I just put individual portions of pulled pork in the fridge."

"I didn't come over here to steal your food," I said. Naturally, my stomach picked that moment to growl.

Lauralee smiled knowingly and handed me a plastic plate from a stack on the kitchen table. "You can be my taste tester. It's an important job."

Yeah, right. "I showed up just in time."

"While you're in there, you can also get Hiram more grapes," she said, pointing to the almost-empty bowl in the middle of a Hot Wheels traffic jam.

"That I can do," I said, wading through the cars. Hiram didn't even notice me as I refilled his bowl. Then I retrieved a portion of pork out of the fridge and leaned against the wall next to the table to eat. It was the only free place in the kitchen.

Lauralee fished around in her refrigerator and pulled out a small container of potato salad. She plopped it on my plate. "Big Tom took the boys to a casting call this afternoon at the VFW Hall. They're looking for drummer boys with lots of energy," she said excitedly, "to lead the Yankee charge. Tommy Junior is just old enough. And he likes to drum. Big Tom got a callback right after he and the boys came home with some take-out chicken noodle soup from the diner. They want Tommy Junior back tomorrow and Tom's going back tonight to try on uniforms."

I jabbed my fork in her direction. "Remind me to ask him for his autograph."

The still-warm pork was tender and delicious. It was the best meal I'd eaten since Melody pretended to cook too much lasagna and brought me over the entire tray, with the grocery price tag still attached.

"Tom called and said the callback line's about a mile long. Word has it Virginia Wydell is overseeing final casting decisions and she rejected a man because the gray on his temples didn't match up right."

"Yikes," I said, finishing my meal. "I guess that's show business."

She paused, holding a wooden spoon. "Tom doesn't have any hair. Does that mean I should worry more or less?"

That earned a snarf from me and a mock glare from my friend. "Thanks. I needed this," I told her. It was more than the food. It was the company.

Lauralee grinned. She knew.

My left side went cold as Frankie shimmered into view way too close. "The smallest one is shrieking. The skinny one decided I'm his imaginary friend. And now they say they're gonna turn the couch into a hideout. As if you could hide from the fuzz in a piece of furniture." He let out a shudder. Frankie could join the mob, but he couldn't hang out with a couple of kids for ten minutes. "We're leaving," he said, as if his word were final.

I was tempted to tell the gangster to shake it off, but I heard the desperation in his voice and saw the way his left eye had begun to twitch. We didn't need him rattled for tonight.

"Sorry I can't stay," I said to Lauralee. I hadn't quite told her about Frankie yet.

She waved a hand at me, as if to say *no big deal,* and went to her kitchen table to grab a large brown sack. "I'm always glad to see you." She proceeded to load fresh bread and tubs of pulled pork into the bag. "You going right home?" she asked casually.

"No. Ellis needs my help."

She didn't approve any more than Melody did, but so far, Lauralee had kept her concerns to herself. She took out the pork and added a brand-new jar of peanut butter and a jar of homemade jelly before pressing the bag into my hands. "Now you listen to me. The Wydells do well enough on their own."

"Not this one," I told her, accepting the food. "It's going to be fine. I promise."

She gave me a long look. "Don't you be too sweet, at least when it comes to Ellis. You know I worry about you."

"I'll be careful," I said, heading out into the family room, past the fort-in-progress. Lauralee gave me another hug at the door before I walked out toward the car. Frankie hovered in the driveway.

"It's about time," he said, when I stashed my bag in the back and slid into the driver's seat. "Now what do we do until ten?"

"That was my solution," I said, waving at Lauralee, who stood at the front door. "I suppose you've got a better idea?"

I glanced at my unfriendly ghost. And at the dashboard clock that read fifteen minutes after seven.

It might not hurt to run past the library and take a peek. Ellis had said his shift started in the evening.

Most of Main Street stood empty, the storefronts lit with security lighting and only a few darkened vehicles parked in front of the vintage-style meters along either side of the street. Shops closed early on Sundays, if they opened at all.

We turned right into the historic square, and after circling around the town founder's statue, we drove slowly along the front of the library building. The first-floor windows blazed with light in sharp contrast to the darkened second and third floors. Police tape crisscrossed the front steps, held tight by the century-old iron lampposts with their glowing glass dome lights.

"Don't look too welcoming," Frankie said as I slowed.

"Yes, but get a load of that." Ellis's squad car hunkered against the curb a little ways down. I didn't see any other parked cars on the square, not even at the town hall. "Let's do this early," I said, speeding up again. "It's not like we need to ghost-hunt only when it's super late and dark."

Frankie leaned his arm through the closed window, catching his fingers on the cool autumn breeze. "It's like you want to take all the fun out of it."

I drove around back, looking for an inconspicuous place to park. "So did you ever haunt anything?"

"On a permanent basis?" he asked, eyeing the old library. "Nah. Too much of a commitment."

I found a parking spot behind the old Episcopal church next door. The single security light at the rear entrance buzzed, casting a weak yellow beam. I purposely pulled the car into the farthest back corner, under the canopy of a large oak tree. It would appear suspicious for me to return to the library when I had no business there. I didn't need my car giving me away.

The green monster didn't exactly blend.

I hurried to cross the parking lots, Frankie's urn clanking in my bag. This should be simple. I needed it to be. All we had to do was talk to the ghosts who were there when Darla was killed and get a lead from them, any kind of a clue as to who committed the crime. Or even better, a ghostly witness who could point us directly to the killer.

Then Ellis would feed it to Marshall. Once we had something for Marshall to latch onto, a real lead in the case, I could leave the rest of this to the police. Most importantly, poor Darla Grace would have justice.

It should be simple. It should be fine. Except when I approached the back door of the library, the place felt...foreboding. Actually, it was the area about ten feet in front of the door. An icy shiver drew up my spine as I edged past the spot. It was more than just cold. It was as if someone or some*thing* stood in the center, just beyond my sight.

And even though it didn't communicate with words, I could tell in an instant it wanted me to leave. Now.

I gathered up my courage. Frankie hadn't even opened me up to the other side yet.

Ignore it. I just needed to put one foot in front of the other. This should be the easy part. Walking to the door.

With a sigh, I edged all the way around the anomaly in the parking lot and approached the same back door Melody and I had used when we discovered the body this morning. It was locked, which didn't surprise me. This was a crime scene.

I could dial Ellis on my cell phone and ask him to let us in, but if things went wrong and I got into some sort of trouble, he'd need to look like my impartial, unlikely ally, not the guy I called at night. I could ask Frankie to handle the entire job for me, but he wasn't very friendly or diplomatic…or reliable, for that matter.

I turned to Frankie. "Can you go make sure the street out front is still deserted?"

"We breaking in?" he asked, with a little too much relish for my taste.

"No," I said quickly. "But Ellis will probably be near those front doors. In fact, you might even want to take a peek. If we can get his attention, maybe he'll let us in early."

"Spoilsport," the gangster said. But he disappeared, so I assumed he went off to do as I'd asked.

That left me standing by myself in the darkened parking lot.

A frigid gust of air seized me. Dead leaves swirled at my feet, prickling my legs. All normal for fall. Or for a haunting. My heart thudded and I had the overwhelming urge to run.

Screw it. Frankie would find me even if I didn't wait.

I took off, sticking to the shadows of the building, afraid to look behind me to see what might follow.

Whatever lingered back there felt dead. It couldn't hurt me. I was safe from the not-so-happily departed when I wasn't using Frankie's powers to reach the other side.

Of course, that was exactly what I planned to do.

I stumbled over the uneven grassy ground, relieved that the air on the side of the building felt warmer. My foot hit another dip and my ankle twinged. I risked a glance behind me and saw only darkness. It could have hidden anything.

"Okay," I said, voice shaky, my arms and legs weak with fright as I made it to the last remaining deep shadow before reaching the lights at the front of the building. I planted my back against the rough, hard limestone and waited.

"Verity," hissed a disembodied voice, right in my ear.

I shot off the wall and stumbled. "What do you want?"

"Oh, I could go for a nice steak dinner, a ritzy babe on my arm"—Frankie appeared in front of me, stroking his chin—"some bathtub gin with a dash of absinthe, and maybe a fresh pack of smokes."

I didn't know if I wanted to hug him or throttle him. Actually, neither, considering it was a bad idea to touch a ghost. "You took forever."

His lip hitched and he looked at me as if I'd gone off my rocker. "I ain't been gone that long." He drew next to me. "Now keep it down. The front door is open and your copper is inside."

"Ellis?" I asked.

He frowned. "That's what I said."

"Good." Some of my tension eased, having Frankie with me and knowing Ellis was near. I shuddered, my body trying to shake off some of the lingering fright. "You know I'm not usually this jumpy. I thought you might be...someone else."

Frankie cocked his head. "Who? The guy in the back? He *is* pretty pissed. Stay away from him," the gangster said as we made our way around the front.

I *knew* I'd felt an entity back there. Even without Frankie's powers I was becoming more sensitive to the other side. "Who is he?"

"Just some fella haunting his death spot." He tried to be casual, but his eyes held mine for a split second too long when he said, "I'm serious. Don't mess around back there."

"I wasn't." Still, it made me curious. "I didn't feel him this morning when I was with Melody."

Frankie frowned. "He don't have to stick around. *He's* not grounded."

Right.

Police tape ran all the way down the sides of the stairs, roped around the lights, and blocked the main entrance.

"Let's do this," I said, ducking under the yellow barrier near the top of the stairs.

Frankie gave one last, lingering glance behind us.

The front door opened easily. I slipped inside and tried not to jump when the door boomed closed behind me. "Ellis?"

"Verity." He appeared around the corner, one hand on his gun belt. The sudden bright lights in the lobby made it hard to see, but all the same, Ellis didn't appear at all happy to find me standing there. "We said ten o'clock."

"I'm avoiding your brother," I told him, nervous and chilled from outside. "Is it a problem?"

As my eyes adjusted, I realized I hadn't mistaken his apprehension. "Marshall said he'd stop back by after supper."

"Oh," I began.

Ellis lifted his head as a car pulled up out front. "Speak of the devil."

Dang. "What do I do?"

"You hope he doesn't see you," he said, moving past me to the door. He cracked it open and I heard a car door slam shut. "Hide. He's coming."

"Hide?" I muttered to Frankie, who had already disappeared. There was nowhere for a mortal human to take cover around here. Lights blazed in the lobby and the main room behind it. There were no dark corners, no bookshelves to duck behind. They'd all been relocated for the party. And I was *not* huddling up under a skirted table like the one where I'd found Darla's body.

But I had to go somewhere. Anywhere. Before I could think on it too much, I opened the heavy wood door to the storage room located just off the lobby. I'd seen them use it as a coatroom for events, and a dented, empty garment rack still stood near the back. Boxes crowded the walls, more donations for the Cannonball in the Wall brunch. Poor Darla must not have gotten through them all before…

I closed the door behind me and kept the lights off, knowing that if Marshall decided to investigate, I was in one of the first places he'd look. But it was the best I could do on short notice.

Marshall's footsteps echoed on the marble as he entered the lobby. "Wydell, here. Brought you a coffee." The detective's voice was warm and relaxed. Thank goodness. That meant he hadn't seen me enter the building. "All quiet?"

"As much as you can expect around here," Ellis said. "I caught Ovis Dupre peeking in the side window, trying to get a picture for the *Shady Oaks Extended Living Center Gazette*."

The detective let out a huff. "I thought he was persistent when he worked for the *Sugarland Gazette*. That guy just can't retire, can he?"

"Guess not. Beatrice expecting you back home soon?" Ellis asked, a note of expectancy in his voice.

Please say yes. I'd do anything. Well, not anything, but...

"She's on the phone with her mother. That could take all night. I thought I'd look around here for a bit. See if I can't make sense of it all."

No, no, no. I couldn't leave my hiding spot with him wandering around the main room. And what if he wanted to see the rest of the exhibits, the ones in here with me?

Ellis didn't know where I'd gone. He might not even try to stop Marshall from opening this door.

Their voices drew closer.

I brought a hand to my heart.

"You know who else stopped by?" Ellis asked, a hint of mischief in his voice. "Alma Sue Holcamp."

Marshall gave a low chuckle. "I had her fudge cookies at the county fair this summer. She more than earned that blue ribbon. Good enough to make a man think he died and went to heaven."

"She tried to bribe me with a double batch. The whole time she's holding out the plate, Alma's peeking past me into the library, like she's about to see the Holy Grail."

Marshall chuckled. "The Holy Grail of gossip."

"I didn't want to bring food into the library, so I put them in the car. Want to sit out there and have a couple?"

"Couple dozen?" Marshall asked. "Sure," he said, after a pause. "Why not?"

"Okay." I could hear the relief in Ellis's voice. "You head on out. I'm going to make sure the windows are locked. For all we know, Alma Sue could be conspiring with Ovis Dupre," Ellis added, only half joking. He knew this town.

The door of the library boomed closed.

Before I could even take a deep breath, Ellis wrenched open my hiding spot. "I swear, Verity," he began, a grin tickling his lips, "you are lucky I like you."

My heart warmed at that. "You like me?" I don't know why I was so surprised. I knew he did. Maybe I just needed to hear it again.

Naturally, he chose that moment to clam up, ushering me out of the storage room with quiet efficiency. "I asked you to come at ten because I knew Marshall would be out of the way by then. Sometimes, you have to do what I say instead of always thinking you know best."

Shoot. I'd been so busy dodging Beau I hadn't even thought about avoiding Marshall. "Okay, so what do we do?"

"Just stay put a minute until Marshall is out of the way. I'm going to stall him with Alma Sue's cookies as long as I can. You do your investigating. Fast. I can hold him for about a half hour, but that's only because we have a big plate and he brought coffee. When you leave, go out the back door."

Oh no. "I can't." I wanted to avoid that frigid spot until the ghost was good and gone. Even if I couldn't exactly see the specter, I sure as heck didn't want to draw its attention. I'd heard of spirits following people home. "Is there any way I can sneak out the front?" I asked, more than a touch desperate. "Maybe use a side window? It was good enough for Ovis."

Ellis's cheeks flushed. "Don't do this to me, Verity. You absolutely cannot get caught in here. It wouldn't go well for either of us."

He was right. Ellis would get into so much trouble. He could even lose his job.

"Fine," I said, forcing myself to accept that he was right. "I'll go out the back." I'd risk a run-in with the ghost that made even Frankie nervous. "But you have to give me that half hour in here. Not a moment less." I needed to concentrate, to focus without worrying about Marshall bursting in the door at any second.

"You got it," Ellis said, checking his watch "It'll be okay. We've pulled out of tight spots before."

True. But sooner or later, we were bound to get caught.

Frankie materialized as the door boomed closed behind Ellis. "That was too close," I said.

The gangster glided to one of the arched windows flanking the door. "Don't matter how close it is, as long as you don't get pinched."

That was one way of looking at it.

My hard, flat sandals echoed against the marble floors as we passed through the lobby and into the main reference room. The tables stood undisturbed, their artifacts eerie in the deserted space, the remains of lives long gone.

"You ready?" Frankie prodded.

"No," I said. I wasn't being saucy. It was the God's honest truth.

Frankie was not amused. "Wrong answer. Clock's ticking."

I knew that. I was strong. I could handle this. "I'm ready." As ready as I'd ever be. "Show me the other side."

Chapter Five

THE AIR SHIFTED, prickling my skin and working a dull throb through my muscles and bones. Sparks of energy spiraled lazily downward like enchanted dust motes.

I held my breath while an unearthly light settled over us, casting the room in an eerie silver glow.

Images slowly came into focus all around me. The row of display tables in the reading room faded away, replaced by military cots. A woman huddled over one of the nearest ones, her long skirts trailing behind her as she bent to whisper over an empty pillow crumpled with the weight of a head. I froze when the apparition turned my way, as if I'd called her, which I certainly hadn't. She had no face. She barely had any form at all, just an outline of a woman.

I heard faint sobbing as she glided toward me. No telling where that came from. I fought to keep my expression neutral, locking my knees lest I show the fear pounding through every cell in my body.

"What do I do?" I whispered to Frankie when it became clear she wasn't stopping. "Frankie."

I turned to find him gone.

My mouth went dry. The woman hovered inches from me, forcing me to stare straight at the churning mist that should have been her face. I could see right through her. I leaned back as the chill of her washed over me.

"Private Baker asked to send a letter." Her lilting voice was sweet, hollow. Haunting. "Will you take it down for him when he wakes?"

She pointed back toward the bed with the crumpled pillow, and I could have sworn I saw a flicker of light over the bed.

Keep it together.

I'd seen ghosts before. I had one living in my house. But these entities seemed...less human. I felt bad for even thinking it.

Still, I wasn't so sure I could even speak to Private Baker if he was a wisp of light on a pallet, and how dare I even hesitate when it came to helping an injured soldier? "Yes," I said, before I could change my mind. He was suffering, and I'd do whatever I could. Maybe Frankie would have some ideas on how to connect with the barely there spirit. If the gangster didn't laugh me out of the building first.

"See to the men," she said, before she faded into nothingness. Her voice echoed in the air around me. "I'm to help the doctor with an amputation."

I brought a hand to my mouth. The library had been converted into a field hospital after the Battle of Sugarland. I'd just never given much thought to what that meant.

When Frankie showed me the other side, I saw the strongest energies that haunted the space. If I concentrated, I could almost see the outlines of the men on the cots, hear moans and chest-deep coughs. They controlled this space.

With a creak and a loud slam that shook the building, the front door of the library burst open. I turned, expecting Ellis, or worse, Marshall. But no. The real door remained closed. Two spirits shimmered through the dark wood. A man in a Confederate uniform staggered into the field hospital, half supporting, half dragging one of his comrades. They flickered in shades of ghostly gray. Even still, I could see the man's leg dripped with blood.

"In here," I said, waving them over.

They disappeared.

I dropped my hand to my side. What was I thinking? I couldn't help them. None of this was real. Not anymore.

Keep it together.

I squeezed my hands into fists, welcoming the sharp sting of my nails biting into my palms. That was real. I was real. They were not.

And as far as my ghost buddy? At least I'd found Frankie. He sat on the floor near the lobby with a group of bandaged soldiers. They appeared to be playing poker.

At a time like this.

I stalked over to him. "What are you doing?" I didn't appreciate being abandoned in a haunted library. Especially for a game of five-card stud. It wasn't like we had all day.

The curly-haired soldier on Frankie's right glared at me with his one good eye. The other was covered in gauze. He quickly drew his cards to his chest. "Are you cheating, Frank?"

"Me? No," the gangster scoffed, as if the mere suggestion offended him. He jabbed a thumb in my direction. "This dame wouldn't know a good hand if it bit her."

We had work to do. "I don't care about your cards and he shouldn't, either." I gave Frankie a pointed look. "Now are you going to help me out, or are you going to sit around gambling?"

"One more, Stoutmeyer," Frankie said to the dealer. He accepted the card and lazily fingered his hand. The gangster threw a card down and the dealer, a skinny guy with bruises all over his face and a chest full of gauze wrap, laid a new one facedown on the table. Frankie scooped up the card. "I did my job. You're the one who wanted to do some investigating. So why are you talking to me instead of trying to find out what happened?" he pressed. "Ticktock," he added, just to get my hackles up.

"Fine." He was impossible anyway when he was like this. "I'll do it without you." I addressed his buddies. "Maybe some of you gentlemen can help. I'm investigating a death that happened in this room last night."

The corporal on Frankie's left straightened his uniform collar. He didn't appear injured at all. If he hadn't worn a uniform, I would have pegged him for a cute farm boy. "Were we here last night?" he asked the others.

"That's a tough one." The man on Frankie's right shrugged a shoulder, not bothering to look up from his cards. "What year is it?"

"1973, I think," the corporal said.

I started to correct him when the dealer interrupted me. "More than a hundred years since the battle and the town still remembers us."

"More like one hundred and fifty," I said, "but let's stay on topic."

"This one here is a real war hero," he said, jabbing a thumb at the young soldier who couldn't have been older than his late teens, or late 170s, depending on how you looked at it. "Lost his head taking out the Yankee cannon position."

The corporal gave an embarrassed shrug. "I put it back on." He touched a hand to the longish dark hair curling at his neck, as if to make sure his head stayed put.

"Thank you for your service," I said. I appreciated it. I did. "One of the volunteers for our Cannonball in the Wall event was killed last night. A woman named Darla. She died right over there." I pointed to the place where I'd found the body. The display table had faded away and in its place, I saw flickering streaks of white and yellow light shining up from the floor. "Oh, wow."

"Would you look at that?" The corporal tossed his cards down and joined me, earning a collective *arggh* from the group behind us. "Soul traces. She *is* new." He cleared his throat and seemed embarrassed. "Not that I didn't take you on your good word." He edged closer to the death scene. "Sometimes, it's hard to focus on anything outside the game."

"You gonna play or what, Owens?" the dealer groused.

He waved them off. "I fold."

"Thank you," I said. I'd needed someone like him to care.

"My pleasure," he said, before he averted his eyes and took a sudden interest in the floor.

Pops of red pierced the white and yellow soul traces. "What are those?" I asked.

"I'm afraid it means your friend Darla did not die easy," he said, a touch of sadness in his voice. "It's most likely a crime of passion. See the purple?" He pointed to the floor. It oozed over the hardwood like blood. "She passed away there on the floor or it wouldn't cling like that."

"Oh," I said, moving to take a closer look.

"Don't touch it," he said. "It'll give you a blistering shock."

I'd take his word for it. "You tried it?"

"Only once," he said with a shudder.

"What are the shadows?" They swirled like smoke, just out of reach of the light.

"Anger. Hers, from the look of it. See how it mingles with the light? Poor girl didn't want to go."

Amazing.

I turned to him. "So you can actually look at a place where someone died and learn things about how it happened?" The implications were enormous. I could use an assistant like that.

"You can do it as well," he said, as if my excitement embarrassed him. "If it's a recent death."

I didn't know if I wanted the responsibility. Although it didn't seem as if I had a choice.

I turned back to the group on the floor. "Did any of you see what happened to the woman who died?"

The one-eyed soldier furrowed his brows. "I think we were at that sock hop last night."

"We haven't done that since the '50s," Owens corrected.

"I almost feel bad about locking the beast in the basement now," Stoutmeyer said. "Almost."

He and the one-eyed soldier laughed.

"You have animals in here?" I asked, a little taken aback.

Owens cringed. "No. He died in the battle, same as us, but he's damaged and angry. He's banished to the basement most of the time." The baby-faced corporal watched the flickering streaks of white and yellow light, Darla's soul traces. "The beast insisted he saw a man use a bayonet on a lady," he said. "She had a discovery that would change everything. We told him he was wallpapered."

"What?" I asked, not catching the slang.

"Wouldn't put it past a Yankee," Stoutmeyer added.

"Now I wonder," Corporal Owens mused.

"He might have killed her himself," the man with the bandaged eye insisted. "I hear he can touch things in the mortal plane."

I exchanged a glance with Frankie. That would be one powerful ghost indeed.

"What else you know, Gregson?" Frankie asked.

The ghost scowled and kept his cards to his chest.

"You have any idea where this beast person is?" I prodded. I really needed to talk with him.

Gregson's expression deepened to one of disgust. "A lady like you shouldn't even look at an animal like that." He pointed to the bloody bandage above his eye. "He's not right in the head."

"The man is evil," Stoutmeyer declared. "If you even want to call that *thing* a man. He's banished to the cellar for a reason."

Lovely.

I hoped he wasn't a poltergeist. I'd dealt with that particular manifestation before, and it had scared the living daylights out of me.

"Down below?" I asked, just to be sure. The basement of the library housed rare books as well as duplicates that had been taken out of circulation. I'd been there once during a library tour. Otherwise, the area was off-limits to nonemployees.

The men nodded, appearing distinctly uncomfortable.

Right. "I'll check it out." I glanced at my watch. Only fifteen minutes left. If I could secure just one lead, one clue, it would go a long way to helping the police investigate. And we'd get Marshall off my back.

At least I knew where I was going. The entrance to the stacks was located in the hall behind the circulation desk.

I didn't even look at Frankie as I left. Either he'd join me or he wouldn't. I couldn't waste time worrying about it. I walked down the center aisle of the hospital. The moans of the sick grew louder.

I opened the pass-through on the desk and slipped behind it, refusing to show my relief when Frankie glided straight through the solid mahogany on my right.

"Don't say anything," he grumbled, pulling out a silver revolver. He opened it up, checking the bullets.

"You can't shoot him," Owens said from behind us.

"We've tried," Gregson added.

I turned to see all three men hovering behind us.

"Don't go down there," Stoutmeyer warned. "I'm serious, Frankie. And if you do, for God's sake, don't take the lady."

Unfortunately, I was the one who needed to go.

"We'll be fine," I said, not quite sure if I was reassuring them or giving a pep talk to Frankie and myself.

We passed through the door in the back marked "Employees Only."

"This isn't my idea of a good time," Frankie reminded me.

"Noted," I said, flipping on the lights to the stark corridor. Straight across stood the six-paneled oak door that led to the stacks.

It had been spooky enough on the library tour. I opened it wide, and as I felt the cold air streaming from the narrow staircase, I fought the urge to run. I'd never been able to understand before why I felt so uncomfortable in the stacks, but now I knew. The ghost didn't want anyone down there.

Now or never. I pulled at the string to illuminate the bare bulb above my head.

"It's a little medieval, don't you think?" Frankie asked, hesitating on the landing. He felt it, too.

"According to Melody, they don't go down here much," I said. "Most patrons want the newer books and the periodicals." No doubt the librarians avoided the place when they could.

We began our descent.

I ran a hand over the rough-cut gray stone wall on my right and felt the coldness of going underground.

This had been the coal pit back when they needed it to heat the building. Melody had talked about renovation plans, but those had been shelved for lack of funds.

I reached up for another lightbulb string and froze at the sound of metal groaning against concrete below. I jumped when I heard glass shatter.

"Somebody's down there all right," Frankie said under his breath.

As if we hadn't known.

I pulled on the light. I didn't need it to see, but it made me feel better all the same.

Frankie cocked his gun.

"Put that thing away," I murmured. "It won't work." Stoutmeyer said so.

"Doesn't hurt to try," Frankie mused.

Or it might just make the ghost angry. "We have to let him know we mean him no harm."

Frankie let out a huff. "Speak for yourself."

There were no more lights on the stairs, and the one I'd turned on only illuminated a pool of gray at the bottom. After that, blackness.

With each step, the air grew chillier. Goose bumps raced up my arms as I fumbled for a light switch at the bottom. Something to escape the penetrating emptiness and despair.

This one didn't work. My eyes flickered up and there, in the ghostly silver light of the other side, I could see why. The bulb had been obliterated.

It seemed the ghost had been counting on a regular intruder instead of me. And what I saw in the underground room surprised me. Rows upon rows of metal bookshelves penetrated the ethereal mist.

"I'm seeing what's really here," I said, trying to process it. Every other time, when Frankie had let me view the other side, I'd witnessed the ghost's view of things.

"This is how he sees it," Frankie said, as if no other explanation mattered.

"Okay." I pressed forward. So we had a solitary, rampageous, possibly murderous ghost who lived in the stacks and saw…books.

I ran my hand along the shelves on either side of me. The books felt solid, real.

As we neared the end of the row, I caught a flicker of light around the corner.

Frankie stiffened. "It's him."

I kept walking. I turned the corner, ready for anything, when I was blasted by a furious wind. The ghost flew at me, a terrifying vision of sharp teeth and snapping jaws. It wasn't even human.

Chapter Six

I SCREAMED AND dodged behind the bookcases. The ghost streaked past, a wall of terror and pain and rage.

It would have slammed right into me.

Obviously, this was not a talking ghost. This was an attacking one, and it was very, very angry.

I braced myself against a row of hardbacks, my heart threatening to beat clean out of my chest.

"Ha," Frankie's disembodied voice said against my ear, the shock of it jolting my last frayed nerve. "Stoutmeyer was right. This one's more animal than human."

It was an easy thing to say—even simpler to dismiss a person without giving them a chance. I had to admit I was tempted to go along with the group's view after what I'd just seen.

Except that Stoutmeyer had said he'd talked to it.

Crazy, rampaging, beastly ghosts didn't stop to chat, did they?

I crept closer to the edge of the bookshelf once more, wondering if I had the courage to peek around the corner.

This ghost had witnessed Darla's murder. He'd been aware for long enough to notice and care about what happened in the living world. That was more than we could say for the poker-playing ghosts or the nurse I'd met.

"Aw, no," Frankie grumbled as I neared the aisle. "Whatever you're thinking, stop right now."

"Shh…" I whispered. I could do this. I could step back out into that aisle. "He's kind of like you."

"Me?" Frankie snorted. "You think he's like me? You're smoked."

I stepped around the corner and saw the apparition straight ahead. It had taken on human form this time, which I took as a positive. The air crackled with animosity and frustrated energy. It pinched at my skin and made my joints ache.

The man glowed fuzzy at the edges, but I could see enough to discern that he wore dark pants and a simple shirt with buttons and a collar. He'd settled himself in an old library chair and curled inward around…a book.

He held a hardback with a gold cover and white lettering. I could even make out some red accents on the letters. And since the book had color, I'd venture to say it was a real volume from the library.

Which meant Stoutmeyer was right. This ghost could interact with physical objects. He was powerful indeed.

The apparition raised his head, glaring at me through empty eye sockets. His jaw grew longer before my eyes, his teeth pointed. "Leave," he hissed, his voice echoing in the isolated old coal room.

A line of sweat tickled my back, even though the rest of me burned. Every cell in my body screamed to run. Run! And never look back.

He drew the book to his chest and snarled.

The ghost was reading *Interview with the Vampire*.

"I love that book," I blurted out. My voice sounded squeaky, shrill. More than a little desperate. "Have you read the whole story? I did. Five times. My roommate in college gave it to me and I went so crazy for it I skipped class for a week and read the entire series straight through."

He glared at me, as if ready to strike. His nostrils flared with breaths he no longer needed to take. He jerked out of his chair and I fought back a yelp.

"I've read it twenty times." He said it like a challenge while holding the book to his chest.

"Wow." He sure had a lot of time on his hands. Wait. Of course he did. "Did you know they made it into a movie?"

He rumbled low in his throat. "Movies scare me."

"Sure," I said automatically, my mind frantically spinning to keep this conversation going, searching for some way to connect. "Some of the casting choices frightened a lot of us, but Tom Cruise was actually good in it."

The ghost came into clearer focus and I could see he didn't quite know what to make of me, either.

"Why are you...speaking with me?" he asked, choosing his words carefully, as if he wasn't quite accustomed to friendly intruders wandering down into his lair and rambling on at the mouth.

"I can see ghosts," I explained, "which is really good because last night—"

He drifted closer. "You realize I'm a Yankee."

Oh. Well, no. "I hadn't noticed."

He stopped. "That's the nicest thing anyone's said to me in a hundred and fifty years."

Poor thing. He must have been banished down here for a long time. Of course he had. The ghosts upstairs said he'd also died in the Battle of Sugarland. It seemed they'd kept to their separate sides, even in death. It hurt me to think of him isolated like that.

"Your side was in the right," I told him. It needed saying. "Maybe the ghosts upstairs just didn't want to see Sugarland burn." It was hardly an excuse. Still, war was ugly, and it seemed these ghosts had been unable to let go of the pain from the fight.

He fingered the spine of his book. "It would be nice to move on," he said, letting out a self-conscious huff, "but, of course, none of us have managed it."

"I'm so sorry," I said, wishing I could give him a hug.

Frankie's cold breath chilled my skin. "What are you doing?" he demanded, teeth clenched, as if he didn't quite want to know the answer. "You're not here to make friends. Besides, you say one wrong thing and this beast could go poltergeist and tear us apart."

"Shoo," I told him. Hadn't he listened to a word this man said?

Yes, our Civil War soldier could still turn into the rampaging, teeth-baring crazy ghost I'd witnessed earlier, but I doubted it. What I saw in front of me felt much more real.

I approached him cautiously, as casually as I possibly could. "I was hoping you knew something about the woman who died upstairs. Early this morning," I clarified, thinking of how many others must have breathed their last in this building over the years.

His features came into sharper focus and I could see his high forehead, prominent cheekbones, and weak chin. He appeared more cautious in his human form, ready to dart at any moment. "Darla was my great-great-niece."

Amazing. "Do all ghosts recognize family, or is that a special talent of yours?"

He dipped his chin as if we'd suddenly ventured into personal territory. "She wouldn't stop talking about how she's related to Myra Jackson, my sister."

Well, wasn't that sweet? Not surprising, either. It seemed all the older families in town were related in one way or another. "I'll bet she bragged about you, too."

"No," he said, with a touch of regret. "They don't talk about me."

It hit me. "You were the only one in your family to join the North?" For many families in Tennessee it had truly been brother against brother, and it seemed men like him were still paying the price.

"I had to fight following my conscience," he said, welcoming no argument.

"Yes, you did." We were glad for it today. "Although I can see how you'd catch hell upstairs."

He let out a huff, glancing at the ceiling as if he could see clean through it. "A lot of the time, they don't even notice me. Or they'll ignore me. They don't bother tormenting me much anymore." He chewed at his lip. "I like the display Darla was putting together. My favorite belt buckle is on one of the tables. Although it's labeled as my father's." He let out a small laugh. "No way my father would wear a flashy silver belt buckle."

Now we were getting somewhere. "Were you watching Darla when she was killed?"

"No," he said quickly. "I was there for a little while, watching her fiddle with the display. Then the head surgeon found me. He chased me back downstairs."

That made me sad. He shouldn't be banished down here. It wasn't right. Still, I couldn't dwell on it right now. Instead, I needed him to tell me, "What did you see?"

He floated upward, as if he could break right through to the room above. "Darla was being Darla. She had such life. Such energy." He ran a hand over the beams above his head. "I was proud of her. I even gave her a cold spot to let her know I was there, but she didn't notice." He gave a small, self-effacing laugh. "She was too excited over a piece of paper. She even said something about a hidden Bible."

No kidding? I drew closer. "What about it?"

He gave a wry grin. "It has to do with an old scandal from the sound of it."

"Show me," I urged.

He gave a quick nod. "All right. But for my sake, keep quiet."

He rose up through the ceiling while I took the long way out, through the stacks, up the narrow staircase and back from behind the circulation desk. I moved fast, worried that I'd lose track of him. That the ghost would be chased away or lose power or simply leave before I could find him upstairs.

I hadn't even asked his name. We'd have to remedy that. For now, at least I knew he was a Jackson. Although if I called out "Jackson!" in the library, I'd be willing to bet about a dozen guys would come running. It wasn't exactly a small family.

Just as I feared, there was no sign of the ghost when I entered the main library reading room. I saw the hospital, the men playing poker, Frankie glaring at me from a spot near the soul traces, but not Darla Grace's great-great-uncle.

"How you holding up?" I asked, searching behind him for the ghost of the Yankee.

"It's a picnic when you suck out my energy to go look for another fella," he remarked. "Let me save you some time. He's in there." Frankie gestured to the storage space I'd used as a hiding spot earlier.

"Thanks," I said, hurrying toward it. On the way, I checked the clock on my cell phone. We had about ten minutes left before Marshall came back, if Ellis could even hold him that long.

I'd better not end up hiding in the closet off the lobby again.

I slipped inside. This time, an unearthly gray light permeated the space. I saw a ghostly operating theater. Rays that mimicked sunshine streamed in through high windows, illuminating a pair of wooden tables streaked with gray blood and gore. A perfectly clean set of surgeon's instruments rested on a nearby table, and I couldn't help but stare at the ragged blade of the bone saw.

"We'll have to be quick," Jackson said, poking his head through the door that I just closed. "Dr. Hays is coming back, and he doesn't like me."

I knew the feeling. "Pete Marshall is coming, and he doesn't like me, either."

Jackson frowned. "Someone has taken the secretary I told you about," he said, leading me to an empty place near the wall. "This is where it stood."

"So I'm sunk." The murderer had covered his or her tracks. I wasn't going to be of any help to Ellis or Darla or anybody.

Jackson knit his brow. "I can show you what I remember," he offered.

I stared at him for a moment. "What are you saying exactly?"

He rubbed a hand along the back of his neck. "I can create things as I remember them. It's a common enough ability here on the other side." He drew his hand down. "That's why the ghosts here see a field hospital."

Wow. "Okay. How much do you remember?"

He thought about that for a moment. "I can call back the paper she touched, the one I saw. She didn't take out a Bible while I was with her, so I can't help you there."

"So you can only show me things you directly experienced." I'd take what I could get.

I watched him as he narrowed his eyes and began to focus. I held my breath as a ghostly secretary shimmered into view along the wall. It resembled the top half of a writing desk and was made to be portable, I assumed. A mother-of-pearl dove decorated the latch.

"You can touch it," he offered.

"I'm good for now," I said, still getting used to the idea.

He nodded, understanding, and opened it. The top folded down into a writing surface, with cubbies above for stationery and other correspondence. "She opened it like this, then drew out a piece of paper. She became quite agitated and even made phone calls."

Interesting. For some people, yakking on the phone wasn't a big event. But Darla getting worked up about a find right before she died, that was something.

"Whom did she call?" I asked.

He shook his head. "I don't know."

"And you won't be able to show me what you didn't see," I finished for him.

From the fuzzy, faded letters cramming the slots and the barely visible packages stuffed toward the back of the writing surface, I could tell she hadn't worked all the way through it.

"It's generous of you to show me this," I said, moving toward the ghostly vision. "I appreciate your spending so much energy to help me."

Trouble was, the top paper lay facedown. I gathered the courage to pick it up myself. I'd been able to hold one ethereal object before, a locket. It had become part of my world for a brief time before it disappeared. I wondered if the same would happen with the paper.

Physical contact with actual spirits had made for a few experiences I'd rather forget.

I fought my hesitation. I didn't have time to dillydally. I snaked a hand out to touch the document. With a sigh of relief, I realized I could.

The paper felt chilly in my hand, yet it had no weight, no texture. In fact, it felt like nothing at all. I turned it over and read the letterhead: *Leland Herworth Wydell, Importer/Exporter*. I straightened. This had to be the first of the Leland Herworth Wydells, whose collection Virginia had hastily lent to the library yesterday.

I scanned the paper, finding it difficult at times to make out the fading type. I read aloud the subject line at the top. "Declaration of Parentage."

That struck me as exceedingly odd. Everyone around here counted on family Bibles and good old-fashioned gossip to know who belonged to whom. Unless... "Somebody was hiding...another somebody."

The single-spaced, typewritten document was addressed to a woman named Rosa, dated September 6, 1951.

My dearest Rosa,

I was wrong. And I fear in my age and current state of health that any correction I attempt to make to the situation at hand will only cause you and my family pain. So I now declare it to the world that Madeline Angelica Learner, born June 12, 1933, is my oldest child, a Wydell, and the heiress to my estate. Leland Herworth Wydell II, my first and only son, born October 3, 1935, will do well enough on his own. He has had my support in life, as dear Maddie shall have it in death.

Do with this as you will. You always did know best.

Leland H. Wydell

"I don't believe it." The document shook in my unsteady hands. "It didn't happen this way. Leland Herworth Wydell II, Ellis's grandfather, was the heir. He got everything."

Jackson cleared his throat, uncomfortable. "Yet it seems there was another." He shifted from one foot to the other. "It happens from time to time, even in the best families."

Of course it did. Perhaps even more often in the rich families.

I gasped as the document dissolved in my hands as if it had never existed. Only now I knew the truth.

Was Madeline Angelica Learner/Wydell aware of her heritage? I'd never heard of her. She might not even be in Sugarland anymore, if she was still alive.

I froze. Maybe she was. Perhaps Darla knew exactly who that person was and was killed because of it. With the letter gone, the secret would be safe. Safe from everyone except ghosts like Jackson. And me.

The entire fortune was tied up in the Wydell Heritage Trust Fund, which was now under the control of Ellis's parents and the source of their entire fortune: the mansion on the hill, acres of land, millions in assets, and the film production company.

"In my time, Wydell family wills were drawn so that the first child inherits everything," Jackson said.

Mine, too. I remembered my grandmother talking about that. "Leland Wydell II kept it all, leaving his two younger sisters practically destitute." Those two sisters were gone now, as was Leland Wydell II. "But this woman, if she's still alive, should have inherited the entire Wydell fortune."

The ghost nodded. "Her heirs would as well."

If we had this document, the real one, it could change a lot of things around here. Leland Herworth Wydell III, who managed his law firm from his beach house in Malta, would have to come back to the real world. His wife, Virginia Wydell, who'd tried to take everything from me, who had never held a job in her life, who ruled every society board and bake sale from her castle-like home on the hill, the woman who now considered herself a star maker and a dream crusher, would be forced to get a job like the real people.

"This Madeline Angelica would be more than eighty now." Clearly no one in the Wydell family had checked the contents before donating the piece.

Darla had. And she'd been murdered for it.

A chill slid down my spine. My almost-mother-in-law would have a darned good reason to wield a bayonet. So would Ellis's brother Leland IV, the most ruthless judge in three counties. Come to think of it, I wouldn't put it past Beau, either.

How was I going to tell Ellis? I was sure this wasn't what he had in mind when he asked me to search for the truth.

I stood. We needed more. "We need to find someone who saw."

"Bully," Jackson said, rubbing his hands together. He dropped them when he saw me watching. "I don't mean to be insensitive, but I haven't had much to be excited about in the last several decades."

I headed out into the lobby with the ghost on my heels. "What about her?" I asked, pointing at the ghost of the nurse in long skirts. She bent over the same bed as before, whispering to the outline of Private Baker.

"That's Millicent," he said. "She's more of a memory now. I doubt she saw anything." He scanned the room. "The poker players from the 12th Infantry might have. Or the surgeon."

The poker players were a dead end; they couldn't even remember where they'd been last night. "Where's the surgeon?" I asked.

Jackson stiffened. "In the ether for now."

"Gotcha." Frankie had told me about the ether. Near as I could tell, it was an in-between plane where spirits could recharge their batteries and get away from daily life on Earth. "I'll just have to come back."

The union officer lit up at that. "Later tonight, perhaps? I have a fascinating theory on how the child vampire, Claudia, in her heart of hearts did not truly want to grow up."

I was more interested in learning about the ghosts in the library. "That woman, Millicent," I said, watching her glide past the cots in the reading room. "She wanted me to write a letter."

He glanced at me. "Yes. For the dead private. She asks everyone. She's been asking it since the war, only nobody can do it." He turned back to her as she glided among the patients. "She's mostly gone now. It happens. Some ghosts run out of steam. The spirit fades and you're left talking to a memory."

"Is Private Baker still aware?"

He shook his head. "I don't know."

I'd find out. Soon. When I had more time.

"Jackson," a grating voice bellowed, "what are you doing bothering that fine woman? Gregson glided our way, one eye hidden beneath the bandages on his head. He raised his hand to deliver a mock blow.

Jackson shimmered and disappeared.

"Aw," Gregson said, looking to me for support. "See? Used to be when you did that, he'd rage at you and give it a good fight."

"Leave him alone," I told the bloodied officer. "He's a good person."

The private opened his mouth to say something I was sure I wouldn't like when the lock on the front door clicked.

Marshall.

"Damn it, Ellis. You spilled coffee on me."

I made a beeline for the back, Frankie's urn clanking loudly against the keys in my bag. I'd just passed into the rear hallway of the library when I heard the front door creak open.

Faster.

I didn't know if they'd seen me, or if I'd closed the door behind me all the way, but suddenly it struck me through my panic that I was heading straight for that sinister-feeling ghost I'd detected earlier tonight.

There was nothing to do about it. I raced down the hall, down the back stairs, and flipped the lock on the door before I dashed outside.

Chapter Seven

"VERITY, WATCH OUT!" Frankie hollered.

I didn't even see it coming. Could barely hear over the pounding of my blood in my ears as I rammed straight into a frigid wall of air. I gasped, my breath leaving me as I fell into the darkness. Needles of ice stung my face and hands. I hit hard pavement with a bone-rattling crunch. My mind swam, screamed. Energy engulfed me and I heard Frankie curse and gurgle.

"I can't snap you loose. You gotta push through it!" His voice rose in pitch. He sounded far away.

Halos of light glowed in the darkness. I could make out the outline of the parking lot and felt the burn of asphalt on my bloodied palms. It was as if I crouched behind a pane of dimpled glass.

"Go!"

I lurched to my feet and willed my legs to move, setting off on a dead run that turned out to be more like a stumble.

Pain shot through my stomach. I kept moving and wheezed as I broke out of the freezing, draining, soul-sucking space.

The chilly night air felt warm compared to where I'd been. I kept moving, putting more distance between me and...*it*. My vision cleared and I could see the parking lot, the lights, and the trees beyond.

Frankie reappeared inside my car. I ran for him as fast as I could, bent over, fumbling for my keys.

I threw open my door and tossed my bag onto the floor of the passenger side. He looked like death warmed over. "You okay?" I asked. He didn't respond. He just clutched his abdomen. "It still hurts?" I pressed. I'd gone from a screaming pain in my stomach to a dull throb the moment I'd broken out of that haze. His legs were missing and his entire torso flickered like a bad electrical connection.

He grimaced, his fingers digging into his stomach. "You trying to kill me?" he demanded. "Again?"

I shoved my car into gear. "Didn't think that was possible." I whipped the steering wheel around and pulled the car out. "At least we're alive and in one piece." Oh, wait. He wasn't either of those things. "What just happened back there?"

He lay back against the seat, catching his breath. "You ran straight through a powerful ghost and dragged me along for the ride. The poor sucker died slow, shot through the stomach."

"That spirit energy was everywhere." I hit the gas. "There was no way to avoid it."

"Yeah, there was," he groused. "Slow down," Frankie cried out. I thought he was overreacting until a tingling surge whipped down my body. I slammed on the brakes, flinging the contents of my bag out onto the floor and planting Frankie firmly into the passenger-side dash.

"Now look what you did," he said, his head wedged up against the windshield, his shoulder sticking out of the vent. "If I could actually feel physical objects, I'd be in a lot of pain," he griped, melodramatic as usual.

I fought the urge to roll my eyes, seeing as he'd only injured his pride. Sure enough, the gangster faded and reappeared in the seat next to me.

"I wasn't expecting that tingle when your power left me." I touched a foot to the gas once more, lightly this time, if only to appear less conspicuous as we traveled up the side driveway of the church.

Frankie yanked his hat out of my glove box and shoved it back onto his head. "Take it easy next time. It's not like you never borrowed my power before."

"I had a lot on my mind," I said, pulling out as casually as I could for a person driving an avocado-green Cadillac.

Ellis's cruiser sat out in front of the library, with Marshall's car behind it.

At least the streetlight was out right there. Darkness blanketed this portion of the square.

Frankie gave his stomach one last rub. "And don't run through any more powerful spirits while you're connected to me." He shuddered. "That one hurt. Makes me squirmy, too, like I'm wearing somebody else's undershorts."

Yes, well, it had been even worse for me. "I felt like I was freezing to death. My mind didn't work right." I'd gotten a mild, icky, watery feeling the one time I'd accidentally touched Frankie. This had been a thousand times worse.

I waited to flip on my headlights until we'd made the turn onto Main Street, glad to see it mostly deserted. Frankie rested an elbow on the window frame and stared out at the shops we passed.

"So how do I avoid run-ins like that?" I asked, exiting past the first row of shops, taking the back way through the residential neighborhoods as we wound our way home.

This particular street dated to the 1940s. Frankie continued to stare out the window for a minute before he turned to me.

"You ever just get a bad feeling about a spot?"

"Sometimes," I said, "even before I met you."

He nodded. "Everybody does." He removed his hat and slicked his hair back with his fingers. "Take tonight. When we were headed in, you didn't have my power yet and you still didn't like the parking lot by the back door." He replaced his hat, adjusting the brim low. "Even if you don't know why, a haunted death spot just doesn't feel right. Everyone has the ability to pick up on that. If you trust yourself, you know when something's off."

I thought back on the times I'd heeded my instincts, and the times I hadn't. One thing still puzzled me, though. "Tonight, when I was tuned in to your powers, I didn't see a ghost in that spot."

Frankie chewed at his lip. "I didn't, either." I could tell it bothered him. "Whoever it is, that's one powerful bastard."

"We'll avoid him from now on," I said as he settled back into his seat.

He aimed a pointed look my way. "We can sure as hell try."

My phone began to ring, so I pulled out my hands-free headset.

It was Melody. I told her everything that had happened since I saw her last, although I did leave off the part about avoiding Beau. He wasn't important, and besides, I had him handled.

Mostly.

I adjusted my hands-free earpiece and fought with the wire because, well, it was an out-of-date, off-brand garage-sale purchase that was probably going to electrocute me the next time it rained. "I need you to see if you can find anything on a Madeline Angelica Learner, born June 12, 1933. Also anything on Leland Wydell I or a woman named Rosa."

"I'll work on it while I'm home tomorrow." She gave a small sigh. "The library will be closed again. Montgomery is going crazy, although he'll be plenty busy advising that movie director."

I understood my sister. She wasn't sad about the library or Montgomery. She was trying to make sense of what had happened to Darla Grace. We all were.

I was about to tell her that when I noticed Frankie staring at me.

"What?" I prodded.

He straightened in his seat. "What do you want to know about Shifty?"

"Who?" I asked.

Frankie huffed. "Leland Wydell," he clarified, mocking the name. "We called him Shifty. He ran our whiskey operation," he added, as if it were no big illegal deal.

Wait. Frankie had said he was Beau and Ellis's great-great-uncle, which meant... "I've got to go," I told Melody. I'd explain later. I turned to Frankie. He hadn't been with me when I'd found the letter. He'd been too busy goofing off. But the generations lined up. Leland I would have been a contemporary of Frankie's, which meant... "You're related to Leland, aren't you?"

Frankie gave a defensive flinch. "I married his sister, Kate. She was the best getaway driver in six counties." He softened a bit. "Not that it's the only reason I went on the lam with her."

So Leland was in their mob outfit. "Beau always said his great-grandfather was an importer/exporter."

The gangster shrugged. "He was, in a sense. When he wasn't breaking heads."

Nice guy. "I learned tonight that Leland had an older daughter, born two years before his son."

Frankie furrowed his brow. "No, he didn't."

I was about to argue when blue and white police lights lit up my back window.

Frankie whipped his head back to see. "It's the fuzz," he announced. "Hit the gas!"

I yanked my earpiece out, getting tangled in the wire. "We are not getting into a police chase." In fact, I would have pulled up against the curb already if I could just get my cheap hands-free doodad to cooperate. Muttering under my breath, I pulled over in front of the quaint bungalows that lined Cypress Avenue.

Frankie stared at me. "You think Marshall saw you leave the library? You weren't exactly subtle."

"I don't know," I said, my throat tight. I didn't know what to think.

I planted my hands on the steering wheel, but the officer was taking his time. I took a chance and rolled down my window, squinting to see past the glaring lights.

Curtains fluttered in the window of the house to our right and I cringed. Everyone in Sugarland would know by tomorrow I'd been pulled over. Nobody else in town owned a land yacht like mine.

I saw movement behind me in my side mirror and turned as Ellis approached the car. He was alone. I hoped. He leaned outside my window. "Hey, didn't mean to scare you."

Too late. "What are you doing here?" Had something bad happened in the ten minutes since I'd left the library?

Ellis frowned and shook his head. "Marshall called in a deputy to take over." A muscle in his jaw twitched. "He seems to think I might have a conflict of interest."

"I'm so sorry. I tried to be discreet." I didn't know what I'd do if Ellis lost his job over me.

"You were good," he said quickly. He rubbed the back of his neck, his biceps flexing. "It's my mom. We pulled up Darla's phone records. It seems Darla called her from the library late last night."

"Wow." Although I couldn't say I was surprised. Virginia Wydell was knee-deep in the business of glorifying the town and her family name, especially lately. "She could have been calling about Cannonball in the Wall." Then again, the letter Darla found could potentially disinherit the queen of Sugarland. What if Darla showed her hand to the wrong person? Virginia could be cold and calculating. I wouldn't put it past her to say or do something drastic. "What did your mom say?"

"I'm not the one questioning her. Marshall's headed over right now."

Virginia Wydell would have an excuse. She always did. The woman was too crafty to get caught in a simple lie.

"Ellis," I began, resting a hand on his. It was no secret how I felt about his mother. She'd tried to ruin my life and render me homeless. But I hated that he had to suffer like this.

And I really didn't want to make it worse by telling him what I'd found. There was no upside. Ellis would feel terrible. He'd feel obligated to confront his mom, who would know the evidence we were trying to find against her. And that I was behind it. She'd turn it all around on me. No doubt she'd enjoy that part. It wasn't like I had tangible proof.

Still… I sighed. This wasn't about me. Ellis deserved the truth.

"Listen," I said, opening the door. He let me and I leaned next to him against the car. The police lights stung my eyes. "I have something to tell you. You mind turning those off?"

"Safety," he answered, as if he had no choice. "I don't want you to get hurt."

I hoped he meant that in more ways than one.

"Okay," I said. This place wasn't exactly private, but at least no one would be able to hear what we were talking about. I drew a deep breath, trying to decide how to deliver information that might very well alter his life, or at least change the way he viewed his family and where he came from. "I found a witness, someone who saw Darla right before she died. He showed me a declaration of parentage signed by your great-grandfather. Your grandfather wasn't supposed to inherit. He had an illegitimate half sister, born before him, who should have gotten it all."

He stood, stunned. "My great-grandfather?"

"It appears he was keeping secrets."

His gaze found the pavement before it shot back to me. "I grant you most of the men in my family don't have the best track record, but are you sure about this?"

"I don't know what to say. I'm only telling you what I saw." He'd asked me to investigate on the other side, and this was what I'd found. "It's on the ghostly plane, so I can't actually show you real, tangible evidence."

Ellis ran a hand through his hair and let out a ragged sigh, but I knew better than to think he doubted me. Ellis had seen enough of Frankie's powers to believe in the other side. He just needed proof in the real world to do anything about it.

"Whoever killed Darla took the letter and most likely the entire antique secretary. Not to mention Darla's record of ever finding it." I hadn't seen anything like it on any of the display tables or in that back room.

He gave a sharp nod. "I'm going home to talk to my mom."

"Do you want to wait at my house until Marshall is done?" It would look bad if he showed up now.

"No," he said, watching me as if he didn't quite know what to think of this, of me.

"I didn't expect to find this," I said simply.

He reached out slowly and took both of my hands in his. "I know." His grip was tight, as if he needed something, some*one* to hold on to. "My mother may be a lot of things, but she's not a murderer."

I hoped he was right. "There has to be more to it." Although whether or not more information would implicate his mother, well, I didn't care to speculate.

I'd only told him about a ghostly revelation, a missing letter, and the fact that someone in his family had motive to kill. On the whole, he was taking it rather well.

He gave my hands a final squeeze. "I'll call you later."

"Do," I said, but he was already walking away.

Damn. I shoved my hands into my pockets. I hated to be the one to tell him, but I owed him the truth, even if it did hurt him. Even if he was on his way to warn his mother.

Of course he wouldn't think she did it. Even if she had cause.

Virginia Wydell might be a conniving matriarch with a mean streak a mile wide, but she was still his mother.

And I'd chosen to date not one, but two of her sons.

I didn't know who was crazier.

"Come on," I said to Frankie as I slid back into my car, my stomach twisting, and not because of a ghost this time. Ellis had pulled out, but now he waited just ahead of me, to make sure I was safely in my car and back on the road before he left. I certainly didn't need him worrying about me.

Frankie leaned his arm on the door, completely unaffected by the fact that his elbow stuck out the closed window. "You told that mug everything he needed to warn your mortal enemy," he said, glaring at me.

"What was I supposed to do?" He deserved to know.

"Hmm…let me think," he said, laying heavy on the sarcasm. "You could have lied, changed the subject, fallen and whacked your head against the pavement. Any of those would have been preferable." He let out a long-suffering sigh. "If I'm gonna partner with you, I gotta know you got some ruthlessness."

"Then you're out of luck," I told him. We hit the end of the street and made a left toward the main drag home. "I *am* glad you care," I added. For what it was worth.

That drew a scowl from the gangster. "Don't flatter yourself."

"Can you tell me anything else about your brother-in-law, Leland?"

"Lots to make you blush, but nothing about a long-lost kid."

Then he'd hidden his secret well. All right. We'd get to the bottom of this. "I'll need you tomorrow."

"And I need you to unground me."

"We're working on it," I told him.

Frankie ran a hand down his face. "Look at me, woman. I have no legs."

"True." But his thighs were starting to come back into focus.

"I need time to recover from the energy drain." He leaned back against the seat. "You took a lot out of me tonight."

"The good news is I don't need your power," I said as we bumped along the dusty back roads toward home. "I just need you to go with me to Virginia Wydell's house and snoop around while I visit."

That got his attention. He eyed me from under the brim of his hat. "You're going to sip sweet tea with the dame that hung you on the hook after her cad son pawed your sister?"

"That's the one," I said cheerily.

He huffed and returned his attention out the window. "I've shot people for less."

I had no doubt.

Trouble was, I hadn't spoken to Virginia since my almost-reception. Hmm...although that wasn't too sticky of an issue. "I'll figure out what to say. I just need to get your urn into the house so that you can look around and tell me if she's hiding that secretary or the letter. We need tangible proof. And I'd like you to keep an eye out for that Bible the Jackson ghost talked about."

Then we'd tip off the police and I'd be responsible for Beau and Ellis's mom being charged with murder.

And possibly disinheriting them.

And giving their childhood home and possessions to an unknown half aunt or perhaps even her heirs.

I gripped the steering wheel harder. I couldn't think that way. If Virginia did it, she'd brought a murder charge upon herself. And if there was another heir, then that person deserved to be recognized. I was only trying to do what was right, to find the truth, and to offer some justice to poor Darla Grace.

Frankie shook his head. "I gotta give you credit. When you do something, you don't do it halfway."

I didn't know if that was a compliment or not.

"Better be the same for me," he added as we worked our way up the long drive to my house. I wasn't sure what he meant until he disappeared from my passenger seat and reappeared near the kiddie pool in my yard. I parked at the back of the house and walked over to join him.

"It's separating pretty good," he called.

I clicked on my flashlight. No, it wasn't. It was a pool of mud. "Give it time," I told him. "The experiment says to wait at least twenty-four hours." Who was I to challenge fifth-grade science?

"Gotcha," he said. "I got a good feeling about this."

"Me too," I lied. We might as well hope.

Frankie appeared tired all of a sudden, and I could tell he was preparing himself for a nice rest in the ether.

"Take care of yourself," I said, watching him disappear. "And remember, I need you back first thing in the morning."

"You're sure bossy tonight," he muttered.

"Frankie," I began. He knew this was important.

"Don't get all balled up." His voice drifted over me. "I'll be there."

And then he was gone completely.

I backtracked to my car to retrieve his urn, along with the extra flashlight batteries. Then I slung my bag over my shoulder and headed for the house.

Lucy scratched on the other side of the kitchen door, no doubt excited to see me.

As I inserted my key into the lock, I saw something far less welcoming propped up against the bottom of the door:

a gold foil box of Godiva chocolates, with a white envelope tucked under the gold elastic bow. Scrawled across the front, in Beau's handwriting: *My one and only Verity.*

Ha. *One and only.* No doubt because I was the only Verity he knew.

My poor little skunk began to grunt on the other side of the door, shoving her nose into the crack at the bottom as if she could crawl straight through and onto my lap.

"I'm coming, sweetie." I picked up the package, fully intending to open the door, when I saw a silver picture frame underneath. "Of all the..." It held a snapshot of Beau and me together. Laughing.

We had been dating for only a few months when it was taken. He'd surprised me with a birthday party in the park.

Later, I'd learned his mother had planned it.

Lucy let out a high-pitched squeal.

"I'm coming." I popped open the box of chocolates and ate a caramel-filled one as I opened the door. No sense wasting good candy.

The minute I stepped through the doorway, a happy skunk assaulted me. I tossed all my junk onto the counter and bent to show her some snuggly love while she turned in circles and whipped her tail up and down. She crawled halfway up my chest as I rubbed her belly and let her snort to her heart's content. "I'm sorry," I said, enjoying her soft, warm fur as well as the taste of the chocolate. "I didn't mean to be gone so long. I know you don't like being alone."

I picked her up and she immediately wanted down. Lucy was a lap skunk, but she had to be in the mood to be carried.

I let her go and put the chocolates up in the cabinet. The card went into the trash. Then I considered the picture. It belonged in the fireplace, along with a few logs and some lighter fluid. The frame, however, appeared to be solid silver, antique, with mother-of-pearl butterflies in the corners. I might be able to sell it for some pocket cash.

Then it hit me. I'd seen that frame before. It belonged on Virginia Wydell's grand piano.

Tomorrow would be the perfect time to return it. Yes, I'd have to tell her that her son was courting me again, but it was better for her to find out from me than from Beau. Who knew what he might say? And besides, the truth should offer enough fireworks for Frankie to search the whole house twice over. Maybe even host a craps game.

If I'd only known how right I was. And how unpredictable Virginia Wydell could be.

Chapter Eight

BY THE NEXT morning, Frankie's legs had come back all the way to his ankles. He'd be getting his feet back soon.

We drove to the west side of town and down the old mill road. Ellis was still working on opening up a restaurant on some property out that way. I doubted he'd gotten much done in the last week or two. I slowed when we passed the stacked white stone wall near the entryway.

A large brick building stood at the end of a narrow dirt road. Tall green-painted windows looked out from the first and second floors, sheltered under red brick arches. Faded letters, hand-painted in white on the brick, read "Southern Spirits since 1908."

"You miss that place?" Frankie asked, leaning to see past me. "I'd thought you'd be hitting the gas."

"I miss them," I said, referring to the friendly ghosts we'd met, not the run-ins with the poltergeist. Although I supposed that had worked out in the end.

I steered the land yacht up the twisting road along the river bluff until we came to a private driveway blocked by ornate iron gates with the letter *W* emblazoned in stylish monogram-style script. Ah, the family homestead.

A black box on a pole stood vigil on the driver's side. I trundled my rickety roll-down window all the way open and pushed the red button on the call box. "Verity Long to see Virginia Wydell."

I hadn't rung in advance to tell her I was coming. I was afraid she'd make an excuse not to see me. Which still could happen.

The machine clacked with static. "One moment," a man's voice drawled.

I planted my hands on the large green steering wheel and glanced at Frankie. "Are we close enough for you to go on up there and take a look, even if I don't get in?"

He squinted, as if he could see all the way up the tree-lined driveway to the house. "Too big a property. If this doesn't work, how do you feel about breaking and entering?"

Absolutely not. I didn't know anything about sneaking or spying. And if we did manage to slink our way into the house and got caught, with my luck Ellis would be the one to have to come arrest me.

I was saved as the gates slowly began to open.

Whew.

"It's not like it would be hard to break into this place," I said, now that I knew I didn't have to. "Over the fence, easy peasy." I gave a shrug. "I could do it if I had to."

The gangster dipped his chin and regarded me. "You're a terrible liar."

Perhaps he'd simply had more practice.

I drove straight through the gates the very moment I was sure my car would make it. No sense giving them time to change their minds.

Towering cypress trees lined the meandering drive that wound past small, carefully tended gardens of native purple passionflowers and American beautyberry.

The Wydells had owned their property even longer than our family had lived in my home. This estate had been in the family dating back to the land grants in the early 1800s.

"Feel like you're coming home?" I asked Frankie.

I'd gotten his urn after Beau had ventured up into the family attic and thought he stumbled on a cheap yet historical-looking vase. He'd given it to me in lieu of something fun and useful. Not that Frankie wasn't useful. Or fun…sometimes.

The gangster shifted in his seat. "I always came up the side drive. We had a hideout in the carriage house, but it was mainly just a place to stash loot and get schnockered."

We pulled past the richly blooming blue and white hydrangea bushes that crowded the circle drive and scattered flower petals over the custom brick.

The white plantation-style house, with its upper and lower porches and towering Palladian windows, had been designed to appear as if it had always been here. In truth, the place had gone up in 1982, after Virginia married into the family. Word had it, she'd been instrumental in razing the family's original home and replacing it with this overblown version of Tara.

She'd also gotten a special permit to bulldoze the old-growth trees on the back of the property. That way, the house looked down on the river, as well as the entire town of Sugarland.

"Ready, Freddy?" The gangster's urn clanked in my bag as I walked up to the porch.

"Don't call me Freddy."

A grin tickled my lips despite the situation, or maybe because of it. I had to admit I liked having Frankie along. I'd barely touched the brass door knocker when Sissy the maid opened the front door, her hair drawn tight into a bun, her round face welcoming.

"Why, hello," she said in a deep melodious voice, acting surprised although she couldn't have been. "It's wonderful to see you," she added, with a twinkle in her eye.

That last part felt real. I'd always liked Sissy and never understood why she stayed working for a woman like Virginia Wydell.

Then again, I mused as she ushered me inside, I didn't know much about the maid. She went out of her way to dodge any kind of social overtures. All I'd ever gathered was that she lived two towns over. And thanks to Melody, I knew she was a graduate student in sociology at a very expensive private college. Perhaps that was the reason she put up with this place.

"How have you been?" I asked, wanting to be friendly and unsure of what else to say.

She gave a slight hum in response as I entered the marble foyer. "It's been a while."

Yes, it had.

The last time I'd set foot inside this house had been as Beau's fiancée the day before our wedding. So much of my life had changed since then.

I'd owned stylish clothes; I'd had a job. Now I was very aware of the hole in the skirt pocket of my pink flowered dress, even if no one else could see it.

"You make yourself comfortable in the parlor," Sissy said, directing me to the richly decorated room on the right. "Mrs. Wydell will be down shortly."

"Thank you," I said as she nodded and left, her white sneakers snicking against the polished marble floor of the hallway leading back to the kitchen.

I sat on the edge of the velvet settee that had been in the family since men and women rode in buggies and took afternoon tea. An antique phonograph graced the window overlooking the drive. A grand piano stood proudly nearby, decorated with gleaming silver picture frames, just as I remembered it.

Perhaps I should have wrapped Beau's frame in plain white drawing paper, made it look nice.

Nothing to be done for it now.

Besides, I refused to feel cheapened just because everything about me didn't gleam like the carved Victorian tea table in front of me.

I was here to do a job, plain and simple.

"Frankie?" I murmured, lowering my bag to the floor. His urn clanked against the picture frame.

"What?" His disembodied voice sounded in my ear. I jumped and nearly spilled the whole kit and caboodle.

"Stop it," I whispered. It would not do to have a burial urn topple out of my bag during a social call.

The gangster shimmered into view, standing in the middle of the tea table, his hands on his hips. "Sure. Okay, I'll refuse to answer you from now on."

He knew that wasn't what I'd meant. I glanced around the room, paying particular attention to the arched doorway leading to the stairs. "Go," I whispered, motioning him upstairs. "Look for the secretary." The sooner the better. Every second he spent trying to find that evidence was one I'd eventually have to endure making chitchat with Virginia Wydell.

Frankie made a face. "She's still in her bedroom."

That didn't matter. "It's not like she can see you."

Frankie recoiled. "I'm not going to be able to concentrate if I'm worried about her running into me."

"Then start in the attic. Work your way down."

The gangster grinned and let out a low chuckle. "You don't know nothing about stealing stuff, do you?" He shook his head and began to explain as if I were a toddler. "Most of the time, people hide the goods in the closet or under the bed."

"Well…" I waved a hand. "Rule out the rest while we wait."

He shrugged and began floating upward. "How about I slip her a cold draft on the neck? For you."

Before I could answer, he disappeared through the coffered ceiling.

I arranged the skirt of my dress on the settee, my only company the imposing men in the portraits lining the wall. I couldn't help but notice them as I kept an eye on the stairs. The paintings of the Wydell patriarchs hung in heavy gold frames and went back seven generations. No telling which of the stern faces belonged to dear old Leland I. The entire window-lined room felt like a shrine to the Wydell legacy.

Any time, Virginia would make her grand entrance.

It shouldn't take long, especially if Frankie gave her an icy nudge.

Then, as if on cue, Virginia Wydell began to descend the grand staircase. Her gold bracelets clicked against the banister; her perfectly rounded and polished nails skimmed the wood. She wore immaculately tailored tan trousers, a gold belt, and a tasteful green-and-white polka-dot silk shirt, top collar button undone, so as to make it casual.

She'd slicked her perennially blond hair back into its usual bob and wore the overlarge pearl earrings that her great-great-grandmother had famously buried under an apple tree in the yard during the war.

Virginia, like her home, held a timeless, museum-quality perfection that couldn't be matched in the real world, at least not in mine.

Her appraising gaze slicked over me and I knew I was judged unworthy even before she crossed the room and wrapped me in a bony hug that lingered like the scent of her expensive perfume. "Sugar." Her voice was warm, her eyes cold. "How sweet of you to visit."

We both sat on the grand settee, as far from each other as possible.

"Of course," I said, smoothing my skirt, vowing to get through this without mentioning the house I'd almost had to sell, the failed wedding, or her attempt to destroy me. Virginia liked seeing me out of control. I wouldn't give her that advantage. Never again. "I'm glad you could take time out for me," I said sweetly, "given how busy you must be with the Cannonball in the Wall events."

"Now, dear"—she brought a hand to her chest—"you're not trying to sweet-talk me for a part in my movie, are you?" She absently adjusted her earring. "If you were a member of the family, that would be one thing, but I'm afraid that ship has sailed."

Frankie needed to hurry up and find that secretary.

"I'm not an actress," I said candidly, wishing I simply had enough talent to appear calm and unaffected. Instead, I'd felt my cheeks flush and my heart speed up the minute she'd walked into the room. "I have to admit, though, this isn't a purely social call. I have something I think you'll want."

She raised a brow, as if she couldn't imagine what that might be.

I pressed on. "Beau contacted me after the reenactment this Saturday." The wrinkles around her thin lips deepened at my revelation. I should let her worry. I should let her rush to the phone and call Beau the minute I left the house. But Ellis didn't deserve that kind of drama. For his sake, I had to make one thing clear. "I did *not* encourage Beau in the slightest. He and I are not seeing each other again."

She clucked, as if I'd said something amusing. "I wouldn't presume he would take you back." She leaned closer, as if we were sharing a secret. "Don't try, dear. It'll just make you look cheap."

With the will of a saint, I kept my posture perfect and my expression neutral. I had my dignity and my pride.

"It isn't me doing the chasing," I corrected. I slipped the picture frame from my simple brown bag. "Beau left this on my doorstep last night," I added, offering it to her.

She took it as if I'd handed her a dirty sock. "Isn't this lovely?" she asked, with about the same enthusiasm. Beau's actions had disturbed her, even if she refused to show it. She turned the gleaming frame over in her hands, as if she didn't even notice the smiling picture of me with her son. "The poor boy must have been rooting through my

Goodwill boxes in the garage." She placed it on the edge of the tea table, facedown. "I'll see that this makes it back outside."

Before I could respond, Sissy entered the room, carrying a tray. "Here we are," Virginia said, directing the maid to place it on the table in front of us. "Refreshments. Although I'd understand if you didn't want to partake. The past few months have done quite a number on your figure." She made a point of staring at my hips. "Of course, it could just be that dress."

Frankie had better be finding the secretary, Virginia's signed confession, and the Hope diamond.

I kept my chin high. My dress was lovely, even if it wasn't expensive. "These look quite delicious, thank you," I said, reaching for a pastry and a china plate. I'd never be skinny, but I wasn't fat, either. And I wasn't about to be shamed out of the only good thing I might get during this visit.

Virginia appeared quite satisfied as she poured us both a cup of tea.

I bit into the pastry and tasted the sharp tang of rhubarb filling. I made a pleasant sound and forced myself to swallow. Rhubarb made me break out in a rash. Virginia knew it quite well. Too bad for her, that little taste should only make me itch a little.

She handed me a cup, truly pleased this time. "I only had two left. I told Sissy we *had* to serve them for your visit."

I tasted the Earl Grey, letting the bite of it take away some of the sting of the rhubarb. "You shouldn't have," I said, meaning it.

She sipped from her cup. "Well, you are a very special visitor."

At that moment, Frankie's head popped through the floor between the tea table and the settee. His hair was mussed, as if he'd been running his fingers through it. "It's not upstairs, not in the attic or the basement." He made a show of pushing himself up through the floor, as if he couldn't simply float. "Hmm..." He gave the living room a once-over. "There's not too many places to hide it in here."

I narrowed my eyes at him, as if he could read my thoughts. Which he couldn't, thank goodness. *Keep looking.*

Virginia placed a chilly hand on my arm. "Are you all right, dear?" she asked, clearly hoping I was about to have an allergic-to-rhubarb reaction.

"I'm fine," I said, agitated as the ghost floated over to the grand piano and stuck his head inside. As if that's where we'd find the missing document.

Virginia set her untouched pastry plate on the table and took up her tea again. "I did want to ask you about that unpleasantness at the library yesterday evening." She sipped from her china cup. "I hope it wasn't too traumatic when you found that woman dead."

Why? Was she hoping I hadn't gotten a chance to talk to Darla and ask about what she found?

"It was a shock," I told her honestly. And speaking of the case, "I hear Darla Grace called you shortly before."

She clucked as if that were the most interesting thing I had to say. "Darla wanted to talk about the luncheon," she said, lowering her voice, probably lying through her teeth. "I'm head of the Cannonball in the Wall committee. It's only appropriate, considering my family's contribution. To think, her last words may have been to praise all the hard work that I do."

"I find it hard to believe she called about a fund-raiser," I stated, inviting no debate. "In my experience if someone calls at three in the morning, it is usually with bad news." Like you're about to lose all of the fortune that has propped up your ego for the last forty years.

Virginia paled slightly. "Oh, it was unfortunate—she discovered a terrible catering error and had to tell me about it right away." She took a long sip of tea and I swore she seemed to be hiding behind her cup. "You knew Darla, the poor woman could never let go of something."

"Like a really good scandal?" I remarked.

She cleared her throat and set her cup down so hastily that it clanked hard on the saucer. "I wouldn't know. I never suffer busybodies, and gossip is so tasteless." She straightened her already rigid shoulders. "Is it true you found her beneath the display tables?"

She couldn't be serious. "I don't think Ellis would want me to say."

I watched as Frankie flickered out into the yard, probably checking the carriage house. I was glad he had enough range from the house to inspect the property. I focused on that, and not the fact that my arm had begun to itch. It was too soon for a rhubarb reaction. I couldn't let Virginia get to me.

"Ellis?" She sniffed, drawing back. "I don't see what Ellis has to do with this."

Virginia Wydell never had forgiven her middle son for pursuing a modest career in law enforcement, and it seemed as if she still clung to denial. He was the black sheep for not toeing the family line, for not playing her games. The way I saw it, Ellis was her greatest achievement.

She waited for me to speak, no doubt hoping the silence would prod me.

Now I understood why she'd let me into her house. "I'm sorry," I said, sweet as a rhubarb pastry. "I don't think I can give you any more detail than that without jeopardizing the investigation."

Her features clouded before she chirped out a laugh. "Look at you, practically a junior detective. Your grandmother would be so proud." She drew the neck of her blouse to the side in a casual gesture and I saw she was wearing my grandmother's cross.

My grandfather had presented the delicate necklace to my grandmother as a wedding gift. I'd always loved it. I'd sit in her lap as a little girl and run my fingers over the gold and silver filigree. She'd gifted it to me on my eighteenth birthday, right before I'd left for college. Said she couldn't think of anyone who would care for it more, treasure it forever. It was my responsibility. My legacy. And I'd sold it to Virginia Wydell as part of my last-ditch effort to avoid losing my family home.

I fought the urge to rip it off her throat.

She wanted me to lose it, to fly off the handle. Virginia Wydell wanted nothing more than to break me. Too bad for her, I was made of stronger stuff.

No. I'd never resort to violence, but in that moment I vowed to get my cross back. I had absolutely no idea how, but I would. I'd take Virginia Wydell down a peg if it was the last thing I did.

She saw it in my face and I could tell my pain gave her energy. Power. She ran her fingers over the silver chain that my grandmother had lovingly polished every Sunday. "I wore this especially for you." She tucked it back under the collar of her cheerful polka-dot blouse. "All told, it's a bit flimsy for my taste. But I thought you might like to see it again."

"Tell me," I said, taking in the antique phonograph on the antique table, the tea set in front of us, the chandeliers dripping with cut crystal. "How much of this is your family history and how much of it have you...acquired?"

"Don't smirk. It'll give you wrinkles. Besides, it doesn't matter. All of this is mine now."

"For now," I agreed.

Virginia lost her plastic smile. "Just because you can no longer be a part of this legacy doesn't mean you should mock it."

She was a greedy parasite and positively ruthless. "I'm just wondering how far you'd go to preserve it." Her precious legacy and her fortune.

Her gaze chilled and for a moment, she revealed the true depth of her ambition and her pride. "No one builds a legacy like this...without getting a little blood on their hands." Her lips twitched at my obvious surprise. "That's something you never quite learned," she drawled, punctuating every word. "For love and family—it's always worth it."

I stared at her. *She might as well have admitted it.*

Unbelievable. Only Virginia would have the gall to tease me with the truth, to play this as if it were a game instead of...murder.

"Are you all right?" she asked, seeming to enjoy my shock. "Could you go for another rhubarb tart?"

"I'm fine," I said, through gritted teeth. I knew who and what I was up against. Now I just had to prove Virginia had stabbed poor Darla Grace in the back. With any luck, Frankie was digging up the evidence right now.

The doorbell rang, and for the first time, I saw a chink in her carefully placed armor. We'd been so busy doing battle, both of us had neglected to notice the documentary crew unpacking a van in the circle drive.

I took advantage of her distraction to look for Frankie. I didn't see him anywhere.

"I'm afraid I must let you go," Virginia murmured, eyes on the driveway as Sissy answered the door.

Not yet, at least not until Frankie found the evidence we needed.

Montgomery entered first, twisting his head this way and that, looking for Virginia, not sparing a glance for the maid. "There you are," he said, opening his arms wide as he approached us. He wore one of his signature tweed jackets with a blue striped bow tie. She didn't move to embrace him, but rather let him pay homage to her on the settee. He bent and made a show of kissing her hand. "The crew wasn't interested in my weather report from the day of the battle. And we ran through the actual mechanics of the cannon shot to the library rather quickly." He straightened, his gaze roving the grand room, startling a bit when it landed on me. "They were anxious to come film the family manor."

Dating all the way back to 1982.

I snickered and tried to care when Virginia shot me a dirty look.

"By all means," she said to her pet historian. "I'll count on you to point out our family's ties to significant events. I don't want to brag."

Too late.

"Hi, Montgomery," I said, since he hadn't addressed me yet.

The historian turned to me. "Hello," he said, as if I'd popped up out of thin air. "I didn't expect to see you here."

Yes, well, one should never underestimate a Southern girl. "I didn't expect to be here," I admitted, "but I had a few things to discuss with Mrs. Wydell. The Cannonball in the Wall Festival is deadly important to her." That earned me a biting glare from Virginia.

"Er, yes," Montgomery said, flustered at the obvious tension in the room. He rubbed a hand over the back of his neck. "I'm hopeful we can get things back on track. That was quite a morning yesterday," he added, in the understatement of the year. I wondered if Darla had to be dead a hundred years for the historian to care about her.

There was a commotion at the door while Sissy let the film crew into the house and I immediately lost Montgomery's attention. "Come in!" he said, going to them. "You're going to find this fascinating. The history contained in this house cannot be overstated."

Virginia gave a gracious smile when she perhaps should have thrown him a liver treat for good behavior.

That was my cue. I stood and gathered my bag. I'd wait out the rest of Frankie's search from the front seat of my car. "Congratulations again on your documentary and your film."

Virginia nodded, as though she were the queen of England and I was being dismissed.

All right, then. I passed two cameramen and caught the eye of the producer on the way out. Poor man. I gave him a quick, reassuring smile. "Ask to see the carriage house." It was the only original building left. Beau had taken me inside once. "It's pretty neat."

"Wait," he called after me. "Miss, are you going to be on camera with Mrs. Wydell?" He glanced at the queen bee. "If so, we may want to put some makeup on you."

"Oh no." Virginia stood, all grace and manners. "She's not part of the family. She didn't make the cut."

I patted the man on the arm. "Good luck." And with that, I slipped out of the house.

The film was for the sake of Sugarland, I reminded myself as I descended the brick patio steps. This wasn't just about the Wydells.

Only it was.

I climbed into the land boat. Virginia would get hers someday. I had to believe that.

In the meantime, Frankie shimmered into view in the seat next to me.

"You done making chitchat?" he asked, like I'd been in there gabbing over pastries and coffee. "Because I found something."

Chapter Nine

"WHY DIDN'T YOU come get me?" I gasped, starting the engine.

"I was waving to you from the front window," he said, demonstrating. "And on top of the piano. I practically slid down the front hall banister."

"I was distracted." Getting Virginia's tacit confession. And now the evidence. It was almost too much. I punched the gas harder than I'd intended. The green monster shot forward and I had to quickly force the wheel left, lest we end up in a hydrangea bush. "Where was it?" I mean, I'd hoped we'd find the secretary, but I didn't think it was likely. "The smart thing would have been to destroy it."

Leave it to Virginia to get cocky.

Frankie chuckled. "I thought the same thing." He leaned back against the seat. "Maybe we're not so different after all."

"So where did you find it?" We'd inform the police and let them handle it from here on out.

My arms ached as I muscled us down the driveway. I'd never missed power steering more than I did at that moment, but Frankie's discovery gave me plenty of motivation to get away from the Wydell estate. As if I needed more.

"It's in the carriage house," Frankie explained. "We used to hide out in there." He smiled, remembering. "We had this secret room underground, with an entrance under the stairs. I swear nobody's been down there since we dropped our card game and ran out of there after Lemonhead botched that drop in 1933."

It made sense. I'd be willing to bet nobody had been down there except for Virginia Wydell. She didn't think anyone would find her trophy, but she hadn't counted on a sneaky ghost. I wanted to kiss Frankie, to hug him. My stomach quivered and my head swam. I'd hoped this would work out, but part of me hadn't dared think it would be this easy. I gripped the wheel as we lurched over a nasty bump—testing the Cadillac's ancient suspension. "Virginia Wydell is a murderer!"

There. I said it out loud.

Yes, the woman was a vicious Southern belle who would smile while she scratched your eyes out. She massacred reputations and ripped into hearts and souls without a thought. But until she'd admitted having blood on her hands, I'd never let myself fully believe she could stab Darla Grace in the back with a bayonet.

Now we had proof. Especially if her fingerprints were all over that document.

"What are you talking about?" Frankie asked, leaning hard as I maneuvered a tight turn around a bend, narrowly avoiding a small garden. "She tell you that?"

Of course not. No. "She didn't need to tell me. You found the antique secretary, with the letter, on her property. And did it have Darla's notebook in it as well?"

That would prove she had a motive and link her to Darla.

I didn't know if I should call Ellis about this or talk to Marshall first and then talk to Ellis. The police would have to get a search warrant.

Frankie groaned as I hit another dip in the road. "I didn't find no secretary."

"Just the letter?" I pressed.

He shook his head no.

I ground to a stop as we approached the guard gate. "But you said you found it in the carriage house." Maybe he hadn't used the words *letter* or *secretary* exactly. "What kind of proof did you find?"

Maybe I shouldn't have been having a terse conversation with the empty passenger seat of my car. Not with security cameras pointed at me. But we had to get this straight.

Immediately.

Frankie shook his head as the gate slowly opened for us. "When I said I found something, I meant our poker game. From 1933." He grinned broadly. "It was still laid out like it was before we had to get out of Dodge." He leaned toward me, as if this were the good part. "I picked up Silvio the Greek's hand and—bam—he had an extra ace. I knew he was cheating! I told him that night. That bastard owes me fifty bucks!"

"Wait. You were talking about a card game?" I didn't need this from him. Not now. "We're investigating a murder here!"

Frankie furrowed his brow. "And I had a life before I met you. Geez."

Unbelievable. "I thought we had real evidence."

He leaned back against the seat. "You want my help, but you don't care at all that I knew Silvio was a cheat. He brought that ace in from another deck. I know because I marked the cards."

I tried to find it in me to care. "Isn't that cheating?"

Frankie waved me off. "You're missing the point."

I rested my head on the steering wheel as my euphoria drained away. "So you're telling me that's it. An old card game. That's what you found."

"Yeah." He glanced behind us. "You want to go back and swipe the evidence for me? I was thinking we should try. Just in case Silvio's ghost is still around. I fully intend to collect. It's not hard to get down there if you know how. I was gonna take you back, but then you got all excited and went barreling down the driveway like we was being chased. I just figured we were. You know, habit."

Oh, Lordy. "We can't go back in there now. I told the film crew to head that way." Besides, he couldn't spend fifty dollars even if he could track down this Silvio guy. Dazed, I started driving through the gate as it lazily swung open.

"That's okay," Frankie said. "We'll break in later."

I checked for traffic before pulling out onto the old mill road. I'd been so happy, but now my best chance at getting a lead for Ellis had turned out to be a complete dud. "I thought we solved the case."

"No, but after you unground me, and after you help me liberate my card game, I may help you with this murder thing."

"Gee, thanks."

As we drove, the countryside opened up and I saw downtown Sugarland in the distance.

I wouldn't say it out loud. Frankie wouldn't understand. But even after this morning's less-than-stellar results, I believed that our whole initial accident—me dumping the urn, grounding him, us being flung together—had happened for a reason, a higher good, if you will. Too many positive things had come of it for me to think otherwise, from finding justice for that poor girl a few weeks ago, to giving us a clue about who might have killed Darla Grace.

But Frankie did have issues. I might be able to help, as long as I did it gently. The gangster wasn't the most touchy-feely person on the planet.

I tightened my fingers on the wheel. "Frankie, do you want to visit your death spot?"

He'd never wanted to tell me where he died, or what had happened that night. The only clue I had was the raw bullet hole in his forehead. I respected his need for privacy, but I was starting to suspect that it came with a lot of pain. The gangster might feel a lot better if he shared the load.

"You don't want anything to do with what happened to me," he said, shutting down. "I don't even know everything that went down before, you know"—he put a finger to his forehead—"boom."

"I'm so sorry."

He shrugged and retreated from me to stare out the window.

I waved at a passing car driven by one of my mom's old church friends.

When Frankie showed no sign of wanting to continue our exploration into his past, I took mercy and switched back to where we'd started in the first place.

"Did you search everywhere you could for that declaration of parentage?" It would be easier to hide than an entire secretary.

He rested a hand over his eyes, appearing tired all of a sudden. "It's not there. I looked into every nook and cranny in that pile of bricks, and the carriage house." He smirked. "Saw more than I ever wanted to see of dame Wydell's personal life. Whatever you do, don't look in the nightstand drawer."

I couldn't help but chuckle. "Perish the thought." My blinker gave a loud *click-clock, click-clock* as I made a right onto Jackson Boulevard. It skirted south around the main part of town and back toward my house. "That document has to be somewhere on the Wydell property." I didn't know where else Virginia would hide it.

I could feel the gangster's gaze on me. "Unless she didn't do it."

"She's the best lead we have." And she was more than capable.

"Then we'll just have to figure out someplace else to look." The gangster gazed out the window at the bare trees dropping the last of their leaves.

I thought about it the rest of the way home—where else Virginia could have stashed the evidence. If she still had it anymore.

I was still thinking about it when I ground to a stop in my driveway.

"Verity," Frankie said, his face coming straight through my windshield at me. I startled. I'd thought he was in his seat. "The experiment is finished." He reappeared next to the kiddie pool as I hurried out of the car. "See?"

"Right," I said, rubbing a hand over my face. I joined him at the edge of the muck-filled plastic toy, and sure enough, a thin layer of ash appeared to be floating on top.

"This is good," I said, grinning at him.

"Get the net," he ordered, following me as I walked over to where I'd left it by the hose. "Get both nets."

"Hold on," I told him. I needed the Tupperware. And some towels from the bathroom. "It's not going to disappear while I go get what I need."

I'd never seen Frankie this excited. He practically hummed with it. "But you will get me separated, won't you?"

Now was as good a time as any to find out.

Chapter Ten

I KNELT BY the kiddie pool while Frankie eyed me expectantly. I'd laid out a large Tupperware bowl and had a fish net in hand. Gently—expertly, I daresay—I skimmed the net over the top of the sludge-filled pool.

Flaky bits of ash stuck to the net, and when I'd gotten enough, I emptied them into the bowl. Sort of. "I still think I should put water in here so I can rinse the net."

Frankie watched over my shoulder. "The kid didn't say to do that."

Bits of ashes stuck to my fingers as I rubbed them up against the bowl. "The kid got a C on this project."

"C for complete," the gangster reasoned.

I glanced back at him. "You didn't pay a lot of attention in school, did you?"

He winked. "I lost interest after I learned how to count money."

Typical. I scooped some more, emptied some more.

"Use both nets," Frankie coached.

"This is barely working with one," I told him. It was a two-handed job.

By late afternoon, my back had started to ache and my knees were stiff from kneeling. I stood when Lauralee's red Ford Focus rolled into my back drive. Frankie groaned.

"Don't worry," I said, careful not to upset our Tupperware bowl. "I'm just taking a little break."

I crossed the yard and waved to her. She got out of her car, toting a brown paper take-out bag. "How'd they like the pulled pork?" I asked.

She broke into a grin. "It was so neat being on set. All the actors were so nice. And then Leon Garber, who will be the next George Clooney, this I promise you...he said my pulled pork was the best he's ever had. I got so nervous I couldn't say anything back."

"Your cooking speaks for you," I told her as she handed me the bag. "What's this?"

"Fried chicken and biscuits," she said with a touch of pride. "I'm on my way to set up dinner service."

"You don't have to feed me," I protested, appreciating it all the same. My stomach growled just smelling the spices in the breading.

"But I want to feed you. I might even be able to hire you next week."

"To work for Virginia Wydell?" I balked.

"Think of it as working for the good of Sugarland. Or helping me. The job's only going to get crazier once they cast all the extras and start shooting the battle." She fanned herself in mock excitement, then turned her attention to my science experiment. "What do you have going on here?"

I'm ashamed to say I considered lying. Lauralee didn't know anything about my Frankie problem, and I didn't feel like burdening her now. But this must look awfully strange.

"I think I might have a ghost," I said, in the understatement of the year. "I went online to see how to release it and...this happened."

"I can see you're trying." She planted her hands on her hips and surveyed the damage. "But if you want to banish a ghost, you need a psychic."

"Really?" How did she know so much? "You've never been haunted, have you?"

She gave me a sidelong look. "Remember that cook at my work with the haunted lawn mower?" She nodded as I began to vaguely recall. Lauralee had a lot of crazy work stories. "Psychic cleared it right up."

Frankie shimmered into view behind Lauralee. "This is great," he said, wide-eyed.

"Then there's the waitress at work who's psychic," Lauralee continued. "She did a séance once in the parking lot and I swear we all saw these little flickering lights."

"Could be fireflies," I suggested.

Lauralee and Frankie both frowned at me. "What?" I asked. I obviously believed in ghosts, but that didn't mean I had to fall for every wild story. Besides, psychics cost money I didn't have.

"What's your game?" Frankie ground out. "You afraid it might work?"

I sighed. "I think I have to give this science fair project a chance," I said, realizing how sad it sounded.

Lauralee gave a slight *tsk* at the mess in my yard. "My waitress friend is looking for a logo for her fortune-telling business. I could talk to her for you."

"That would be lovely," I said, mainly to get Frankie off my case.

"Great, then," my friend said, as if that solved things. She gave me a nice, long hug. "I've got to go. Enjoy your supper."

"I will," I said, letting her go, "thanks to friends who don't know when to stop."

She grinned at that and got back in her car. I waved to her as she drove away, ignoring Frankie, who stood watching me.

"I like the idea of bringing in an expert," he said.

I returned to our backyard experiment. "I seriously doubt she's ever dealt with anything like this before." The sun would begin to go down soon. We had about a handful of ash from the entire pool of water. Not enough to even justify one of the measuring cups.

I took the Tupperware container with what we assumed were bits of Frankie. "Let's hope this does it," I suggested. "We'll return these ashes to your urn, and maybe we won't even have to worry about the psychic."

Frankie frowned. "It doesn't look like all the ashes."

Truth be told, it didn't. I remembered dumping a lot more into the rosebushes. There had been at least three solid inches of ash in that urn.

We returned to the kitchen and I used my funnel to guide what we'd scooped into Frankie's urn. The ash clung in wet clumps, and it took some pounding of the urn on my counter and some nudging with my finger, but we transferred what we had into the urn.

The gangster stood, hands at his sides, as if he were unsure of what to do next. I shared a glance with him. I knew the feeling.

The magnitude of the moment weighed on me as I placed the urn on the counter. This was it. "Okay. Try to leave."

He wet his lips and gave a quick nod. "Right." He adjusted his Panama hat. "This is only my afterlife we're talking about."

My stomach went a little hollow. If this were truly it...I'd miss him. I hated to admit it, but I'd kind of gotten used to the jerk.

He locked eyes with me. "If this works, I'll come back and say good-bye."

It wouldn't be the same as having him here. But I had no right to hold him back anymore. He deserved to be free.

I gave him a weak smile and a nod. "Good luck," I said as he disappeared.

Chapter Eleven

OH, MY WORD. Frankie was gone. We'd actually done it. I let out a small laugh, then a bigger one, giddy, amazed...and a little sad.

Frankie was gone.

He'd promised to return for a final good-bye, but as I looked over my empty kitchen, I wondered if he would. He wasn't exactly the most reliable person on the planet. And he'd been trapped here for the last month and a half.

My eyes grew a little glassy. I was going to miss that jerk.

"Don't cry any tears of joy yet, princess," a dry voice said from behind me.

"Frankie?" I turned to find him hovering near my kitchen sink, arms crossed.

"I didn't get no farther than the driveway."

Oh. Shoot. "That's better than before, though. Right?"

He looked at me like I had two heads. "No. Why are you always okay with the fact that I can't leave your property? Science is a crock."

The way we'd done it in the backyard? Yes.

"We did make some progress," I said, trying to see the bright side. "We do have more of you in the urn." At least I hoped that was Frankie. "It will give us more to work with when we try again. And I do want to unground you," I promised. "I really do."

"You keep saying that." He removed his hat and placed it on the counter. Actually, it hovered about an inch above. "But what's the plan?"

Oh, gee. "Let me think." Perhaps Melody could do a search.

He let out a huff. "I say we call the psychic."

"Really?" I hadn't pegged him as the psychic type. "You believe in that?"

He stiffened. "There's all kinds of hokum I can't explain," he shot back, "like how I ended up stuck with you."

Charming.

"All right," I said, notching up my chin, refusing to let him get to me. "Let's do it."

I called Lauralee. When she didn't answer, I left a message while Frankie watched, fuming. Because his bad attitude would certainly help get things done. And then I clicked over to my voice mail and fielded seven messages from Beau.

This day was just getting better and better.

You know what? I couldn't do a thing about the dead gangster in my kitchen, but right now, I was going to put an end to Beau's insane attempt to win me back. I gathered up my courage, punched in his number, and prepared to lay out the facts in no uncertain terms.

Instead, I got his voice mail.

"This is Beau Wydell. You know what to do," he drawled.

I certainly did.

"Beauregard Buford Wydell, this is your ex, Verity. 'Ex' meaning someone you do not call, you do not gift with old photos, you do not contact or even speak with unless we meet on the street and then I will greet you with a pleasant hello." This wasn't as harsh as I'd planned. "That is it. Good-bye," I said, hanging up quickly.

Frankie stifled a laugh.

"Can it," I ordered, pointing the phone at him. Just because I wasn't ruthless didn't mean I deserved to be ignored.

I'd done all I could for the moment, so I unpacked my yummy chicken dinner and tried to forget about ghosts, exes, and psychic visitors.

All three would find me soon enough.

Chapter Twelve

THE NEXT AFTERNOON, I was giving Lucy a bath in the kitchen sink while my resident gangster hovered over the counter and watched. Frankie's right foot had reappeared, although I didn't think he'd want to hear any congratulations from me.

"Why don't you go sit out by the apple tree?" I suggested as my skunk struggled to climb out of the soapy water, away from Frankie. Lucy usually loved bath time. No doubt Frankie was making her uncomfortable.

"Nah," he muttered, idly passing his hand back and forth through my purse, which lay next to him. Poor guy couldn't even pickpocket anymore. "I'm too hopped up. If that psychic was any good, she'd know to hoof herself over here."

He was worse than a three-year-old. "Lauralee's passing the message along."

Suddenly, my bag began to buzz and vibrate.

"Jesus!" Frankie shot away from the counter.

"Relax." I dried off Lucy's face so no soap got into her eyes, then reached past the hovering gangster and pulled my cell phone out from under his urn. "I forgot I set it to vibrate before I went to see Virginia yesterday."

He settled back down slowly, still a bit out of sorts as he regarded the phone. "I don't like those things."

Yes, well, I didn't enjoy the fact that a wet skunk was currently making a run for it down the other side of my counter. I shoved the phone in my pocket and grabbed for a towel. "Here, baby," I said, gathering her up so she could get comfortable and dry. The poor thing was shaking. "I've got you."

I barely had her towel-dried before she started struggling to escape. I let her, knowing she'd dart straight for my bed and blankets. It was where she felt the safest. I supposed I owed it to her—and my sheets would dry before bedtime. I hoped.

"Was it the psychic?" Frankie asked as I retrieved my phone. "Call her back."

I hit the redial button. "Relax, it was Melody."

Luckily, she was better at answering her phone than I was.

"Tell me you're taking care of yourself," she said.

Static shot through the line. "I went and saw Virginia Wydell yesterday," I said, walking toward the back porch, hoping for a better connection.

"Why on earth…" she began. "Never mind. I want to hear about it, but listen, I have to tell you. I found Madeline Angelica."

Thank goodness. "Is she alive?"

"Yes. And she lives here in town. Never left." My sister hesitated, which was uncharacteristic of her. I stood on my back porch and waited, the breeze stirring my hair. "Verity, you know her," she said, as if she wasn't quite sure how to say the next part. "Madeline Angelica Learner…well, Wydell. She goes by the name of Maisie Hatcher."

I stood in shock for a moment. Maisie Hatcher. Most people knew her as a fiercely independent woman who rarely left her farm. She had been my grandmother's friend, not a close one, but she'd been a fixture at carry-in dinners, church luncheons, and sewing parties since I had been old enough for Maisie to slip me candy from her purse. She'd fallen on hard times recently and I'd used my ghost-hunting skills to find some money hidden on her property. Then she'd turned right around and given me a loan to help save my house.

She hadn't had to do it. But she was a good person. Eccentric, maybe, but she had a good heart. Maisie had suffered a lot over the years with a bad marriage and health issues, so she'd earned the right to be a little unusual.

And now she was heir to the Wydell fortune.

As long as we could prove it.

I retreated straight back into the kitchen to grab my bag and my car keys. I had to go see Maisie. "Do you think she knows?" I asked Melody, motioning for Frankie to join me.

"I doubt she's aware," my sister said as I locked up and hurried for my car. Frankie grumbled, but he stuck with me. "I had to go through marriage records to find her. Her birth record is nonexistent and nobody else knows about the document you saw."

Except for Daila's killer. Even without my sister's research skills, that person could track down Maisie eventually. My heart thudded in my chest. We might already be too late.

I fired up the engine. "I'm heading over there right now."

Melody's voice hitched. "I know you've got to do it, but please be careful."

"I will," I assured her. "Let me get off the line. I'm calling Ellis."

I took the main road until I reached a smaller side road that snaked through the woods. I turned onto the road less traveled and cringed as my car bottomed out on a pothole.

Ellis would know the best way to approach Maisie. He liked to stop in on her and make sure she had what she needed. He'd done it out of the kindness of his heart, because he was a good person.

Unless he knew she was kin.

No, I couldn't think that way. There was no reason to suspect he'd keep that sort of information hidden.

I also needed Ellis to know where I'd be just in case someone with evil intent beat me to Maisie's house. Or arrived after I did.

My car bounced past the overgrown entrance to Johnson's Cave. I steered while fighting with the wire of my hands-free system. It had gotten tangled up with my phone again. One of these days, I was going to chuck it out the window.

But Ellis didn't answer his phone, despite my repeated attempts.

Frankie didn't seem to care one way or the other. "Just so you know, I'm not here 'cause you ordered me," he pointed out. "I'm here 'cause I want to see what happens."

"Like an impartial observer?"

He trailed a hand out through the window. "More like a rubbernecker at a seven-car pileup."

I'd take it.

We drove farther into the backwoods where Maisie lived. I made a right onto the near-deserted road to her house, all the while hoping with everything I had that I'd arrive soon enough and that I'd find her alone.

Chapter Thirteen

MAISIE'S HOME SAT far back in the woods. The rough-hewn pine planks, gray with age, blended into the surrounding trees and underbrush. She'd lived here as long as I could remember, probably since she married back in the '50s. Her redneck husband had passed a long time ago, which was good, because I'd heard he hadn't treated her well.

My tires crackled against the rock driveway and I prayed I wasn't too late, that Maisie was safe inside.

I didn't want to imagine the alternative.

The windows stood dark. Wind rushed through the trees, scattering dry leaves and whipping up a small dust storm. The dry boards of the house creaked under the assault, but nothing else stirred.

Perhaps Maisie was out walking her property.

I knocked on the rough plank door. "Maisie?" I pounded again for good measure. "It's me, Verity."

After our last adventure, I told her I'd come see her again. That was nearly a month ago, I realized with a twinge of guilt. I'd only dropped by once since then, and she hadn't even been home. I should have tried again.

"Hello?" I called as the front door creaked inward, all by itself. I smelled a hearty mix of beef and vegetables with rosemary and garlic. But I didn't see anyone.

A dark couch and coffee table hunkered in the shadows. The only light filtered from a kitchen window in the back. It illuminated a beat-up wood table and 1960s-style gold-and-brown flowered wallpaper.

I fought the urge to duck my head inside. Maisie owned a shotgun and wasn't afraid to use it. I'd learned that the hard way last month when I'd trespassed on her property.

"Maisie?" I asked, louder this time.

What if she lay dead inside? Injured? The killer might still be here.

Or I might just need to rein in my imagination. I took a deep breath. It wasn't as if I could have envisioned a good majority of the surprises I'd received lately. In fact, most of them had turned out far worse than I could have predicted.

I tugged a hand through my hair. Dang me, I had to stop giving myself pep talks.

All right. Something was definitely wrong if Maisie had left her house unlocked and unguarded. Yes, I didn't always bolt my doors, but I lived near people. And I wasn't as paranoid as Maisie.

She might have left in a hurry.

I made my way around the side of the house, my fingers skimming the rough, cracked wood. I kept an eye out for anyone lurking along the tree line—although it wouldn't be hard to hide.

Maisie's blue beater truck sat on a rocky patch at the back of the house, with Ellis's squad car parked haphazardly next to it.

There was no sign of either one of them.

The light bar on the top of his car sat dark. Perhaps this was a social call. Ellis treated Maisie like a favorite aunt.

Still, I'd gone and riled Virginia up. I practically implied that I knew she would lose her fortune. What if I'd driven her here? She'd as good as admitted she would kill to keep her fortune.

Just beyond the cars, a single gardening shoe lay near the woods. My mind snapped back to the image of Darla's white pump, motionless and half covered by the display table.

Oh no. Not Maisie, too.

But I didn't see a body. At least, not yet.

My heartbeat sped up. Sweat slicked my palms as I made my way toward the shoe.

Voices sounded in the trees beyond the small clearing that made up Maisie's backyard. From this distance, it was impossible to say who it could be or what they were saying.

One thing was for certain: I was not going to call out again. I wouldn't betray my presence or my location, not yet at least. Good thing I'd never taken my cell phone off vibrate. I stuffed my keys into my pocket and clutched my bag to my side to silence any clanging of the urn.

If it was Maisie or Ellis, they'd be glad to see me, even if I sneaked up on them. If it was the killer?

Then I'd run faster than I ever had before.

Quietly, carefully, I picked my way through the trees, avoiding the dry leaves on the ground and any sticks that might snap and betray my location. I kept to the right of the voices, finding the cover of thick trees, my movements precise.

I remained hidden away until the exact moment when a hand grasped my right arm.

"Ha!" I spun away and jammed an elbow straight into my attacker's rib cage, just as I'd learned at YMCA self-defense classes, levels one and two.

"Oof." Ellis took the hit. He bent over, closing both his arms around me, pressing my back into his chest. "What the hell, Verity?"

"It's you." I slumped against him, relieved. Boy, he felt good. And warm. "Sorry about that," I added, a bit guilty to be enjoying his embrace after elbowing him as hard as I did.

He loosened his grasp and turned me around.

His blue waffle shirt set off his eyes. "Nice ninja moves." He stayed bent over a little, even as he tried to play it off. Poor guy. "What were you doing trying to sneak up behind me?"

"Thought you might need saving," I said honestly.

He smiled at that, even though he was tall and strong and gorgeous, and I was still short even when wearing heels. "Thanks. Good to know you have my back."

"And your front," I added, relieved, happy, and mortified as soon as the words slipped out. My hands ran down his chest for a second before I pulled them back like I'd been stung. "Whoops."

"You're fine," he said, his attention following the movement of my hands, his voice gravelly all of a sudden. He cleared his throat and leaned closer. "Just keep your voice down. Maisie's over here. We have something to show you."

"I can't imagine what," I whispered.

"It's a surprise," he said, placing a hand on the small of my back and leading me deeper into the woods.

I was willing to bet the surprise I had for them was just as big. I wanted to break the news to each of them in different ways, one at a time. They both deserved that consideration.

I'd have to think on exactly how to accomplish it.

Ellis picked his way through the underbrush even more quietly than I had. I didn't see much of a trail as we ducked around a fallen log and skirted past a copse of old-growth pines.

"Here," he said gently, and I saw Maisie crouched at the base of one of the larger trees, her old hunting boots digging into the loose soil. Her wild auburn hair stood out like a beacon. Her olive-and-brown plaid shirt and woolen trousers blended into the autumn brush. Low, heavy branches skirted the ground, which was covered with rich green needles.

She smiled, showing her crooked teeth, and motioned me forward.

I crouched next to her as she lifted the branch.

Four tiny baby bunnies huddled together in a pocket of grass. Their eyes hadn't fully opened and their perfect little ears lay tight against their heads.

"Oh, how precious," I gasped. Their mottled brown fur, flecked with black, had to be so soft. I couldn't get over their little pink noses. The smallest one reminded me of Lucy when I first found her. She kept tilting up her head, as if she had to know what was going on.

Maisie sat back on her haunches. "Had a rabbit eating up my winter garden. Ellis and I were setting no-kill traps until we found this."

He chuckled. "Now Maisie's ready to let them eat this year's harvest and next."

She replaced the branch and stood, wiping her knees off. "You get rid of those traps? That nursing mama doesn't need us to hassle her."

"Consider them gone." He grinned, reaching out a hand to help me off the ground.

"Let's pull two of the winter cabbage and plant them at the edge of the tree line. Make it easier for them to get. In the meantime, I'm going to fetch some dryer lint and leave it for them to find. I hear it makes good bunny bedding."

"It's like she's done this before," Ellis mused. Maisie waved him off as she trudged through the woods toward the house.

I couldn't help but smile. "You two realize there are bound to be other little furries eating her garden, not just these rabbits."

"True." He shrugged as we followed Maisie back. "But if she's happy feeding every critter in Sugarland, I don't mind helping."

I clapped him on a broad shoulder. "You're a good man, Ellis Wydell."

He kept his eyes on the ground, shaking his head. "I'm just glad you're still talking to me after you went and saw my mother."

"She told you." I silently berated myself. Of course she did. And Ellis would know exactly what I'd been up to. "Frankie didn't find anything," I assured him.

He met my eyes then. "Did you honestly think he would?"

Yes. But my answer would only hurt Ellis, and he of all people didn't deserve that. So I kept my mouth shut.

As far as I was concerned, Virginia had the means and the motive. She certainly had the temperament. Some irrefutable piece of evidence would turn up soon, I was sure.

It would be painful enough for Ellis when I found proof of his mother's guilt. So in the meantime, I wasn't going to argue. Instead, like a good Southern girl, I changed the subject. "Tell me, Sheriff Wydell," I began, drawing out his name, enjoying the sound of it, "are you taking up bunny raising as a side job or merely a hobby?"

He laughed at that, and I found myself joining him. I liked the way his eyes crinkled at the corners, how he smiled without any pretense. He pressed his lips together, eyeing the forest. "I came here to look at her heater, but we got distracted."

"I didn't realize you were so handy."

"Maybe I'm not," he said as we stepped out into Maisie's backyard. "I thought I fixed the thing last year."

"Ouch."

He began picking up several traps at the edge of the yard, simple metal cages with narrow, funneled entrances. "I'm all she's got, though. She can't afford a repairman. Or"—he held up a trap—"critter control."

He popped his trunk and began storing the traps inside. "She won't let me spot her the cost. Says she doesn't want charity." He shrugged. "I get that. So I figured out how to do these things myself." He closed the trunk and faced me, as if he feared my reaction. "It's good for me, too."

To have someone appreciate him, respect him for who he was. I understood better than he realized. Ellis liked to help people, and he cherished his independence. It only made sense he'd want to help Maisie hold on to hers.

"No work today?" I asked, leaning up against his squad car.

He reached down and pocketed his keys, but not before I saw the frustration flicker across his face. "I took off. Marshall's not letting me work on the murder case anyway. Figured I'd try to cool it."

Then this certainly wasn't his lucky day. "Ellis," I said, my voice hitching on his name, "I have to tell you something and I'm not sure how to do it, so bear with me."

"Okay," he said, facing me, prepared for whatever I had to say. That was Ellis. Hit it head-on and deal with it.

"Melody did some research into county records and discovered the identity of your great-aunt, the woman listed in the document I saw."

He watched me carefully. "You're acting like this isn't good news."

"It is, mostly," I said quickly. It meant he shared blood with someone he already cared for. It also meant she was in danger. "It's Maisie."

He stiffened and took a step back.

"You had no idea," I said, reaching out to try to comfort him.

He eluded my grasp. "Why would I?" he asked, stopping for a moment, stunned. "How can you be sure?"

"She listed Madeline Angelica Learner on her marriage license. Same birth date. Same year as on the document I saw. She's the same person, Ellis," I said, as gently as I could.

"Give me a second." He pinched his fingers to the bridge of his nose. "This is a lot to take in."

"I know." I tried to close the distance between us, to offer him some kind of support. "I'm sorry."

He dropped his hand. "You didn't do anything."

Except dig up secrets from the past. "I have to think this is going to be a surprise for Maisie, too."

Ellis hitched a thumb under his belt. "She isn't going to take this news easy."

"I'm not even sure how to tell her," I admitted.

It would have to be done delicately. Ellis believed me about seeing ghosts and projections of documents, even though he couldn't experience them himself. Maisie might very well think I was bat crazy, and I wouldn't blame her.

Ellis lowered his hand. "We can't keep that kind of a secret from her, especially when it puts her in danger. And we're sure not going to leave her alone."

"Okay, good." We had a plan of sorts in place. "So how do we approach this?" He knew her best.

Ellis glanced at the small shack. "Together," he said, taking my hand, giving it a slight squeeze. "We go in there, find the right moment, and do this together."

"And hope she doesn't shoot us," I added, glad to have him on my team.

His lips quirked. "That too."

Chapter Fourteen

ELLIS OPENED THE door for me and together we walked into the kitchen, where Maisie stood over a bubbling pot on the stove. The scent of rich broth, garlic, and onions made me miss my grandma's cooking.

"You're staying for dinner," she said. It was a statement, not a request.

"Yes, ma'am." There was no way I'd pass on an offer like that, even without a killer on the loose.

I surveyed the kitchen. I'd been mistaken before about the state of this room. Yes, the style harkened back to the 1960s, with an original almond defrost fridge, crocheted yellow kitchen curtains, and a linoleum floor patterned to resemble red brick. But Maisie's home was bright. Loved.

A sun catcher in the shape of a star hung over the window overlooking the yard, and pots of fresh herbs crowded every available inch of counter space. She suddenly reminded me of a mad scientist cook.

I was about to shatter the illusion of a peaceful evening. Maisie was in the path of a murderer. We had to figure out a way to keep her safe. It would be like trying to lock a bear in a garden shed, but it had to be done. I didn't have high hopes that this would go over well.

Ellis inspected the pot, vying for a taste, while I stopped to smell a particularly full and gorgeous rosemary plant. "This reminds me of the kitchen garden my grandmother used to grow." She'd passed the plants to her friend Annice when she'd grown ill.

"Your grandma and I used to share sprigs from our best plants," she said over her shoulder while batting Ellis away from her stew. "I'm pretty sure that one came from her."

I drew a finger over the stiff leaves. "Maisie, we need to talk."

"Talk away," she said, adding spices to the pot. "This'll be the first good meal I've had in a week. I don't bother fixing much if it's just me."

And she certainly wouldn't feel like eating after what I had to say.

"Maybe this can wait," Ellis began.

Maisie turned to him. "Can you be a dear and check out that heater? It's gonna get nippy in here when the sun goes down."

"Right," he said, sharing a glance with me as he headed downstairs.

Maisie lifted her chin. "You're acting funny."

Didn't I know it. "Can I help with anything?" I asked, remembering the manners my mother taught me.

Spoon in hand, she directed me to a seat at the kitchen table. "You can keep me company." She dipped a piece of bread into the stew and tasted. "Just needs a little more basil." She reached for a pot on the counter and broke off a few healthy green leaves. "This is one of my best plants. When you're ready to start your own kitchen garden, I'd be glad to give you a starter sprig."

"Thanks," I said, imagining what it would be like to cook real food with my own fresh herbs. "I could use some help. With what I know about herbs, I might pick poison ivy instead of basil."

She huffed. "You'd only do it once," she said, dropping the basil into the pot. "I know how it is. A lot of young people today don't want the bother."

"No," I said, savoring the smell of the kitchen, "I like this."

She smiled, giving the stew one final stir before replacing the lid on the pot. "That's what I like about Ellis, too. He understands."

We heard him banging around down in the basement. "I had no idea he was handy."

She retrieved a pitcher of tea from the fridge. "He uses YouTube videos. Doesn't think I know." She poured us each a glass. "Ellis wasn't on the force two months when I tripped and fell coming off my porch. I hit my hip pretty hard, was afraid I broke my ankle. Couldn't afford an ambulance. Didn't want to get anybody out of bed. Figured the police could help me get situated." She placed the glass in front of me and joined me at the table. "Ellis did. He was frustrated when I wouldn't go to the doctor, but he wrapped up my ankle and made sure my hip was okay. Lectured me for leaving the porch light off."

"That sounds like Ellis." The man was never without an opinion.

She took a sip of her drink. "Then he realized I didn't have any lights. Couldn't afford the bill that month. Wasn't about to admit that to a Wydell, of all people."

"Let me guess. The lights came back on." Ellis was a fixer. He cared.

"He still won't admit it to this day," she said, glancing out the window at the sunset behind the trees. "But yeah, it was him."

"Stubborn," I added.

A grin formed on her lips. "Not that you or I would know anything about being pigheaded."

I was about to respond when Ellis tromped back up the stairs. "All fixed," he said, closing the door to the basement. "We hope," he added with a wry grin. "Dang, it smells great in here."

"Wash your hands real good and we'll eat early," Maisie said, pushing up from the table. "You worked hard today."

Nobody argued as she dished out three heaping bowls.

The homemade stew was delicious, the best I'd had since my grandma passed. When we'd all finished, I couldn't put off the inevitable any longer.

I placed my spoon next to my empty bowl. "Maisie, you know I care about you." I folded my hands on the table. "And even though we've only known each other for a short time, I'm here to help you in any way I can."

She placed her spoon in her bowl. "This doesn't sound good."

I was going about this all wrong. I glanced at Ellis.

He cleared his throat. "Verity did some...research around the library after Darla was killed."

"Good of ya," she murmured warily, as if she were afraid of what Ellis or I would say next.

"I wanted to know why," I explained. "What motive could someone have to kill Darla Grace, who only ever wanted to help people." My breath hitched. This was hard, but I forced myself to keep going. "Right before she died, Darla discovered a document written and signed by Leland Wydell that names Madeline Angelica Learner as his legally acknowledged first daughter."

She flinched as though I'd struck her. "I don't go by that name anymore."

I nodded. Her past was painful. Still, something good had come of it. "You're an heiress, Maisie."

She stood, her napkin dropping to the floor. Then she blinked in shock for a moment before giving a sharp nod, as if deciding something. "No, I'm not." She hastily gathered our bowls and spoons.

"It's true," Ellis said. "At the end of his life, he tried to set things right."

She violently dumped the stack of dishes into the sink and slammed on the water, ignoring the hard spray. "I don't wanna be no damned heiress. I don't need that. I don't need you telling me who I am when I know goddamned well who I am."

"If it's true, it doesn't change who you are," Ellis said, his voice reassuring. "It could give you some resources, some help you never had before."

"Too little, too late." She slammed the water off and began dumping dish soap over the mess in the sink. "My mama told me who my daddy was, said we could never tell. She worked as his secretary for thirty-eight years, up till the day he died. She would have done anything for the high, mighty Leland Wydell." She banged the soap down on the counter. "But I'm different. I don't care about a man who couldn't even bother to lay claim until he was almost dead in the ground."

"I can see your point," I said. I'd expected the glare, but not the raw pain in her eyes. "But your daddy did the right thing in the end. Doesn't that count for something?"

"The right thing would have been to claim me as his when I still gave a damn." Her breath came hard. "It was hell growing up as a bastard. My mama and I, we survived it. She taught me how to fight. I held on after she died. I held on being married to that asshole, Oskar."

"There's nothing we can do to make this right," Ellis said, approaching her. "But we need to try. If you're part of the family—"

"Don't you dare!" She grabbed a spoon and threw it at his head. Ellis dodged sideways and it struck the floor behind him. "I got my land and my place and I own my life. I ain't about to pretend I'm any society now."

He held his hands out in surrender. "Just think. If this is true, it means you're my great-aunt."

She flinched before the corners of her mouth lifted for a brief moment. "That's the only good that would come of it." Her chest heaved as the energy drained from her. "I need to sit down."

Ellis pulled a chair out for her, but she skirted him and slid into a seat across the table, away from us.

I sat opposite her. "This must be hard."

"I learned about my pa when I was five, after some kid in church called me a bastard and his mama took the time to explain what that was." She scoffed. "Nobody knew who my daddy was. Mama told me when I was older, but it didn't make no difference. He could've made my life a lot easier if he'd claimed me then. But now? *Now?*" She let out a huff.

"It could still change your life," I told her.

She rubbed a hand over her face, processing it. "The entire time Mom and I grew up outside of town because I had no proper papa, the whole time I was married to that jerk because no one else would have me, that whole time, I watched that pretty house up on the hill and thought about how things would be easier if I were in it." She dropped her hand. "At the same time I hated it, and the gates and the walls and everything it stands for. I'm heir to nothing."

"You *are* an heiress," I told her, "and if someone thinks you're after the Wydell fortune, they might come after you."

Her mouth twisted in a wry smile. "Don't worry, sugar. I got my shotgun." It was hard to miss. She kept it propped up next to the fridge.

"No way," Ellis said, scooting into the chair next to me. "You're not shooting anyone."

"Try to stop me," she said matter-of-factly. She looked at him for a long moment. "You realize this news is going to give your mama a duck fit. Why do you want to bring all of this out in the open?"

He stared at his hands for a moment, resigned. "Because it's the right thing to do."

And Ellis always stood up for what was right, even if it was hard. I touched his warm, solid arm and felt the muscles quivering underneath. This had to be one of the most difficult things he'd ever do. If Maisie gained control of the Wydell fortune, it would wreck his family. And if the murderer did come after her, it would be proof that someone close to him was a killer.

Maisie realized it, too. "I don't want your money, darlin'. I just want to be left alone on my land."

Ellis leaned his elbows on the table. "Maisie, the situation isn't as simple as you're making it out to be. Choosing not to come forward isn't going to keep you safe." He shook his head slowly. "As long as you have a legitimate claim, you won't be left alone. The people who killed Darla will want you dead, too." He said it plainly, but I could feel the pain behind his words. He cared about Maisie and about his immediate family, too. The Wydells would be suspect if anything happened to Maisie. And Ellis would have to enforce the law.

"I can take care of myself," Maisie said, waving him off. "You act like it's easy for people to change. Well, it's not. That's what your generation don't get. Some things are best left in the past."

Ellis gave a small nod. "I know. But not this." He stood. "We'll work it out. If it makes you feel better, think about how this is going to tick off my mother," he said, trying for humor and failing.

I understood his mixed feelings. Despite her black heart and her sins, Virginia was still the only mother he had.

Maisie's voice was frosty. "All the Wydells can rot in a barrel." She nudged her shoulder at him. "'Cept for you."

No doubt this could make her life easier, though. She'd been buried under some hefty medical bills the last time I'd helped her out. And she was getting older. She couldn't keep growing her own vegetables and hunting her own meat forever.

"You might be able to use a little financial freedom," I told her gently. "It's not like you'd have to move into the big house on the hill."

"No way, no how." She folded her hands over her chest. "And you, let's see the proof you found of that man actually claiming me."

Ellis and I exchanged a glance. "It's not something we can show you yet," he said.

She gave him a stony look. "Why not?"

I pressed the tips of my fingers to my forehead. "Well…"

"Out with it," she ordered.

I let out a long exhale. "Right now, what we know came from the ghostly plane."

She scrunched up her face. "Ghost planes? You're talking gibberish."

"I'm talking about supernatural, spirit-world information," I said, trying to explain. It sounded unbelievable, even to me.

She barked out a laugh, slapping her hands down on the table. "You got me all worked up over spirit-world talk? And people think I'm a loony."

Ellis leaned forward, his hands fisted on the table. "Maisie—" he began, "what Verity's trying to say is—"

"I see ghosts," I said quickly. There. It was out.

She looked at me like I was barking mad.

"We have conversations," I added, starting to babble as my nerves got the better of me. "And I have a gangster named Frankie who follows me around and sometimes introduces me to the spirits of the dead. Unless I find the dead people first."

Her eyes narrowed. "Is this some kind of joke?"

"No," Ellis said. "Darla left a message saying she discovered something. The ghosts were able to show Verity what Darla had seen. It was a document from your dad, saying he felt bad about how you grew up and that he claimed you as his own."

She wrapped her arms around her chest and her eyes became glassy.

"Whoever killed Darla took the documents she discovered. That's why we think you're in danger."

Maisie leaned back in her chair. "Show me a ghost."

Dang. "They can't always make themselves visible, but I can certainly ask," I offered. I went to retrieve my bag and set it on the kitchen table, along with the urn. If there was ever a time for Frankie to cooperate, it would be now.

Maisie scrunched up her nose and regarded the whole thing dubiously.

"Watch," I said, hoping there'd be something to see. "Frankie." I rubbed the outside of the urn. "I need you to come out now." When there was no response, I rubbed a little harder. "Frankie!"

"How many times do I gotta tell you?" His voice echoed in my ear. "I'm not the genie in the lamp."

"Sorry," I said, more relieved than truly contrite. For a second, I was afraid he wouldn't respond. "I need you to prove to Maisie that you exist."

"Is that all?" the gangster asked as he shimmered into view directly in the middle of her kitchen table. "And how, pray tell, would you like to accomplish that? You want me to read from Shakespeare? Perhaps do a song-and-dance number? Because I'm still missing part of my left foot."

He could have done well on stage. The man liked his drama. "Just...blow a cold breeze at her or something."

"Sure. Let's use more energy," he said, gliding toward the old woman. His form melted into a single orb of light, which wove around her.

I watched for Maisie's reaction, but all she did was frown at me.

"There," Frankie said, hovering near her left shoulder. "Happy?"

Maybe. "You feeling anything?" I asked Maisie.

She rubbed her stomach. "Now that you mention it, I think I ate too much stew." She looked me up and down, as if she couldn't decide if I was truly crazy or not. "You're a cop, Ellis. I never thought you would go in for all this voodoo-hoodoo."

Great. Now even Maisie, the notorious crazy old cat— make that bunny—lady thought I was nuts.

"I'm going to finish the dishes," she said, heaving up out of her chair, leaving Frankie behind.

"I'll help," I said, joining her. Ellis and I exchanged a glance. It was clear Maisie was done with the ghost talk, but maybe we could still convince her to take precautions against the living. "So, do you usually lock your doors?" I began.

She tossed me a dish towel. "Not exactly subtle, are you, sport?" When Ellis chuckled, she glanced back at him. "Neither are you, boy." She shook her head as she turned on the faucet. "You're two peas in a pod."

The sun was fully down now, and it was hard to see anything in the pitch-black yard.

Maisie plunged her fingers into the water. She pulled out a bowl. "Yuck. I was so mad I didn't even prerinse these."

"Here," I said, "let me—" A gunshot shattered the window, spraying glass. I screamed. Maisie rocked backward. I grabbed Maisie and dragged her to the floor.

Chapter Fifteen

OH MY GOD. "Someone shot at us!"

"Stay down!" Ellis ordered.

He helped me off Maisie. Heavens, I was crushing the poor woman. Broken glass littered the floor. "Call the police!"

"I am the police." Ellis brushed broken glass from my shoulders and hair. Maisie sat on the floor next to me, stunned, but alive.

His warm breath ghosted my cheek. "You're fine." His relief was palpable. He moved into a crouching position behind the counter, just high enough to glimpse out the broken window.

"What do you see?" I whispered.

"Stay here." He reached for the gun in the holster at the back of his belt. "Lock the door behind me." He headed out into the yard.

I kept low as I crossed over to the door and threw the bolt.

Meanwhile, Maisie grabbed her gun and pointed it out the window. She fired, the kickback knocking her into the kitchen table.

"Maisie!" I rushed to her. "Ellis is out there!"

"Somebody's up on the hill!" She aimed again.

We both ducked as the shooter fired, shattering a bowl on the counter. "Run!" I grabbed her arm and we dashed into the living room as another shot exploded the plate rack on the far wall.

I couldn't leave Ellis out there to handle this all alone. We needed to call 911. My phone was in the kitchen. So was Maisie's wall phone.

"Get down!" Frankie stood with his shoulders to the wall next to the front door, revolver drawn. He peered out the window. "The shooter's coming down. He's moving around the side."

"How can you possibly know that?" I demanded.

"Take this," he said, reaching into his suit coat and tossing me a pistol.

I jumped out of the way of the ghostly weapon and let it skitter across the floor. "I can't touch that." Well, wait. Maybe I could. I'd been able to pick up the paper at the library, and last month I'd held a ghostly locket and brought it into the mortal plane...

"This'd be the time to try something new," he barked, ready to fire.

Maisie took cover behind the furniture grouping at the center of the room. "We can take 'em," she said, cocking her gun and hunkering bunker-style behind the couch.

I went for Frankie's pistol on the floor at the same time gunfire shattered the front window. I changed direction and dived behind the couch. "Take that, ya bastard!" Frankie hollered, standing in front of the window, returning fire. I was glad I hadn't continued toward the gun. Frankie's ghostly bullets didn't do a thing to the remains of the glass window, much less anything else.

Maisie aimed.

"Don't!" I ordered. *Think.* "Ellis is out there. One wrong move and you could shoot *him.*"

"Or we can shoot the sucker that's shooting at him," she snarled, pulling the trigger. Half the buckshot went straight through Frankie and slammed into the wall.

He spun around. "Jesus, woman! Learn to aim!"

Like he could get hurt.

I turned to Maisie. "I locked the rear door. Tell me you locked the front."

"I don't need locks," she scoffed. "I got my gun."

Another shot hit the house, spraying wood through the broken window. At this rate, a locked door wouldn't make much difference anyway.

"Here," she said, reaching into the back of her pants and handing me a pistol.

"What? Is everybody packing?" The gun felt heavy in my hand, but not at all unwelcome. Dang it. These people were corrupting me.

"Hey." She cocked her shotgun. "I guess this proves you right. I think somebody *does* want to kill me." She took aim and fired. "Still don't buy that ghost baloney."

"I *can* see ghosts," I muttered, bracing my gun on the upper edge of the couch, pointing it toward the hole where the window used to be. Was I really going to pull the trigger?

Outside, an engine started up.

"He's getting away!" Maisie shouted, struggling to her feet. She made a wide-eyed dash for the front door, crunching over shattered glass, passing straight through Frankie.

"Whoa. Hey! Tell your friend to show some respect!" he hollered as she ran out into the driveway. I dodged him and followed, steps behind.

Ellis's car roared to life and sped off in pursuit, his police lights blazing white and blue against the black of the night.

"Now we've lost 'em!" Maisie groused.

"Not if Ellis has anything to say about it." I just hoped he'd be okay. "We can't stay here," I told her. I wasn't sure how many shots had gone into the house, but the front porch light hung by its wires, the entire front window was gone, and I'd lost track of the damage in the kitchen.

Besides, we didn't know if—or when—the shooter might return. "Pack a bag. You're coming to my house tonight."

"No." She frowned. "Feels like running."

"We're sitting ducks right here. You remember my grandma? She wouldn't want me around if something else happens. And I'm not leaving you."

"Damn it," she groused.

"This'll work out great," I said, while she went to pack a bag. "You'll see." I hurried to the kitchen and found my bag among the shattered glass and pieces of linoleum and wood on the floor. I dug out my phone and texted Ellis: *Maisie is coming home with me.*

If the police wanted to question us there, then so be it. We weren't sticking around a shot-up house in the woods after dark.

Maisie returned sooner than expected with a half-full plastic shopping bag and a shotgun. Just the essentials, I supposed.

I didn't even argue with her about the gun. In fact, it gave me an idea. I pulled my house key off the ring. "Go ahead of me. Lock yourself in. I have one thing I need to check out."

"I'll help ya," Maisie said, with more energy than I'd seen from her this entire day, and that was saying something.

"No," I said. "It involves the ghostly plane."

She blew out an impatient breath.

"Yeah, I know I'm crazy," I said, handing her the key. "Mind the skunk. Lucy is a bit skittish around strangers."

"Don't worry. Little critters adore me," she said, heading for her car.

I nodded. "I have no doubt." I just hoped the spirit of Jilted Josephine would be happy to see me.

Chapter Sixteen

I STEPPED OUT into the night. It felt chillier than I'd expected, without the lights of other houses to hold off the dark. I watched Maisie pull out of the driveway and breathed a sigh of relief.

"Frankie?" I called. I knew he was around.

"That was *great*," he said, appearing next to me, a wide smile on his face. "Almost as good as the shootout at the Kitty Kat Lounge in '34." He gave a fist pump. "I owned that one."

"So I take it you're feeling better," I said.

He shrugged, his hands down at his sides, one still holding a gun. "Still missing the toes on my left foot, but that fireworks show kind of made up for it. Did you see that second round of shots I got out the window? Classic."

"Something like that. Listen. We need to learn more about what happened. The first shots came from the direction of Josephine's house. I want to ask her if she saw anything."

"You're killing me," Frankie groaned.

I resisted the urge to remind him he was already dead.

He reholstered his pistol. "I'm gonna lose my legs again, ain't I?"

"I'm sorry." I realized he'd just gotten them back. "This won't take long," I promised. "You know it's important, or I wouldn't ask."

"Fine," he said, loosening his shoulders, as if he were prepping to play a sport. "I'm doing this for me, not for you," he added. "Last thing I need is you dying before you get me ungrounded."

"That's the spirit," I said, tucking his urn back into my bag.

My skin prickled as I felt the air around me shift. Frankie shivered as a dull light settled over us, casting the forest in an eerie silver glow. "This is it," he muttered. "No more."

Before I could respond, he set off ahead of me, toward the haunted house on the hill.

He put quite a distance between us, and I hurried across the yard to catch up, digging for my iPhone. When I found it, I hit the flashlight app to illuminate my way.

Frankie passed through a spindly bush and disappeared into the woods. I had a tougher time of it. The underbrush grew thick and I didn't see a clear trail. Frogs croaked and crickets called to each other. I stepped over logs and dodged grasping tree limbs.

The gangster flickered in the distance, and my heart stammered when I glimpsed a presence lingering just beyond the thick trunk on my left. If it were Josephine, she would have approached me. This spirit hid in the dark.

"Frankie?" I called, yanking a branch out of my face and tripping on a root.

I'd lost sight of him.

Oh my word. He must be too far away to even hear me. I suddenly felt very vulnerable, especially with this...*entity* so close.

I gathered my wits and my courage. "Hello?" I called.

The physical presence faded into the autumn woods, but it didn't fool me. I could still feel it watching.

"Frankie!" I hissed.

"Shh..." he whispered in my ear so suddenly I gave a little scream.

I splayed a hand over my chest. "Someone's over there."

Frankie slowly came into focus next to me. "He took off."

"How do you know?"

He gave me a long look. "Come on. We're getting close."

"If my heart holds out," I muttered, following him. I didn't like how exposed we were, how anything could be lingering nearby. This time, we both made sure I kept up. The ground underneath my feet grew steep and rocky.

A creaking noise sounded among the trees.

"What *is* that?" It didn't sound like anything in nature.

"Don't look up," Frankie murmured.

I lifted my eyes and saw a thick ghostly noose swinging from an old oak tree. The rope hung heavy and stiff, as if it held a body.

My breath left my lungs. "Oh my." A hard-edged shadow skittered among the high branches and I gave a start, stepping back into a soft, spongy spot of dirt. I felt it move under my feet.

"Steady," Frankie warned. "Josephine's crazy mother is just trying to scare you."

"It's working."

We cleared the rise and saw an old family graveyard surrounded by a silvery fence. The ground moved underneath the headstones, as if the dead struggled to break free. I sincerely hoped they'd stay put. I had enough to deal with counting just the ghosts I wanted to see.

The old Hatcher place sat farther back in the clearing. The rough wooden boards of the two-story staggered under the weight of time and neglect. Darkened windows peered out of the mist, and the front door leaned haphazardly on its hinges. It felt twisted, cold as the poltergeist who controlled it.

Weeds had long ago taken over the path to the house. They snaked around my ankles and crunched under my feet. And I forgot them in an instant when I saw a candle flicker to life in the upstairs window, in Josephine's room.

"She's here." I gave a small wave.

A chill wound through the air as the ghostly embodiment of Josephine launched out the window and dived straight for me.

"Watch out!" she hissed as she passed overhead and rose up into the night. "Ma is coming…"

"I ain't scared of no dame," Frankie said, trying to look cool as he scanned the property for any signs of the mad poltergeist.

Yes, he was. Ma Hatcher had run us out of here when we'd first met Josephine. Frankie and I had both gotten quite a rattle that night, but we'd come too far to back down now.

"Josephine," I called, "I need to talk with you." The spirit of the young woman retreated into a round, glowing orb and shot back toward the house. Her ghostly hound barked like mad and pressed up against one of the lower windows. "We can meet in your room if you'd like."

"Oh, hell no," Frankie said. "I ain't going in that house."

"Afraid of ghosts?" I taunted, trying to work up my own courage.

But I had a feeling Josephine didn't want me in there, either. She made an arc over the leaning stone chimney and hovered midway between the house and me.

"She's angry," her voice whispered in my ear.

"Of course she is. There was an intruder on your property tonight," I said. "Did you get a good look at him?"

An unearthly wind whistled through the trees. "He invaded our house. Just the parlor. Ma drove him off. She's resting now, but she won't be for long."

I focused on the glowing orb in the center of the path. "He tried to shoot at me and Maisie through a window." The orb disappeared and, for a second, I feared the worst.

"Josephine?" I asked, bracing myself for the wrath of her overprotective mother.

She appeared in full-body form on a small outcropping of rocks overlooking the woods. "He stood on this hill." Her voice sounded in my ear, even though her body hovered a good twenty feet away.

I refused to think about that as I rushed to join her.

Josephine's skin shone translucent. She appeared almost angelic with her old-fashioned nightgown flowing white around her bare feet. She wore her long hair in a thick braid down her back, baring her neck, which was raw and torn where the rope that had killed her cut into it.

When I joined her on the outcropping, I gasped at the sight laid out before me. I could see straight through the trees, down to Maisie's house, into the lighted window where I'd stood washing dishes. We were about two hundred yards out, a tough shot, but not an impossible one for someone who knew what he was doing.

Josephine gave me a shy smile. "I would have welcomed you here if you died."

"Thanks," I said, aware she'd meant it as a compliment. I cleared my throat, still not quite used to this type of casual conversation with the dead. "What did the shooter look like?"

She folded her hands in front of her. "Just a man."

"You gotta give me more than that." Especially since I knew Virginia Wydell was most likely behind all this. "Was it a woman dressed like a man?"

"A man," she repeated, in no uncertain terms.

Okay, so maybe Virginia had an accomplice.

The ghost startled and drew a hand to her mouth.

"What?" I asked. "Do you remember something else?"

She gazed at me for a moment. I noticed then that the frogs had quieted. The insects had ceased their calling.

Her image began to fade. "There's another spirit lingering here. He seems almost...familiar." Her eyes widened. "Oh no. Ma sees him, too." I heard a low rumble in the distance, not unlike a growl. "It's not safe for you here." Her orb darted back toward the house. "Run!"

She didn't need to tell me twice. I took off like a shot down the hill. Loose dirt and rocks made me stumble, but the cold blast of air on my back zapped me into moving faster than I ever thought possible. I had to get off her property, right now, before Ma Hatcher found me.

Frankie zoomed ahead. I ran past the noose, over the spongy, shifting ground. I was almost to the property line when a wall of energy smashed into me from behind, nearly toppling me. Fire seared through my veins. My spine crumpled and my limbs went slack. I lost all sense of where I was as I fell headlong into an open pit.

I landed hard, my cheek slamming into cold, wet dirt. My body throbbed from the impact of the poltergeist. It had to be Ma. I hadn't made it off her property. Not quite.

I pushed myself up, stunned, as dirt pelted me from above.

The ghost of Ma Hatcher loomed over me, wearing a high-collared dress and wielding a shovel. Her eyes glowed red, the bones of her face stark and skeletal. "Good girls don't snoop," she chided, shoveling dirt down on me.

"I'm a friend of Josephine's," I pleaded, scrambling for a way out of the hole.

She sent another pile of dirt raining down on me. "Naughty girl. I sent her to her room." I had dirt in my hair, dirt in my mouth, and more spilled down over me. "And you, you'll stay put and stop prying into our business."

Whatever her business was, I wanted nothing to do with it. I held my hands up as I scrambled to stay on top of the growing pile of earth. That put me closer to Ma Hatcher, which scared me even more. "I won't say anything." I had no clue how to get out of this. "I don't even know anything."

Frankie slammed into her. "Beat it, you old broad!" He set off a shock wave of energy so fierce it knocked me to my knees.

She whirled and effortlessly tossed Frankie away. Then she directed a hateful sneer at me and pointed her fingers straight down at my head. A bright flash of light blinded me, throwing me back, before everything went dark.

Chapter Seventeen

A COLD HAND brushed my shoulder and I was overcome with the sick, watery feeling that came from touching the dead. My gut twisted with pain. I lurched away, my face mashing into the dirt of the hole. The musty odor made my stomach curl.

"Easy there," a genial voice said, while a clammy hand patted my back, sinking down through my skin, driving a chilling stake straight through me. "You had quite a scare, young lady."

I rolled away from it, ignoring the tingling in my limbs. This ghost's touch was a thousand times worse than Frankie's. It felt as if I'd run through that ghost outside the library again. But it wasn't as if I could hide. It knew I was here. I forced myself to open my eyes and turn over.

A face stared down at me. This wasn't Ma Hatcher. The high forehead, sunken cheeks, and intense expression belonged to the Yankee officer I'd met in the library. Jackson, the Anne Rice superfan. He floated mere inches above me—way, way in my personal space.

"It's you," I croaked. "What are you doing here?"

He came into such clear focus I could see the stubble on his chin. He wore a cavalry officer's jacket this time, with the bars of a major. He also gave me no room to move. He didn't kneel next to me or stand. He hovered, taking up every bit of space, not even bothering to pretend he was anything but a specter.

"I've been following you," he said, his energy imprint tickling my chin. "You didn't come back to the library tonight."

I scooted around him and struggled to lean up against the edge of the grave. Oh my word. I was sitting in a grave. I shook the dirt from my hair and wiped the tears from my cheeks and eyes. I hadn't even realized I'd been crying. "What happened to the poltergeist?" Stars dotted the night sky. There was no sign of Ma Hatcher.

"I got a jump on her," Jackson said, excited. He hunkered down next to me. "Knocked her hard from behind." The delight drained from him. "Just like a sneaky, conniving Yankee, right?" he added, a bit self-conscious.

"More like the hero who saved me." Even so, I scooted a few inches away. "Ma was ready to—" I didn't even want to think it.

"Bury you alive," Jackson finished.

"Yes." My body still hadn't stopped shaking. "In fact"— I struggled to stand—"I need to get out of here."

"Sit," he said, reaching for me. "You're in no shape to walk. Besides, the poltergeist isn't coming back anytime soon. I made sure of it." I shrank away and he couldn't quite conceal his wounded expression.

"It hurts me when you touch me," I explained.

"Really?" He withdrew his hand and stared at it as if it would throw off sparks or something. "So that's why you made a fuss when you ran through me behind the library."

"That was you?" I asked, my mind scrambling. Of course it was. I'd felt it the second he touched me tonight.

He glanced away. "I was feeling vulnerable after we talked. Returning to my death spot helps." He forced himself to meet my gaze once more. "Besides, I wanted to make sure you made it home all right."

I didn't know what to think. Poor man. "You died in the parking lot," I said, trying to get a grip, "outside the library."

He gave a small shrug. "It was just an open yard back then, out behind the building. I was too far gone. It wasn't worth taking me to the surgeon."

"I'm sorry." That must have been a frightening, lonely way to die. And now, more than one hundred and fifty years later, he was still alone. "I'm just surprised you didn't feel it when I ran straight through you." I looked him over. His body was relaxed, his expression intent. "Frankie got the heebie-jeebies the one time we accidentally touched, and he won't let me forget it. But you really are fine."

"I'm different," Jackson said, in the understatement of the year. He could touch the living. He could banish the dead. He shrugged, embarrassed. "It's one of the reasons they keep me in the basement."

I wondered if he had any idea how much power he held.

I brought my knees to my chest and wrapped my arms around them. "I have to know, what did you do to scare off a poltergeist? My usual method is panic or fleeing, and frankly I don't recommend either."

He smiled at that. "I've had a lot of practice defending myself. I can knock a ghost like Ma into the ether for a while."

"Nice trick," I said. I didn't know what I would have done without him tonight.

He dropped to a sitting position next to me. "It doesn't make me very popular." He leaned his head against the back of the grave. "I've lost my temper and done it to the Johnny Rebs when they've ticked me off. That was all the time in the early days."

"Not the best way to make friends," I agreed.

He shook his head. "They wouldn't be friends with me anyway." He turned his head toward me. "You're so very nice. I realize we've only known each other a short time, but we have so much in common." He smiled "I've been wanting to talk again, just the two of us. And perhaps, if you already own it and it's not too much trouble, I was hoping you could lend me Lestat's book. I read the preview chapter, but the library doesn't have it in my stacks."

"I'll find it for you," I said, struggling to stand. I'd buy my copy back from the used bookstore. "But first, I have to get out of this grave."

"Of course," he said, taking a sudden interest in the clumps of dirt at his feet. "I hope I wasn't asking too much. I know I must seem odd to you." I felt a twinge of guilt as he rose up out of the grave. "I'll try to remember my place."

"No," I called to him. "Wait." He lingered at the edge, right where Ma Hatcher had stood. I managed to reach a few sturdy tree roots and haul myself out by a leg thrown over the side, then a roll, and then a clumsy stand. A lady does what she must. "I do want to talk to you," I said, out of breath. "I like you," I added, and was rewarded when his face lit up. Poor guy. "It's just that we're in a haunted forest, and I don't know where my ghost friend, Frankie, is. He's not in good shape. I'll bet he's lost his knees by now and probably a good portion of his mind."

"Then I shall help you find your friend," he said, offering me his arm.

"Erm…"

"Sorry," he said, dropping it.

"I'm glad for the company," I told him as I began walking toward Maisie's house, grabbing nearby trees for support. My knees felt weak, but that wasn't going to keep me from moving. "I also appreciate your help with Ma." Hopefully he could keep me safe until we arrived at my car.

"We can talk while we walk," he said as I stepped over another mushy part of ground. I didn't want to risk falling into another grave. "I have some fascinating theories on whether Louis really knew about Lestat's desire to turn Claudia. Because when you think about it…"

I shrieked and stumbled backward when Josephine appeared right in front of me, with absolutely no warning.

"What are you still doing here?" She wrung her hands. Her long hair streamed out behind her, as if held by an invisible wind. "Ma won't stay gone."

These ghosts were going to give me a heart attack one of these days. "Major Jackson sent your ma to the ether," I told her, "for now at least."

My new ghost friend stared at Josephine, openmouthed. She jumped when she saw him, and immediately began fidgeting with the lace edge of her ghostly white gown. "It was you?" she stammered. "In the woods? You?"

"Major Jackson, this is Miss Josephine Hatcher," I said, making the introduction. "Josephine, this is—"

"Matthew," she gushed. I swear if she'd had blood running through her veins, she would have gone pink in the cheeks. "Matthew Jackson. I knew you." She dropped her gaze. "You didn't know me."

"I knew you," he said, stumbling over her words and his. "Prettiest girl in church."

Her image grew stronger, more defined. I could see the wisps of hair at her temple, feel the intensity of her gaze. "I was sorry when you…"

"When I joined the Yankees," he finished for her.

"No," she said earnestly, "when you died."

They stared at each other for a long moment.

"This is great, you two," I began. I really hated to break up the moment. "But Josephine, you said your ma is coming back. The major saved me once, but I'm not going to push my luck."

"Oh, wow." She tucked a stray wisp of hair behind her ear. "Thank you," she said to him. "Verity is the only friend I have."

His lips pursed. "Not anymore," he said, giving a low bow.

She giggled and disappeared.

"As much as I want to pinch your cheek right now, we have to keep moving," I said, picking up the pace.

He dragged behind, staring at the empty space where Josephine had appeared. Oh, brother.

I'd never been so happy to see Maisie's house. "We made it," I said on a sigh. I dug for the keys in my bag. "Thank you for the escort. I think you saved my life tonight." Quite literally. "I've got to go, but you should stick around here. I think she likes you."

He let out a huff. "You are imagining things."

"Trust me," I said, heading toward the front of the house and my car. "You got her flustered. I've never seen her just disappear on a guy like that." Never mind that I'd never seen her talk to any young man, period.

He fell in next to me. "It's too late for me. I'm a monster. You saw me in the basement of the library. I'm hideous."

"You are not." He'd merely spent too much time alone and angry. A century and a half of bullying would do that to anyone. He needed confidence and the company of a sweet girl like Josephine. "You should court her."

He let out a huff. "That would be highly improper, especially given how I treated her mother when she tried to kill you."

"Josephine knows what her mother is like," I told him. "Besides, you also saved me and I'm her friend. Friendships mean a lot to a girl like Josephine."

I breathed a sigh of relief when I saw my car. There didn't appear to be any damage from the shoot-out tonight. What kind of life did I have when I actually had to worry about that?

The ghost of Frankie illuminated the front passenger seat. Thank goodness. We were getting out of here.

But before I put the key in the lock, I turned back to the major. "Ask her to go for a walk. Tonight, before you chicken out."

He ran a hand through his longish hair. "But—"

"You don't know if you don't take a chance. And wouldn't it be nice to get out of that library and talk to a pretty girl?"

He appeared distinctly uncomfortable. "I think she'd rather have me protect you."

"I'm fine now," I assured him. "You can do this."

He glanced back toward the haunted house on the hill. "I'll consider it," he said, before he disappeared.

It was all I could ask.

I heaved open the door to the land yacht and found only the top half of the gangster inside. His body had disappeared clear up to his chest. "Frankie, you poor thing. I hope you're okay," I said, sliding into my seat and depositing my bag on the floor of the passenger side.

He barked out a laugh. "Now you worry about me," he said, adding in an eye roll just in case I didn't get the point. "I need a vacation."

Him and me both. "We did good tonight," I said, trying to focus on the positive as I started the car. "We learned where the initial shots came from. Ellis can look there for shell casings. We learned the shooter is a man. I didn't get buried in an unmarked grave in the woods."

Frankie glanced down to the empty space where his lap should be. "Yeah, well, I'm missing some important parts you can't see."

Oh my. I put the car into gear and started down the driveway. "Give it time. Everything will come back." It always had.

The gangster ignored me. "This is a sacrifice no man should have to make."

"Just rest up," I said, preparing myself for the sizzle as we headed down the driveway that led off Maisie's property. Soon, we'd be disconnected and he could recover. I'd make sure of it. And after that? Well, one step at a time.

When I returned to the house, I found Maisie's rusted pickup truck parked out back and her sitting on my porch steps, talking to a blonde woman wearing tight-fitting jeans and a peasant top. The yellow light near my door gave off a warm glow.

They were both petting Lucy, who lay in Maisie's lap with her belly up. That critter could charm just about anyone.

The unfamiliar woman stood as I closed my car door. "You must be Verity," she said, closing the distance between us. "I knew you'd be here soon."

"That's 'cause I told you," Maisie said, ruffling the underside of Lucy's neck. The skunk arched her back and stretched out all four legs, overcome with bliss.

"Avery Connor," she said, holding out a hand. "Lauralee told me you need a psychic."

"And you're it?" I asked. As soon as the words came out, I worried they sounded rude. It's just that Avery wasn't what I was expecting. She was young, perky. She looked more like the waitress she was than the psychic she claimed to be.

Frankie straightened a bit, and if I wasn't mistaken, he actually sucked in his stomach. "Nice stems," he said, checking her out.

If she noticed the reception she was getting, she ignored it. "I was going to call, but I'm working at the diner the next three days straight. I only had today off because I had a speaking part in the movie."

"You got me a psychic who's also a waitress *and* an actress?" Frankie asked, gliding backward, clearly impressed with her range of talent.

"Congratulations," I told her.

She shrugged. "The part was small. And Virginia cut me when she found out my third cousin was a Jackson." She held up her fingers and did a mock Virginia impression.

"We wouldn't want to make this a star vehicle for the wrong family," she intoned.

A fellow sufferer. "I can relate."

"Show her my urn," Frankie pressed.

"In a minute," I muttered.

Avery's silver earrings gleamed in the moonlight. "Lauralee showed me some of your work, so if you can do a logo for me..." she began.

"That sounds great," I said, relieved I could actually afford her.

Meanwhile, Maisie had come within eavesdropping distance as she stroked my blissed-out skunk.

"Why don't you head on into the house?" I asked the older woman. "Maybe treat Lucy to a banana."

"And miss this?" Maisie huffed. "Not on your life."

Great. Fine. Maybe I could get Maisie some proof and unground Frankie at the same time.

Avery closed her eyes and took a deep breath. Then another. "This is going to sound wild, but I think you have a ghost near you right now."

"Hallelujah!" Frankie shouted, loud enough to wake the dead. "She's both pretty and smart."

She gave no reaction. Her eyes remained closed. "It gives off a strong feminine energy."

"Wait. What?" Frankie asked.

"And she's weeping," Avery continued.

"I don't cry," Frankie protested. "Ever."

"Maybe she's talking about someone else," I suggested.

"I'm the only one here," he said, holding out his hands.

"She's trapped here," Avery said, dismayed, "like a weak, fluttering bird."

"Poor birdie," I said, for Frankie's benefit. Then for mine: "Do you know how we can free this weeping, fluttery, girlie presence?" I asked the psychic.

Avery concentrated for a moment. "The sweet little spirit must do this on her own," she murmured.

I grinned at Frankie's expression of horror.

He pointed a finger at me. "Don't even think you're getting out of this."

"All right, sweetheart," I told him.

Frankie looked ready to blow a gasket. "You think this is funny?" he demanded, throwing his arms out to the sides.

Fluttering, I daresay?

"How can the spirit do this?" I asked the psychic as he stared daggers at her and began muttering in German.

She stiffened. "It's not your journey, Verity," she said, opening her eyes. "The ghost has to solve her problem on her own."

"Even if I helped cause it?" I asked. I didn't want the story getting out about this, but if it would help Frankie... "You see, I had this urn that I thought was a vase..."

"Doesn't matter how you found your ghost," she stated. "This is a lesson for the spirit to find her way."

"You are rather good at solving mysteries," I said to Frankie.

"Shut up," he grumbled back.

"Is there anything else you can tell me?" I asked Avery.

She paused for a moment. "Yes." She pressed her fingers to her temples. "Patience. You're going to need plenty of patience with this one."

Well, you didn't need to be a psychic to see that.

Chapter Eighteen

"SO WHAT DO we do now?" Frankie demanded.

I stood for a moment, unsure. "She said it's up to you. Do you get any stirrings or ideas?"

The gangster opened his suit jacket and caressed the handle of his revolver. "You don't wanna know what I got an itch to do."

"Well, you're too late. Avery is probably home by now."

"What makes you think I mean her?" Frankie mused.

Very funny.

Maisie had also retreated to the house, convinced I was the colorful one.

"She knew you were standing right here," I told him. "I think she does have some talent, so we should listen to her idea. It can't hurt to try."

He yanked off his hat and drew a hand through his hair. "This is all balled up."

"What's your first instinct?" I prodded. "Tell me what you would do, right now, to fix this."

He thrust his chin back and forward a few times, really thinking. "I'd get my ashes together."

"Good," I said. "How?"

"I'd take everything you dug up, including the dirt, and I'd put it in one spot that could hold all of it. Something I could take inside and keep."

"Okay," I said, going with it. "We can get everything out of the pool and we'll hold on to it." In fact...I had an idea. "Wait here."

I had a black plastic trash can at the side of the house that I used for yard clippings and sticks. It even had a big caved-in spot at the bottom, kind of like the dent in Frankie's urn, which should make the gangster feel right at home. I ran back and emptied it out onto the ground. "Look at this," I said, hoping Frankie would understand the appeal.

"I'm not garbage," he said as I dragged the trash can back to our science experiment.

"Don't be so picky." I turned it upright so he could appreciate it. "This is clean and it's big enough to hold everything."

Frankie stared at it for a moment. He rubbed the back of his neck as he thought it over. "I don't mind the color..." he mused. "I tell you, it don't feel half bad."

"Okay," I said, starting to feel pretty good about it. "I like this, going with your gut." I grabbed the shovel. "We're going to put all of you in one spot."

"With my urn in there," he said, getting excited. "And that fat rosebush."

I stopped. "That's my favorite rosebush." I backed down at his zealous glare. "Got it. Urn, dirt, trash can, rosebush. It'll look great in my parlor."

"You missed a spot," Frankie corrected as I shoveled dirt.

We kept at it until the trash can was almost too heavy to drag. At that point, I went to recruit Maisie, but she had fallen asleep on my futon. So I dragged the trash can into my kitchen and set it up there, transferring the rest of the dirt by Tupperware container, along with my humongous red rosebush, until we had a shrine to Frankie next to my kitchen island.

"It looks good," he said as I eased his urn into the dirt at the base of the rosebush. "Don't get any dirt in the urn or we'll screw up the ashes."

True. We didn't have many ashes left. I kept the urn upright and dug it down until about half of it disappeared into the dirt. But the top remained open and you could still see the hideous artwork on the side.

"Do you feel any different?" I asked, dusting off my hands over the pile of dirt.

"Not yet," he said, easing down onto my kitchen island, his attention lingering on the trash can, waiting.

"I'm going to go check on Maisie," I said, forcing my stiff body to move. I felt like I'd been gardening all night.

Maisie lay snoring on my futon in the parlor, her shotgun nestled nearby, along with an old camping lantern turned down low. I was not all that surprised to see her cuddled up with my skunk. Not many people warmed up to Lucy so fast. Then again, I supposed the little critter had a head start with Maisie. There wasn't that much of a difference between a skunk and a baby bunny.

Lucy stirred when I approached, the white stripe on her head twitching as she tried to bury her nose deeper into the crook of the old woman's arm.

She knew who had been petting her, and who had been hanging out with ghosts instead.

"Good girl." I stroked her soft little head. "You two take care of each other."

Lucy jerked to attention, and a second later I heard what had earned her notice. A car crunched over the gravel driveway at the back of the house.

"Stay here," I said as she wriggled out of Maisie's grip and followed me. The older woman sighed and rolled onto her back, letting out a loud snore.

I took my cell phone from my bag and stuffed it into my pocket as I peeked behind the edge of my kitchen curtain.

Ellis was just cutting the lights to his police cruiser. Thank God and hallelujah.

Lucy and I headed out onto the porch. I rushed down the steps to greet him as he exited the car. "You're okay!" I said, throwing my arms around his neck.

"Oof," he protested as he caught me, but he didn't move away. "Your neighbors might see," he said, glancing behind him.

"The backyard is large," I told him. And dark. And if I did have a crazy neighbor with binoculars and a Peeping Tom attitude, he or she would have seen much stranger happenings than me hugging a Wydell. "How are you?"

He looked tired, rumpled. Gorgeous.

"It was a hell of a chase," he said. One arm wound around me; the other touched the curve of my neck. "You're pretty scraped up."

"I am?" I suspected most of it was from digging out a thorny rosebush. Although my knees probably looked pretty bad after falling into that grave. It had been a busy night.

He ran his fingers over my bare skin and I felt it down to my toes. "I'm sorry I wasn't there with you."

The police radio crackled from inside the car: *Confirmed location of suspect.*

It was Marshall's voice.

Ellis closed the door. "Let's go inside for a minute."

"What was that?" I asked, glancing back at my darkened backyard as we headed into the house. From the sound of it, he was still in the middle of a manhunt. "You found the shooter? Who is it? And why are you here instead of arresting him?"

"Give me a second."

Ellis and I entered the kitchen silently. "Maisie's asleep," I whispered.

"She could sleep through the Normandy invasion." He stopped when he saw the trash can rosebush. "What is this?"

"We're trying to unground Frankie." The gangster still sat on my kitchen island, gazing at our trash can monstrosity as if it were a museum display.

Ellis's gaze caught on the urn sticking out of the dirt. "Is it working?"

"Not yet," I said, watching the gangster roll his eyes at me as he disappeared.

Ellis turned to me, suddenly uncomfortable.

"I can't stay," he said. "I just came because..." He stood in front of me, somehow at a loss for words. "I needed to see you, make sure you made it home safe." He sighed. "What you heard on the radio... I was able to ID the car I pursued."

Fantastic. "And?"

He dipped his chin. "I can't tell you any more."

"Then why are you here?" I asked, my words coming out harsher than I intended. I touched him on the shoulder and felt him stiffen. Something was wrong. I knew that slant of his mouth, the regret in his eyes. "Ellis? I didn't mean that. I'm sorry."

He appeared torn, and I positively ached for him. If he'd just learned it was his mother or even one of his brothers... I wanted to help.

"I'm sorry too, Verity. I've got to go in to work." He touched my cheek. "I just wanted to stop by to let you know...you're going to be okay."

"Of course I am," I assured him. He worried too much. "Is there anything you *can* tell me?"

"Just that we'll get through this," he said, drawing close. He brushed a kiss over my lips.

It was brief. Simple. It also gave me warm fuzzies and butterflies, and it scared me to death.

"Now I'm really worried," I said, enjoying the warmth of his skin. "The only other time you kissed me, you thought we were dying."

He played with a lock of my hair that had curled near my neck. "We're not dying," he promised.

"No?" I teased.

He kissed me again, just as sweet and sexy as before, the way every girl wanted to be kissed. I found myself positively lost in it until I heard a pounding at my front door.

"Verity," a harsh voice demanded.

Beau.

Ellis pulled away as if one of us were on fire. "What's my brother doing here?"

"I don't know," I said, heading for the front door, "but he's about to wake up Maisie and get a shotgun pointed between his eyes." Not that he didn't deserve it.

"Verity," Beau called, "I know you're in there."

Icy panic seized me. "Sneak out the back," I told Ellis.

It was the wrong thing to say. I could tell by the way Ellis immediately bristled, as if I'd straight-up told him he was the one who didn't belong. "Not a chance," he said, passing me in the hall as he strode for the front door. "I want to know why he's showing up at your house at ten o'clock at night."

"He wouldn't stop calling." Ellis had seen how clueless his brother had been. "So I did call back and leave a message." It certainly shouldn't have prompted a visit.

Then again, this was Beau.

Ellis turned. "You…what?"

"Calm down," I assured him. "I only told your brother to stop contacting me."

He glanced back as Beau started pounding on the door again. "I don't think he got the message."

I slipped around him. "Let me go first."

This isn't awkward and uncomfortable. No, not at all, I told myself as I opened the door to Beau with Ellis standing right behind me.

Chapter Nineteen

BEAU DREW ME out onto the porch, hugging me before I had a chance to think. "I missed you, pumpkin," he said, enveloping me in the familiar scent of Tom Ford Tuscan Leather. "I'm so glad you called."

"Whoa." I jerked back, knocking his chin with my head. "Did you listen to the message? I said don't talk to me anymore." This was way worse than talking. This was showing up and manhandling me.

He drew back, still holding me. "My mom said you visited her." He wore a Confederate uniform with dirt on the sleeve and a stylish streak of blood highlighting his left cheekbone. He saw me noticing and grinned. "I know we're forbidden to see each other now, but I think that makes it hotter, don't you?"

"No," I said, ducking out of his grip.

He straightened his shoulders. "I'm playing Colonel Vincent Wydell. Mama says I'm good enough to be a soap opera star if I want."

Oh, brother.

"My mom told me what happened at the house," he said, with a slight wince. "Then, when you called, you sounded different."

"Harsh." That's what I'd been going for.

"Flustered," he answered.

Great.

To be fair, he appeared more concerned at that point than cocky. Guilty, from what I could tell in the glare of the yellow porch light. "I had to see if you're all right."

"I'm fine," I said, putting some extra space between us. "You can't come by every time your mom is out of line." He'd never leave. "You do realize it's over."

His gray-blue eyes held pain, regret. "It doesn't have to be."

"Get a clue, little brother."

Beau's head whipped up and he went slack-jawed when he saw Ellis leaning against my doorframe like he owned the place. "What the hell are you doing here?"

When Ellis didn't make a move to explain, I did. "Maisie had an...incident at her house tonight," I said, telling him as little as possible. "She's staying with me. Your brother was here just checking up on us."

Ellis shifted his stance, as if he didn't appreciate my toned-down assessment of the situation. Well, tough. We'd agreed to keep our relationship a secret.

And he was the one who'd worried about what my neighbors might see.

"Okay," Beau said, rubbing a hand on the back of his neck. "For a minute, I thought..." He smirked. "Never mind. It would never happen."

A horrible snarl echoed throughout the house, making all three of us turn. Maisie. She snored like a lumberjack.

"Maybe I should take you to a hotel," Beau mused, innocently enough.

"Do it and I'll remove your liver with a fork," Ellis said.

"Relax." Beau scoffed. He shot me the same sweet expression he'd used often when we first started dating. "You don't have to protect me from my girl, big brother. Mom is wrong." He doffed his wide-brimmed uniform hat and gave a slight bow. "Verity's a sweetheart. Always was and always will be."

Before Ellis could swallow his tongue, the police radio on his belt went off. He grabbed for it, but not before we heard, *We got a camera team for those shots fired at Maisie Hatcher's house.* He turned and spoke low into his radio. "Hang tight. I want to be there when they go in."

"Shots fired?" Beau choked out. "Holy hell, Verity. What sort of mess are you involved in this time?"

Requesting an ETA on the arrest.

I couldn't believe it. "Why are you here when you're supposed to be on the verge of an arrest?"

"Good question," Ellis muttered. He cursed under his breath. "I'll be there in ten," he said to his team. Then to me: "I have to go."

Beau's eyes narrowed as he looked from his brother to me. "Well, I'm not leaving you alone, pumpkin. He might, but I won't."

Oh, Lordy. "Beau, I don't need—"

"I don't care," my ex said. "This isn't even about winning you back anymore. I'll sleep out front in the car if you don't want me in the house. Hell, I'll even sleep on the lawn. I had no idea you were in real danger. Please let me stay."

"I hope you two lovebirds can work it out," Ellis growled before heading back through my house, toward his parked cruiser.

"Damn it, Ellis." His temper tantrum practically screamed "jealous boyfriend." He might as well hold up a sign: *We are dating.* "Stay right here," I said to Beau as I ducked inside and closed the door.

Then I locked it.

By that time, Ellis was already halfway down the hall. I understood he needed to leave immediately, but before he did, we had to make one thing crystal clear. "I don't know what that was with your brother back there," I hissed, catching up with him, "but this"—I pointed back and forth between him and me—"what we have going on between us, this can't come out. I don't want it to come out."

Ellis looked mad enough to spit nails. "I don't either, but I don't have to stand here and watch him touch you like he owns you."

"He didn't—" I began.

"He did." He stood over me, his features shadowed in the pale light streaming from the kitchen. "You do realize that if this is going to happen"—he glowered, mimicking my gesture, pointing from himself to me and then back again—"eventually it's going to come out."

Eventually, yes. I didn't even want to think of the consequences when it did. "But not now," I insisted. "It's too soon and you know it."

He ran a hand through his hair, leaving it spiky and unkempt. "I get it. I do." He shook his head before dropping his gaze to the floor. "We just need to catch a break. A normal date would be nice."

"We had dinner tonight," I said, trying to shake him out of his mood. "That's kind of a date."

He rolled his eyes.

"What?"

I considered it a victory when he took my hand and dragged me toward the kitchen. "Nights where you get shot at don't count as dates."

I trailed along, enjoying the contact. "If you put it that way, then we've hardly gone out at all."

He stopped me near the door. "I want to keep you safe," he said, brooking no argument.

Well, then he was in luck. That's what I wanted, too. "I do feel safe with you," I said, trailing my hands up his chest.

We met halfway for a kiss. It was sweet at first, reassuring. I nipped his bottom lip gently and he groaned, kissing me harder.

I opened myself to him, enjoying his warmth and affection, even though I knew our time was limited. "I'll call you when I can," he said against my lips.

"Please tell me where you're going." I needed a clue as to what was happening. It would at least give me something concrete to worry about.

Ellis squeezed my hand and brushed his lips against mine one last time. "Stay here," he said, heading out.

I couldn't promise that.

"Keep my brother outside."

That I could guarantee.

He looked back at me as he got into his cruiser. He'd schooled his expression, kept his handsome face carefully blank, but that only worried me more. I wish he could have confided in me. It wasn't like I would have followed him.

Well, maybe I would have.

Yes, Ellis was the one who should pursue Darla's murderer. It was his job, not mine, to put his life on the line. But I didn't like it.

Meanwhile I had Beau on my porch, ready to stay the night. My stomach twisted into a familiar knot. I'd somehow ended up with the wrong brother again.

Ellis pulled out of my back drive and I was surprised to see Frankie standing in the spot where the police cruiser had been parked.

The gangster hadn't quite grown back his chest, or the part he claimed to miss most. Yet he grinned, happy as a pig in a peach orchard.

I drew in a sharp breath. "Are you ungrounded?"

"Not yet," he said, surprisingly upbeat.

I threw open the back door. "What's going on?"

He disappeared and reappeared behind me in my kitchen, still grinning like a fool.

"What?" I didn't have patience for games.

"Tell me how brilliant I am."

"Frankie—"

He threw his hands out to the sides. "Tell me how I can double-cross the fuzz."

"You say that like it's a good thing."

He winked. "I'm a sly dog. The best." He drew his Panama hat on with a smooth flick of the wrist. "Because I know exactly where your copper is going."

Chapter Twenty

"WHAT DID YOU do?" I demanded.

"I lived out a fantasy," the gangster said. "I spied on the heat."

"*That's* your fantasy?" At least it didn't involve stealing or shoot-outs.

Frankie shrugged. "Better than what used to happen to me in the back of a squad car." He grew serious. "The point is, I listened in on their private radio broadcasts. They're going to arrest your sister."

I couldn't have been more shocked if the earth swallowed me up right where I stood. "Melody didn't do anything. There must be a misunderstanding. I have to call Ellis. He'll straighten it out." And then it hit me. No wonder Ellis had been all worried. "He knew about it."

"He's the one who found the evidence. He's going right now to put your sister in cuffs," Frankie said.

"Where is she?" I asked, searching for my bag and my keys. Where had I tossed them?

"Your sister's working late to reopen the library."

I'd abandoned my stuff in a heap by the door. "I don't see what he could have found to incriminate Melody." I grabbed my things and stormed out the back. Ellis had kissed me and then gone off to arrest my sister as if nothing had happened between us. How dare he not tell me? Part of me understood it was his job, but another part, the protective sister part, wanted to kick him in the shin.

Frankie stopped me cold on the porch. "Hold up," he ordered. "What you gonna do about the person who wants to kill your friend in there?"

It was the only thing that could have stopped me.

As if on cue, Maisie let out a loud, rumbling snore.

I couldn't help it. I had to go. "I'll lock her in," I said, trying to work out a solution, the guilt gnawing at me. "She has her gun." She was a grown woman, for goodness' sake. If she even knew I was wrestling with the idea of letting her hide out here by herself, she'd laugh in my face. Still, I wouldn't forgive myself if something happened to her. "On second thought, you'd better stay."

"Hell no." Frankie held up both hands. "As soon as I get ungrounded, I'm out of here."

"Please stay," I prodded, wondering what on earth I'd do if I returned to find him gone.

"I ain't no babysitter."

"You're not," I agreed. "You're her bodyguard."

He drew back. "I ain't falling for that."

Fricking mercenary gangster. "You're the only one I trust with this. I need you. In fact, I'm going to put your urn here in my bag."

"Don't you touch that!" he ordered.

"I'll put it back later," I promised, digging it up and shaking it off over the trash can. "But for now"—I deposited it in my bag—"you can zip straight to me if she's in danger. I can also call you if there's trouble at the library."

"It's not a two-way radio," he ground out.

True, but it was our connection point, and I intended to use it.

"This isn't ideal." None of it was. "But I have to go. Ellis could very well be arresting my sister right now."

I skirted Frankie and locked Maisie in the house. Then I raced to my car, praying I could get off the property without Beau following. The land yacht wasn't the stealthiest of vehicles under the best conditions, and I groaned under my breath as it started up with a loud rumble.

There was no way I'd be able to go out the front, so I adjusted the plan. I heaved halfway off the seat as I turned the oversize steering wheel all the way to the right and began driving out through the backyard.

My old Cadillac lurched over the uneven ground, the ancient suspension clanking and groaning with the effort. I passed the apple tree in the back and the small pond beyond. I bottomed out twice before coming up on the cornfield, cringing at the way the spent husks scraped at my undercarriage. It wouldn't take much for my muffler to go spinning off like a tiddlywink.

But I'd rather chew nails than let Ellis take care of things, especially when he didn't trust me enough to tell me he was about to arrest my sister. I sat rigid in my seat and kept going.

Now I understood the regret in Ellis's eyes tonight, the guilt he'd tried to hide. I'd figured he was worried about me, and I'd been right to a point. Only it had been much, much more.

Damned Ellis and his savior complex. Intellectually speaking, I understood why he did it, why he couldn't tell me. But at the same time, unreasonable or not, I felt betrayed.

The back road to Charlie Johnson's farm opened up past the cornfield and I took a hard left, my thick tires grasping the hard pavement. Then I outright gunned it for the library. To hell with anyone who tried to pull me over.

I raced through town and arrived at the library faster than I ever had. But I was too late.

Ellis's squad car was parked out front. Behind it, Marshall's blue detective's vehicle sat with the rear door open. The gray-haired officer held on to Melody's shoulder as he deposited her, cuffed, in the back of his car.

This was a nightmare. Even under the glow of the streetlights, I could see how scared she was. I pulled up right alongside them.

"Melody," I called, grateful I remembered to shut the engine off before I dashed around my car.

"Stay back," Marshall ordered, slamming the door on my sister. He held up a hand, as if that could stop me. "Verity, I'm warning you."

"What did she do?" Whatever it was, we could figure this out.

He appeared tired, strained, as if he didn't want this to happen any more than I did. "Get going or I'll arrest you too."

I lit up at the thought. At least then I'd be in the same car with her. We could talk.

Marshall must have guessed where my mind was going. "No," he ordered as he got in his car and slammed the door.

I watched helplessly as he drove away. What was I supposed to tell my mother? That I'd just watched my sister get arrested? On evidence that my almost-boyfriend brought against her?

Speak of the devil. Deputy Sheriff Wydell himself walked down the darkened stairs of the library, approaching me as though he were facing a firing squad.

"What the hell, Ellis?" I demanded.

He was cold, closed off. I met him halfway up the stairs.

"What are you doing here?" he asked stiffly.

Yeah, from the guy who had been kissing me in my kitchen not a half hour ago.

I ticked my chin up. "Usually, I just hear about it through the grapevine when the Wydell men double-cross me. Figured this time I'd come down and watch it happen for myself."

At least I got my reaction. He appeared as if I'd stabbed him in the gut. "Verity, that's not fair."

I knew it wasn't, but I was pissed. "You couldn't give me any warning at all?"

His eyes burned hot. "That's not how it works." He let out an exasperated snort. "How did you find out, anyway? I knew the Sugarland grapevine was good, but this is truly impressive."

"Frankie spied on you."

He let out a curse.

"Don't be a hypocrite, Ellis. You think it's plenty fine when you're the one who needs information from that ghost."

"You want to know what happened?" he demanded. "I didn't have a choice. I put out a warrant for your sister because when I chased down the shooter, it was her. Or rather, someone driving her car."

I took a step back and almost lost my balance on the stairs. He reached out for me, but I held him off. "You can't think it was her."

"I don't," he said, stepping down to face me. "I refuse to believe that. But it doesn't change the fact that I chased her car with her plates out of the woods tonight. I lost the car when it crossed the railroad tracks and nearly got flattened. It was headed straight into downtown, right here toward the square. I called in the model and the plates and it came back as hers. We put out an ABP and found her and her car at the library."

I stood there, with the outside lights buzzing, struggling to put it all together. "So someone took her car."

"That's the kicker," he said, moving closer. "She says they didn't. She claims her keys were in her purse the entire night."

"Then she's wrong."

He looked as frustrated as I felt. "She was working with my mom and Montgomery Silas all evening. Only Mom and Montgomery were busy rewriting his speech for the evening. Melody could have easily driven off."

Ha. Says Virginia Wydell. "It can't be Melody. Jilted Josephine said the shooter was a man. The casings from the gun are on the top of the hill and Melody doesn't even own a gun!"

"I know," he said quickly.

This was all too much. I stared back at the darkened library, then out over the deserted town square. "Where are they now? Virginia and Montgomery?"

Ellis motioned up the hill, keys in his hand. "They're headed up to the Cannonball in the Wall midnight salute." I could see the lights on the hill overlooking the town. "Ovis wanted him for pre-event pictures, and we both know Montgomery's the star. He gave me his keys and asked me to lock up."

Yikes. I hadn't realized it was the sixteenth, the night we commemorated the October 17 battle by gathering at the original cannon on the hill as the clock changed to 12:01 a.m. "It doesn't even feel that late."

"It's not, but he was anxious to get away. It's a media circus up there and this is his event."

His and Virginia's.

"I need to get into the library again."

"Verity—"

He knew it as well as I did. "The ghosts might have seen something." If he cared for me at all, he'd do this. "You owe me, Ellis."

He ran a hand over his face. "You said yourself they don't keep track of time. They're not going to know when your sister left." He caught himself. "If your sister left."

But I couldn't let go. This was the only plan I had. "I just need to figure out who took her car and why."

Ellis cringed. He wanted to help me, I could tell. "I'm supposed to lock up and help with the questioning."

"I need you," I told him. He'd used a judgment call earlier, and now I was making one. Only his was to follow the rules and mine was to bend them. "I can't do this without you."

"All right," he said through clenched teeth.

His cooperation came from guilt, but I'd take it. "Be fast," he said as we hurried up the steps of the library.

"If we get caught, I'll tell them I lost my sweater," I promised.

"I'll tell them I lost my damned mind," Ellis said, twisting his key in the lock.

The doors boomed open. The lobby stood dark, the only light coming from outside. I searched for a switch. "Oh, frick. I can't see."

"Hurry," Ellis said, ushering me inside. He flipped the security lights on and closed the door behind us. "I swear this town has eyes."

The foyer appeared eerie in the weak overhead security beams, as did the reading room beyond. There were no Confederates playing poker, no field hospital. I hadn't brought Frankie. I needed him to open my eyes. But if I did that, Maisie would be all alone.

Beau would have taken off the second he realized I was gone—which wouldn't take long.

I was still deciding what to do when Major Jackson slowly took form right in front of me. "Matthew," I greeted him, surprised.

He'd removed his officer's coat and appeared as I'd seen him before, in a simple homespun shirt and trousers. He tilted his head shyly. "I walked Miss Josephine home tonight." There was an edge of excitement in his voice.

"Good for you," I said breathlessly. It still wigged me out that I could see him without help.

"I really hoped you'd stop by," he said. "Did you bring your copy of *The Vampire Lestat*?"

"Unfortunately, this isn't a social call," I said, glancing at Ellis, who stood near me with a hand on his holster. "Can you...see him?" I asked Ellis.

"No." He cleared his throat. "But it feels cold all of a sudden," he said, his breath coming quickly. It was a start.

"You're much more open to me," Matthew said, clearly meaning it as a compliment.

"I'm glad," I said. "Listen, I'm hoping you can help. My sister was arrested and I need to know what happened at the library tonight."

He glanced behind him. "I haven't really seen anyone or anything tonight."

"Can you show me the other side so I can ask around?" It was a big favor, but we were sort of friends.

Major Jackson thought for a moment before nodding. "I think I understand what your gangster did. It's highly irregular."

"That sounds like Frankie."

"Brace yourself." He closed his eyes and focused. As he did, I began to see the ghostly room take shape around me. Only this time, it was different. Groans came from the field hospital, only the beds lay empty. I saw no ghostly nurse. No friends playing poker. The lobby lay abandoned. "I've never done this before," Jackson said, his eyes closed, his cheek twitching as he held the connection. "I don't want to hurt you."

"Me neither," I agreed. I didn't see much in the main area of the library, but the door to the coat closet glowed white at the edges. "I think it's working."

"Tell me if it gets to be too much," Jackson said. Sweat formed on his brow. "This is dangerous."

"Then you're doing it the way Frankie would." I heard banging inside the coat closet. Someone let out a loud curse. "Do you know who's in there?" I whispered.

"The surgeon," Jackson said, with a slight shiver. "He doesn't like anyone in his operating room unless you're on the table."

I remembered. The surgeon had chased Jackson out of the coat closet on the night Darla was murdered. I'd been hoping to talk to him about that. And tonight, he might have seen who took Melody's keys.

Jackson watched me, worried. "Are you still all right? You couldn't even touch me without hurting yourself, and this is much more personal."

"I feel fine," I assured him. The others might call him a beast, but from what I'd heard he only lost control when they harassed him, or when he felt painfully alone. He was neither of those things right now. We'd forged a connection that we both needed, and I knew in my gut that he'd do his best to protect me. "Can you hold the connection steady enough for me to talk to him?"

He swallowed visibly, the man who'd faced down a poltergeist. "Yes." He focused on the coat closet, on the glowing light beyond. "I will stay here and give you small bits of power. I will not get emotionally involved and I will not hurt you." He said that last part like a vow, as if he had to convince himself.

"I trust you," I said to the ghost. His eyes widened at that, but I didn't have too much time to think on it. Instead, I watched the old wooden door open wide for me.

Chapter Twenty-One

A HOLLOW SCREAM echoed from the room. I exchanged a glance with Ellis, who stood with his back straight and his hand on his gun holster. He'd seen the door open by itself. Despite the fact that we both *knew* what had done it, he seemed as startled as I was.

"I'll go in there with you," he said, his voice gruff.

"No." I approached the room slowly. He couldn't help with what lay past the darkened doorway. "I'll handle the ghostly threats. You tackle the human ones." I needed him to stay outside and keep watch. They'd arrested the wrong person, which meant Darla's murderer was still out there. I'd do my job much better if I didn't have to worry about the killer sneaking up on me.

A faint silver mist streamed from the room and curled over the floors. It felt cool against my toes. I walked straight into it, letting it flow over my ankles, my shins, my knees. I saw the other side in glowing shades of gray and white, and a flicker of movement inside the claustrophobic room caught my attention.

I stepped through the open doorway and straight into a pool of blood, thick and almost black.

Keep it together.

Lanterns blazed in the room, and white light streamed in from small high windows near the ceiling. Below, a heavily bearded man in a butcher's apron and white shirtsleeves wiped down a surgeon's saw. Blood stained his front, his sleeves, and the rag he tossed into the corner with a pile of others.

"Bring in the next patient," he ordered, bracing a hand on the bloody table, his head lowered, as if he craved some small release, a brief respite from the never-ending carnage that was his afterlife.

I cleared my throat. "I'm not a nurse," I said, cringing at the way my voice wavered.

His head whipped up. His expression was pained, his eyes piercing. "Then get out!"

"No," I said, taking a step forward, tripping on an empty coatrack that someone should have at least put away in the corner. "I need to talk with you."

He sneered as I rolled the coatrack to the side. "They use my operating room as a dumping ground. Boxes and coats and garbage!" He shoved at a tall box that stood between him and his surgical instruments, but his hands went straight through it. "How am I supposed to concentrate?" There was an edge of desperation to his voice. I couldn't imagine his life. This. Standing here in a storage closet and being expected to operate, to chop off arms and legs to save lives. I was sick and sorry for all of it.

But I couldn't do anything for him or his patients.

I could help Darla, though, so I focused on that. "A woman came in here several nights ago," I told him. "She discovered something in a wooden secretary with a dove on the lid. It had been kept in here." I scanned the boxes stacked against the wall, two more beneath his operating table, and a box full of rolled-up posters blocking the lantern he used to light his table. "Do you remember? It was right before you chased off Major Jackson."

He ran a hand through his hair. His eyes were bloodshot. I wondered when he'd slept last. Probably in 1863. He appeared almost lost for a moment before he shut down hard. "I don't need any damned Yankees in here, and I don't need you."

The front door of the library crashed open with a loud *boom*.

Cripes. I hurried to the doorway and peered out. Ellis stood guard at one of the long windows by the library entrance, his eyes trained on the street. A Confederate infantry soldier entered the lobby behind Ellis. The soldier's muscles strained as he supported the weight of his injured comrade. It was the same two men I'd seen the night I met Jackson.

"The doctor's in here," I called.

The uninjured soldier turned to me. "He took a round ball in the shin."

I motioned them forward. "Get him on the table." I stepped outside to let the soldiers past.

"What's going on?" Ellis asked, joining me.

"I'm going to need you in a second," I told him. "Hang tight."

Inside the operating room, they were hoisting the injured man onto the table. "On the count of three," the surgeon ordered, "One, two…" Together, he and the other soldier lifted the injured man.

"Okay." They were settled. "Ellis, we have to get all the junk out of this room."

He looked at me like I was crazy, and maybe I was. "You realize it's a junk room."

"And a coat closet," I added as Ellis and I ducked inside.

The soldier gripped his friend's hand and the man winced as the doctor examined the bloody hole in his leg. The young soldier was frightened and in pain. And there was nothing I could do for him or the poor doctor whose eternity had become one bloody mess.

Except for one thing. I could help in a small way.

I'd explain later. "We can start with these," I said, pointing to the boxes by the door.

"Where?" he asked, searching for the electrical switch. That's right. He needed light to see. When he found the switch, he flipped it on and grabbed an armload of boxes. "Where to?"

"Out in the lobby for now." Melody would have a better idea where to put them tomorrow. I refused to believe she'd be in jail tomorrow.

"Excuse me," I said to the surgeon as I scooted the box of rolled-up posters away from his operating light. He grunted, focused on his work.

When I got them out to the lobby, I saw Ellis stacking boxes by the arched doorway to the reading room. "Not there," I called. "The guys need room to play poker."

He stood. "Okay. Sure." It was sweet of him to trust me like this, and I found my earlier anger softening a bit. He pointed to the corner nearest the door. "Anybody needing this spot here?"

"No," I said, scooting the box that way. "That should be fine."

"Leave it," he told me. "I can get it."

"Sounds good," I said, relieved to hand part of the job over to him as I headed back for the rolling coatrack.

It took some doing, mostly on Ellis's part, but we managed to get everything out of the doctor's way and out into the lobby.

"Thank you," I said, my back aching a bit. I reached for Ellis's hand and squeezed.

He held on. "I'm sorry."

I gave a quick nod. "I know."

He leaned in close. "You about done in there?"

It depended on what happened next. "I hope so."

I watched as two orderlies carried the young soldier out on a stretcher and headed for the makeshift recovery area in what was now the reading room. I didn't see as much of it as I had last time, but it was there.

The soldier who had burst open the door lingered behind. I approached him gently. "Your friend is in good hands. That doctor in there might be gruff, but it's only because he cares so much."

The young man nodded, lost in his thoughts.

I turned and saw the doctor watching me from the doorway.

It was as good an invitation as any.

When I let myself back into the room, he headed to the corner with a table that held a bowl of water. He stood over it, rinsing his hands in the already bloody bowl. He made no move to toss me from the room this time. I took it as a good sign.

"Thank you," he said. "I don't know why people can't leave me alone to do my work. If I'm not at my best, patients die." He turned, wiping his hands on a linen cloth. "Do you have any idea what that's like?"

"No," I admitted. "But I understand what it's like to feel powerless." I shook my head, trying to keep frustration from taking hold. But it settled in my gut, winding through me. "A good woman died right outside and I can't do anything about it. She discovered something in here and it made someone angry enough to kill her. But I can't prove anything."

He threw the towel over the bowl with more force than necessary. "You helped me with the junk, so I reckon I can help you with that."

"Really?" I tried not to sound so eager, but I needed this break. "Did you see her that night?"

He stood, as if taking my measure. "She found a letter in the wooden secretary. It's gone now. I don't know who took it."

I rubbed a hand over my eyes. "I know. I've been chasing down that lead and it hasn't led me anywhere useful."

He narrowed his eyes. "I'm not talking about the letter Jackson showed you."

I dropped my hand. "You saw me with him?"

"I always know who's in my operating room."

The doctor walked over to where I'd stood with Jackson, and the image of the antique secretary shimmered into view on the table, exactly as it had before. He was remembering the same thing, recalling it from the ether. He caressed the mother-of-pearl dove inlaid on the wood and opened the lid to reveal the foldout writing table and the cubbyholes stuffed with letters. But then he lifted the leather lining on the writing surface and reached underneath.

"I fear this will make us look bad," he warned. "The men who died here deserve glory. But not if it lets a murderer go free. There is a higher morality at play here." He withdrew an envelope with large, scrolled handwriting across the front. "This is it," he said, offering it to me.

I didn't want to touch it. "Can you open it?"

The doctor frowned, and I decided not to press my luck. "It's fine," I said, reaching for the letter, hoping to heaven I could remove the paper from the envelope. This was more complicated than simply picking it up or turning it over.

It felt ice cold against my fingers, but I had it. I could touch it. It felt real enough.

Breathe.

The envelope glowed silver gray in my hands. The outside was addressed to Jeremiah Hatcher in careful, flowing script.

There was already a slit at the top. With shaking fingers, I withdrew the letter.

Dear Mister Hatcher,

It is with my deepest regrets that I write to inform you that I must end my engagement to your daughter, Josephine. It is not because my affections have ceased. Rather, the unfortunate circumstances that have come to light regarding the events of the afternoon of October 17, 1863, have forced my hand. I know you were not in favor of our union, so perhaps for you this will serve as a silver lining in an otherwise painful situation.

My father still considers you his dearest friend, and was honored to receive your personal Bible when you feared for your life at the battle of Eads Creek. However, your written confession about the Battle of Sugarland, which I found inside, cannot be forgiven or forgotten by me.

I confess I am shocked and dismayed by your account of the events of that day, as I had believed this a great victory for the South and for Sugarland. In light of this deception and your role in these shameful proceedings, I cannot in good conscience marry your daughter or join your family. I shall return your Bible, with your confession, for you to do with it as you wish. Your secret will go to the grave with me.

Yours,
Jonathan Conway

Impossible. The Battle of Sugarland was our finest moment. Nothing shameful had happened on that day. Had it? I gripped the letter so tight that it stung my fingers. Our town based its identity on that battle. Virginia Wydell had pinned a good part of her legacy on that one historic day.

And now it seemed the Hatchers were involved in this as well. I needed to learn more. I turned to the surgeon. "Did you know a Hatcher who fought here?" I wondered if Josephine's dad still haunted the house on the hill, along with his poltergeist wife. Josephine had rarely spoken of him. "Do you have any idea what he could have been hiding?"

The surgeon began organizing his instruments. "I was here the whole time, patching people together. The town burned down around me, and I didn't leave this room. My job is the same no matter what happens on the battlefield.

But the woman who died found the letter quite distressing. She left this room, eager to spread the word to the living."

"Did you see who she told?"

"No," he said, wiping his hands on a dirty rag. "I had an amputation to perform, but when I came back out, she was dead and the secretary and all of its contents were gone. A shame. There's been more than enough death around here."

"There has," I murmured. Enough lies as well.

We had to find that Bible.

It had been the property of Pa Hatcher, and according to the letter, Jonathan had returned it to him. I wondered if it was still somewhere in the house, hidden.

Maybe that's why Ma's ghost guarded the place with such a vengeance.

The more I thought about it, the more I warmed to the idea. Josephine had said the shooter tried to break in tonight, but he'd been run off. I hoped he hadn't found the Bible first.

The doctor and I watched as the letter disintegrated in my hands, just like the one before. That was okay. I didn't need it anymore.

"Thank you for your help," I said to the doctor as I made my way out of his operating room.

He nodded and returned to his instruments. He'd given me a great new lead. Now I just had to use it.

Chapter Twenty-Two

OUT IN THE lobby, Ellis had just hung up his cell. "We have a problem," he said, returning the phone to his pocket. "Somebody ransacked Maisie's house tonight after you left."

"I think I know what they're looking for." It had to be that Bible.

Whatever confession Pa Hatcher had unburdened on those pages, it was causing a lot of trouble now. Who else would be implicated, and how many more people would have to die to keep the truth hidden?

"We need to go to Maisie's," I told him, glancing around for Matthew. I didn't see him.

Ellis headed for the door. "We'll pick her up at your place on the way," he said, grabbing his keys.

"No, wait. I don't think we should involve her until we know what we're dealing with." We made it outside and Ellis began locking up the library. "Maisie is old and frail. And she's way too fond of that shotgun. Let's see what we have first."

He glanced at me. "We'll need her permission to search."

"She said we were welcome anytime," I told him, cringing.

Maisie would want us to do what was right. Plus, I really didn't want to wake her up to explain another message I'd found on the other side.

Ellis shook his head as we hurried down the stairs toward his squad car. "You aren't much for rules."

"True," I admitted. People were more important. And Ellis would do what he could to help Maisie. I wasn't above using that to our advantage.

"We'll go in if we have probable cause," he cautioned. His radio chirped and he took the call as we slid inside his car. "What do you got, Marshall?" He pulled out as I slammed my door closed.

"Melody Long claims somebody must have stolen her vehicle," the detective said, his voice dripping with doubt.

"That was my first thought," Ellis said as we raced, lights blazing, back to the Hatcher homestead.

"I'm not sure I believe her. What car thief in their right mind returns the vehicle?" He huffed out a breath. "Did the suspect drive like a woman?"

"I don't think you want to go there," Ellis remarked, giving me a "keep quiet" look.

He was asking a lot.

Main Street was more crowded than usual. Everyone was climbing the hill toward the midnight Cannonball in the Wall celebration. Spotlights shone on the lectern and the VIP stage. The cameras and lights of the documentary film crew weaved in and out of the growing crowd.

Ellis's grip on the wheel tightened. "You ever think Melody might be telling the truth that she doesn't know anything?" he asked Marshall.

"She's acting wild as a june bug on a string. It's suspicious."

Probably because he *arrested* her. Guilt washed over me. I should be with my sister. Although, heck, they wouldn't let me see her. I'd be more of a help to Melody if I could just put this together and point the police to the true killer. Then Marshall would have to let her go.

Ellis ended the call, which was just as well. I didn't know how long I could stay silent.

We drove away from the crowd, toward the rural east end of town. Fewer cars passed us heading toward town, simply because not many people lived out this way. Ellis's car hugged the road, going at top speed as we switched from the highway to the back roads.

We took the winding drive through the woods and pulled up right out in front of Maisie's house. It was trashed. Police spotlights lit up the front yard, glass-strewn from the earlier gunfight. Through the broken front window, I could see someone had taken a knife to the couch. The slashed cushions bled foam filling all over the floor. The side-table drawer hung open. Magazines, knitting yarn, and VHS tapes lay scattered.

A young lieutenant greeted us at the door. "It's a mess, and there's no sign of the homeowner."

"She's sleeping at my place," I told him, ignoring his surprise.

I didn't have time to explain. Not when it was all starting to make sense.

The shooter hadn't been trying to kill us. He just wanted to drive us out so he could get to the Bible. Only it wasn't in Maisie's house.

Ma Hatcher was guarding her husband's secret with all the power of a poltergeist.

Josephine had said the shooter tried to get in and failed tonight. No doubt he'd be back.

"We've got to go to the old Hatcher place," I told Ellis. "That's where the killer will go next."

The lieutenant balked. "Who said anything about a killer? This is a simple vandalism case. Probably kids attracted to the police tape."

There was no time to explain, at least not to him. But Ellis didn't protest. He trusted me. "Let's go."

We got back into his car and I told him the whole story as he took the overgrown drive around the property that snaked up to the haunted house on the hill. He tapped a finger against his steering wheel as I got to the part about the Bible.

"So you're saying this has to do with the cannonball in the wall," he said, working it through.

My shoulders stiffened as we crested the hill and the house came into view. "Something bad happened that day. When we figure out what, it's going to explain a lot."

Ellis stopped the car in front of the haunted house. "Here we are." He killed the lights, and I shivered as the sudden darkness washed over me.

The last time I'd been near the old Hatcher place, I'd almost been buried alive trying to escape. Ma Hatcher's ghost would kill to keep her family's secret.

Poor Josephine seemed caught in the middle.

"At least I don't see any evidence of a live killer up here," Ellis muttered, not comforting me in the least.

But he was right. We saw no other cars, no signs of life.

Frankie would be able to tell us more. "Hey, buddy," I said, taking the urn from my bag. Come on. He had to have some energy left. "Frankie," I asked.

When that didn't work, I tapped at the urn. That would surely get a rise from him. I could hear him now: *There ain't no doorbell, sweetheart.*

The ghost didn't answer.

He might have gotten ungrounded and split, although I still had the urn. At least some of him was still with me. I rattled it a bit and felt the ash inside shift. Maybe it wasn't enough to keep him around.

I shared a glance with Ellis over the glowing lights of the dash, trying not to let my disappointment show. "Maybe he wants to stay with Maisie." I'd rather not think of the alternative.

He gave a sharp nod. "Right," he said, pushing his door open.

I joined him outside. The Hatcher place stood dark and foreboding. I saw no light in Josephine's window, no sign of Ma. It was as if the house itself held its breath, waiting for us to make our move.

Ellis clicked on his police-issue Maglite and I fired up my dollar-store cheapo. If we could pull this off, if we could make this quick, I promised myself I'd never set foot in that place again.

The bare trees stirred as we made our way to the front door.

"Josephine?" I whispered.

Maybe I could spot her on my own. Lots of people had seen a candle glowing in her window. But tonight, it remained empty.

Ellis hung close to me. "Is she gone?"

"Seems so." I hadn't even realized she might want to leave. But she would have given me a sign if she were here. We were friends. Sort of.

Ellis took the lead as we approached the house, and I'm not ashamed to say I let him. I watched the darkened windows, looking for any sign of life...or afterlife.

He closed his hand over the front doorknob and the house let out a low, chilling groan.

"Jesus!" He jumped back. "Has it done that before?"

"No," I said, my voice an octave higher than it should be.

He steeled himself and reached for the knob again. This time, the door opened easily.

"So far, so good," he muttered.

I didn't trust my voice to respond.

The inside lay dark. Goose bumps shot up my arms the second I stepped through the entryway. The temperature had plunged at least twenty degrees in the span of two feet. I could see my breath as I struggled to stay calm. I'd been inside this house before. Once. With Frankie, who had helped fend off Ma when she attacked. But he wasn't with me now.

Stay calm.

The walls crackled as Ellis nudged the door closed behind us.

It felt as if the house itself wanted to spit us back out into the yard.

Believe me, we'd go. I'd be out of here in a red-hot second as soon as I closed my hands on that Bible.

"Where is it?" Ellis asked.

His light illuminated the rectangular first floor, its rough wood walls tangled with thick cobwebs near the ceiling and floors. They trailed over a broken table toward a cold fireplace hearth streaked with soot.

"Um." It occurred to me that I hadn't let him in on that one important detail. His flashlight beam caught the rickety staircase leading to the second floor. "I don't know exactly *where* to find the Bible. I'm just pretty sure it's here."

"You gotta be kidding me," he muttered. His Adam's apple bobbed as a small breeze stirred his hair—one that should *not* have been there because we were shut completely in the house.

The hair on the back of my neck stood up. I could swear I felt someone behind me.

Cold breath tickled my skin, hovering near the curl of my right ear. I froze. "Josephine?" I whispered, hoping against hope. Darkness curled in my stomach. She didn't answer.

Floating lights danced in the fireplace. "You see that?" Ellis hissed, pointing as the ashes under the old iron log holder caught fire.

"Oh yes," I said. I saw it. Without any help at all. We needed to run. Instead, I urged him deeper into the room. "It's not in the fireplace."

His arm was stiff under my hand, and he resisted my tug. "We don't know until we check it out." I held on to him tight, so glad to have him in here with me. "It's trying to chase us away," he whispered. "Whatever is the scariest room in the house, that's where we need to go."

At that exact moment, a low growl pierced the air. It came from the second floor.

"Now that could be something," I said.

Ellis squared his shoulders. "Okay." He took my hand and together we walked toward the stairs. The snarl intensified, halting us in our tracks at the bottom. "This is good," he said, shining his light up as we began our ascent.

"The best," I agreed, ignoring the shaking of the stairs. I heard the low *whump-whump-whump* of an object rolling toward us on the landing above.

"Bowling ball?" Ellis guessed, startling slightly as the object crashed down on the uppermost stair.

I was thinking more like *cannonball*. "You hear it?" I could have sworn it was on the ghostly plane. My light showed nothing. I braced myself.

Ma Hatcher had gathered enough power to try to scare the bejesus out of Ellis and me. The question was whether the poltergeist had harnessed enough rage to hurt us.

"Get ready to run," I urged as the heavy object rolled down to the next step, and the next, slamming into the wood, echoing hard, coming straight at us as we stepped up one more stair, and another, and another. "Steady." I held my breath, ready to bolt.

The sound ceased.

Oh boy. "Let's just…" I began.

"Yeah," Ellis said. Together, we raced up to the second-story landing.

This was it. We were officially out of our minds.

The landing stood dark, eerie.

Ellis let out a harsh breath. "Is this what it's always like for you?"

"No," I said, shining my light over the faded wallpaper. "When Frankie helps, I see things like he does. Everything is illuminated in tones of silver and gray. Places appear the way the dominant ghost on the property sees them. This is like walking in blind."

I stood in a narrow hallway, a long stretch of wall broken apart by three solid doors. We had no idea which way to go, but I had a sinking feeling we'd learn soon enough.

Ellis and I stood deathly still, hands in a firm grip. Waiting.

A low cackle sounded from the door on the far right end. The hair on my arms prickled and my heart slammed hard in my chest.

"That's Josephine's room," I whispered.

We advanced on it. "You think that's her?"

"No." Whatever rustled inside was dark, evil. This was Ma Hatcher's doing, not her daughter's.

We still hadn't seen any sign of Josephine or her dog, Fritz. I hoped they were all right.

I pushed open the door and stepped inside. Hot, prickling energy inched over me like a swarm of ants. I resisted the urge to scratch. It wouldn't help, and I refused to give the spirit the satisfaction. "This is definitely the worst room in the house."

Yay for us.

Ellis's grip on my hand tightened. "No. That is."

He shone his light toward the closet. The wooden door was bent, charred, and blackened around the edges, as if an evil energy had sealed it closed. I let out a gasp as the door began to rattle on its hinges.

He pressed forward. "I'll open it. You cover me."

"I'm the ghost hunter," I said, pressing past him, closing my hand over the ice-cold knob before I lost my nerve. It sent a chill through me that had nothing to do with the frigid temperature inside the house. This was it. I could feel the spirit of Ma Hatcher grasping, snarling as it clamored for me *not* to touch that door.

I swung it open.

Inside the closet, on the dusty wood floor, sprawled the body of a man.

His skull stared up at me, the front shattered. He wore the tattered remains of a gray uniform and his bony hands clutched a Bible. A single-shot revolver lay at his side.

I sucked in a breath. "I think we found Pa."

Chapter Twenty-Three

WARM BREATH GHOSTED over the back of my neck. For a second, I thought it was Ellis. Then I realized Ma Hatcher stood next to me. Her cold, gravelly voice chilled my skin. "Get. Out."

She was a fully formed ghostly presence. I could see her without Frankie's help. Which meant she was right there with us. I turned quickly and stared straight into her burning red eyes. The closet door slammed closed, nearly striking me.

Ellis stood nearby, stiff with shock. The ghost loomed over us, completely manifested. Livid. She grabbed for my neck, hot energy radiating off her.

"Move!" Ellis seized me at the last second and we headed for the stairway.

"Not yet." I broke from his grasp and ran back to the closet. This time the knob burned hot in my hand. We had to get that Bible.

Ma hissed and reached for me.

Ellis swore. "Over here!" he hollered from near the window. He ducked as the phantom shot a blinding stream of energy straight for him. I could see it. Feel it. Like lightning in a bottle.

The poltergeist was firing off pure rage.

It was also missing its legs below the knees.

If we played this right, we could use it to our advantage.

First, I had to be sure. "Did she have legs before?" I pleaded. I tried to remember what she'd looked like when she trapped me in the grave outside. Her dress had swirled down to the ground, hadn't it? I couldn't be sure.

Ellis looked at me like I was nuts. "How the hell should I know?"

"Get out!" the phantom screamed as she fired another round. Ellis didn't move quickly enough. He let out a cry of pain and went down hard.

Oh my God. "Ellis!"

His teeth chattered and he shook all over as if he'd been hit with an electric charge.

I realized with a start that Ma had lost her legs completely. Ellis stared at me through the poltergeist, understanding dawning in his eyes.

"Over here!" I called, trying to draw her off, but she'd homed in on him.

He rolled sideways as she fired a hot blast of energy. He barely cleared it. The room shook as the wall absorbed the impact.

She lost her hips.

"Oh my God. Ellis." I didn't know what to do. The poltergeist was going down a lot faster than Frankie did when he lent me his energy. I had to think it was because she was sending out direct, devastating shots of energy while manifesting on the mortal plane.

She controlled more energy than I'd ever seen a ghost— even a poltergeist—handle before. And she aimed it straight at Ellis.

"We'll go!" I protested. "Just leave him alone!"

She glared at me over her shoulder. "Even my husband regretted it in the end," she snarled, "but a secret's a secret."

I could actually see the energy leave her hands as she fired at Ellis, scoring a direct hit. His body seized. I stared in horror. The room smelled of burned hair and flesh.

"Josephine!" I screamed for my friend, the only person I could think of who might be able to help us.

Ma hissed and sent a heavy stream of hate my way. I dropped to the floor.

Heat sizzled the air above me, charging it, making my hair stand on end. It hurt to breathe.

Ellis didn't move. There was no way I could get around the ghost to help him, unless I went straight through her mostly missing body. Were her legs still there, even though I couldn't see them?

I had to risk it. I couldn't let Ellis take another shot. It would kill him.

She reared, ready to attack as I rushed for Ellis, scrambling headlong underneath the ghost.

I made it.

He looked awful. I grabbed his limp body, shoving it back against the wall, yanking my hands away when I felt the energy hit.

My muscles seized; my mind blanked with pain and rage. I felt the shock of it like a thousand volts.

"Silly girl." She loomed over me, now just a disembodied head, her face pinched with rage. "Don't you know they always betray you in the end?"

Her ghastly features twisted as she gathered the energy for what could very well be a death blow. I screamed. I didn't think I could take another hit. She must not either, because she shot me a feral grin.

A red spark rippled up her neck and zipped straight through her head before I heard a pop, like a burned-out lightbulb.

Ma Hatcher had disappeared.

The room grew strangely quiet, the dark overwhelming. I panted hard, not even sure when I'd stopped screaming. Ellis didn't stir. I didn't even know if he was still breathing.

My light shone on the floor a few feet from me and I scrambled to retrieve it.

"Ellis, can you hear me?" I asked, my voice hoarse. I knew better than to ask if he was all right. He wasn't. "I think the ghost is gone."

Ellis lay on his side, a hand over his eyes. "You're the expert," he said on a groan.

He was alive and conscious. "Thank God." I took his face in my hands and kissed him.

His eyes remained closed. "This is not a date."

"No," I said, a giddy laugh escaping. "How do you feel? Can you move?"

I helped him into a sitting position. "I can't even describe it," he said, working to recover.

"I understand." My muscles felt stiff, my body ached, yet I felt electric down to the core. As if the energy had welded itself to my very bones. She could have killed us both.

"I think we beat her," I said, searching the room for any sign of the poltergeist. "For now."

That said, we needed to get out of here before she regained her energy and came back. I had no idea how long that would take.

Ellis retrieved his Maglite from the floor. He appeared shaky, but determined. "Help me stand. We need to take another look at that skeleton in the closet."

We did. And a few minutes later, after a bit of struggling with the door, Ellis shone his beam down on the body of Pa Hatcher.

Now that I was able to get a closer look, I could see the spiderwebs tangled in the skeleton's empty eye sockets. The rotting remnants of dress gloves clung to his fingers. I cringed at the way his bony hands gripped the leather-bound Bible.

I placed my light on the floor and braced myself on the doorframe as I reached down to pry the Bible from the man's cold, dead hands.

Chapter Twenty-Four

THE CORPSE RELEASED the book, crumbling away as if it, too, had been waiting to be freed from the secret.

Ellis's light illuminated the cracked and aged Bible. On the inside cover, generations of Hatchers had scrawled a hand-inked family history dating back to 1758.

"Where does one write a confession?" I asked, opening to Genesis. Might as well start at the beginning.

The thin paper felt stiff with age and I feared for the fragile book as I turned the pages.

"I have an idea," Ellis said, so I handed him the book.

His fingers trembled as he paged to Proverbs 28:13.

I didn't get it. "What makes you think...?"

Oh, my word. Black ink underlined one of the verses.

"I went to Sunday school, same as you," he said, running a finger over the line.

Evidently Ellis had paid more attention.

It read:

He that covereth his sins shall not prosper: but whoso confesseth and forsaketh [them] shall have mercy.

Scrawled in the side margin, in black ink, was a missive that took up almost all of the white space on the page:

I, Lieutenant Colonel Jeremiah Hatcher, under the command of Eli Jackson, do hereby solemnly swear to the truth of what happened the day of October 17, 1863. While we were charged with manning the cannon overlooking the town of Sugarland, we left our posts.

Colonel Vincent Wydell challenged Colonel Eli Jackson to a duel over which Sugarland family should indeed guard the cannon. In the midst of the duel, Yankee cavalry came upon the cannon and fired a shot into the town, which lodged in the wall of the library.

The town, believing itself under attack, panicked, sparking the fire that burned the square. We then charged down to save the town from itself, thereby abandoning the hill and the cannon once more to the Yankees, who used it to defeat the main Confederate force on the battlefield overlooking the town.

We were not heroes that day, but prideful men who neglected our duty and the safety of our families. May God forgive us.

Lieutenant Colonel Jeremiah Hatcher
May the Lord have mercy on my soul.

Mercy indeed, on all of us.

I read it again, just to make sure. "I don't believe it." The Battle of Sugarland was one big lie. Our town celebration meant nothing. And Virginia Wydell's entire extravaganza was based on a humiliating moment in Wydell history, not a success.

Ellis huffed out a breath. "It would be bad enough for Mom to lose her fortune to Maisie, but her entire reputation? This is worse. At least for her."

That was right. She'd never live this down. That cannonball in the wall wasn't a symbol of town and family glory. It was a permanent reminder of her family's pride, arrogance, and greed.

I stood for a moment, taking it all in. "I still can't believe we fought each other and then we burned down our own town."

We'd based a big part of our identity on this moment, just as Virginia had. We held festivals, took pictures, sang songs. We were in the Tennessee guidebook.

Right now, people were gathering by the old cannon overlooking the square, getting ready to celebrate our historic military victory.

It was all a lie.

He studied the passage again. "When you leave a major position unguarded, the enemy will take advantage."

The Battle of Sugarland had been bloody and brutal hand-to-hand combat. And it had been completely avoidable.

"So tonight, up on that hill, they're celebrating internal fighting, a lucky shot, and town panic."

And now that I knew the truth, I couldn't help but see it. "Didn't you always wonder how our militia all ended up in the town and not on the battlefield?"

Ellis shuddered out a laugh. "There's an old family story about how Jackson and Wydell fought a duel before the battle. The Wydells always liked to say Eli Jackson's battle wound was really just a shot from Great-Uncle Vincent."

"Sounds like it was more truth than family pride," I told him.

He closed his eyes for a moment. "I want to tell her. Alone."

I wanted to give him that, but… "You can't." His mother had already seen to it. She'd made an extra-large spectacle of the midnight celebration tonight, and now it was going to come back to bite her. Because we couldn't let it go on. Not now.

"I understand. Mom set herself up for this." He winced. "She won't even see it coming."

She might if she was the one who killed Darla. But I didn't say that. It would only hurt him more.

The room had grown quite warm, at least in comparison to the bone-soaking chill I'd felt when we entered the house. I looked back to Pa Hatcher's skeleton lying crumpled on the closet floor. "I'm surprised Ma Hatcher didn't destroy the Bible."

Ellis shook his head. "I don't think a God-fearing woman of her time would dare."

"So she locked the body in the closet with the evidence and guarded it until her death."

"And afterward as well," Ellis added. "But she must not have known about the letter hidden in Jeremiah Hatcher's personal secretary, the one that talked about the Bible."

"I doubt Leland Wydell found it, either." Even after he'd bought the piece and used it for his personal correspondence. "That aging leather trim must have made it easier for Darla to pry the letter from its hiding spot."

Ellis simply nodded. "Can you walk?"

We leaned on each other as we made our way out of the dark, abandoned house.

I clutched the Bible to my chest. I'd never been so glad to step outside, until a gunshot sounded and Ellis dropped to the ground.

Montgomery Silas stepped from the shadows and aimed a revolver at my chest. His forehead shone with sweat. "Hand over the Bible, Miss Long."

"Let me at least see if Ellis is okay," I gasped, raising my hands in the air.

"Give me the Bible first."

I stared at him, and suddenly everything clicked. "Virginia Wydell didn't kill Darla Grace. It was you."

His expression hardened as he pulled the trigger.

Chapter Twenty-Five

HEAT SEARED THROUGH my shoulder. My eyes felt gritty as I came to on the musty floor of the old Hatcher house. "Ellis?" I croaked.

I could barely hear over the loud crackling noise that surrounded me.

The room had grown hot, and I smelled smoke. A hand gripped my good shoulder and shook me hard. "Stay with me, Verity." Ellis crouched over me. "I'm too hurt to lift you and we need to get out of here."

I opened my eyes. Flames rose from the wall directly in front of us, disappearing behind churning black smoke. The roar of the fire grew louder.

"How are we going to get out?" I pleaded.

"Look for a door or a window," Ellis said, covering his mouth and nose with the top of his shirt.

I couldn't see anything that would tell us where we were. Choking smoke surrounded us. I coughed, fighting a wave of dizziness. The house was ablaze, and old wood like this wouldn't last long.

I grabbed my cell phone from my pocket, hoping to call for help, but a black screen greeted me. Ma Hatcher had fried it.

It wasn't fair. It wasn't supposed to turn out this way. Sweat beaded on my back and ran down from my hair. The house groaned around us.

"Come on," Ellis said, leading me as we crawled across the warm floorboards. "I think I see the door."

I clung to him, my eyes watering from the smoke. And I swore it wasn't an illusion, but I could almost make out the form of Josephine shimmering into view directly in front of us. It could have been the smoke...but no. It was her! I didn't understand how I could see her, and then I realized she was kissing Matthew.

"Josephine," I cried.

The couple jolted apart. Josephine covered her mouth with her hands and Matthew stared down at us in shock.

"The house is on fire!" My throat burned with the smoke I'd inhaled.

Matthew's eyes darted about to take in his surroundings. "So it is. I hardly noticed."

Josephine was crying now. "My house!" She darted up through the ceiling. "Oh, Pa!"

The door stood directly behind the couple. Ellis found the knob and twisted. It didn't budge. He began wrestling with it. Desperate. Montgomery must have barred it.

I stared at Matthew. "Get us out!"

A calm came over Major Jackson, as if he went into battle mode. "Stand aside," he said, not giving us any time to do so before he blasted the door open.

Fresh air streamed in, stoking the fire. Flames shot up around us with renewed vigor.

Oh my word. We couldn't make it out that way. We were going to die in here.

"This way!" Matthew commanded, gliding in the opposite direction, toward the stairs.

No! He was going to get us killed. We had to stay low and get out the door or a window on the first floor. Only they were all on the front of the house, behind that wall of flames. I wanted to cry. I was already dizzy and...

"Quickly," Matthew pleaded. "I can see. You can't!"

"Come on," I said, attempting to lead Ellis farther back into the house.

He clutched his bloody right side. "Stop. No…"

"The ghost says to go this way," I choked out. "We can trust him," I added, praying I was right.

Ellis cursed, and for a second, I didn't think he'd go into the fire with me.

But he did. He believed in me. Together, we crawled toward the stairs, farther into the burning house, every instinct screaming at me to go back the other way.

The stairs felt hot underneath us, threatening to collapse with every creak and moan. We pressed forward. We didn't have a choice.

From the top of the landing, we heard Josephine weeping in her room.

"My house," she wailed, tears streaming down her face. Fritz ran in circles around her, agitated and barking. "Do I even exist without my house?"

"Yes," I told her. "You have us. And Matthew. And Fritz."

She didn't appear to even hear me.

Ellis hurried past her and tested the window. "She won't have us for much longer if we don't get out of here."

He was right. The house would collapse under us. We couldn't make it out downstairs, and we had no exits up here. No matter where we went, we were trapped.

The window opened without the rush of flames we'd endured downstairs. The fire hadn't reached the second floor.

Matthew materialized and pulled Josephine into his embrace. At the same time, he pointed out the window to a sturdy pine that grew at least ten feet away. It wasn't burning, not yet. "Go, Verity. I'll push you along," he urged. The thought of jumping out the window terrified me. It was a long way down. The alternative was smoke inhalation and death. No alternative at all, really.

"Okay," I said, trying to gather my wits. "We have to go out the window. Jump for that tree. Matthew's going to push us," I explained to Ellis.

"Who's Matthew?" he demanded. He couldn't see.

"A friend," I explained, making my way toward the window. "Get Josephine out of here too," I said to Matthew.

I crouched near the edge of the window.

Ellis grabbed hold of my shirt. "Verity, don't." He was having trouble focusing, the same as I was. We'd both be passed out from the smoke in less than a minute.

I untangled myself from his grip. "Matthew!" I hollered, launching myself at the faraway tree.

I fell sharply, and then I felt the smack of power against my back and a gust of air that threw me straight into the branches of the tall pine. I grabbed for the nearest branch I could reach and hung on for dear life. I wrapped my legs around the one lower and managed a clumsy fall against the rough bark. Shinnying, I made it to the trunk and turned back to Ellis.

"Jump!" I screamed.

I didn't see him at the window.

He'd been shot. He was suffering from smoke inhalation. He might have passed out.

"Ellis!" I hollered. He had to make it. I couldn't get back to him. I didn't even hear sirens. Whenever the fire trucks did arrive, they would be too late. "Ellis!"

He clawed his way over the windowsill, dripping with sweat, his side bloody, his face and arms stained with soot. "Jump for the tree!" I pleaded.

We locked eyes and he launched himself out the window.

I screamed as he plummeted, and then choked out a sob as an unseen force drove him straight into the tree below me. The old pine shook with the impact. If he fell, I didn't know what I'd do.

But I saw him catch hold and start shinnying down.

Before I could think on it too much, I forced myself to follow. I didn't worry about the height or the fire or the tears stuck in my throat. I headed down to solid earth.

The fire blazed, consuming the house, illuminating the ground below. I briefly spotted Josephine in her bedroom window, panicked, before flames took over.

We ran to Ellis's squad car.

We slid in and he reached across the console for me. He wrapped a hand around the back of my head and kissed me hard, like he couldn't quite believe we'd gotten out of there. I returned the kiss, scared and grateful and happy to be alive.

"You're okay," I said, cupping his cheek.

He closed his eyes hard for a moment before giving me a bold, beautiful look that said it all. "We're both going to be just fine."

"You're bleeding," I told him. I couldn't see it from where I sat, but it had looked bad when he went down.

He looked over at me, his skin streaked with soot, sweat, and blood. "You too."

Now that some of the adrenaline had begun to wear off, I felt the throbbing pain in my shoulder.

Ellis grabbed for his police radio as he started the car. "Fire at 11 Rural Route K. The house at the back of the Hatcher property."

The radio had been fried, too. He tossed it down.

"Hold on. We're going to the hospital," he gritted out, keeping his focus on the road. His sweaty, blackened uniform clung to his chest and arms.

"Let's skip it for now," I croaked, coughing. It felt good to breathe clean air. "I'm okay if you're okay."

He clutched the wheel tighter. "You're delirious."

Yes, my shoulder screamed and I'd been shot and I was probably out of my mind. Still, we couldn't go to the hospital. "We have to go after Montgomery."

Ellis jerked. "What does he have to do with it?"

"You didn't see," I said, wheezing in a breath. He'd been passed out. "Montgomery shot us. He killed Darla. He's behind all of this."

Ellis bit back a curse.

We couldn't call in backup. We couldn't tell anyone, not until the hospital. By then it could be too late. Montgomery could learn we'd survived and make his escape. But right now, we had the element of surprise. We could end this once and for all.

We could get justice for Darla Grace. And for poor Josephine. She might not survive the burning of her house. How many more lives could be ruined if we didn't stop Montgomery now?

"Verity," Ellis warned, but I could see him cracking.

"You know I'm right," I pressed. "This is our chance." We could intercept Montgomery at the midnight celebration. It was about time to start. This was our one shot.

"If you weren't with me, I would." He ran a hand over his face. "You're sure you're okay?"

Truthfully, I wasn't. I was in more pain than I'd ever been in my life. Scared, too. But we couldn't think about that right now. We had a job to do. "Let's go get him."

Chapter Twenty-Six

ELLIS AND I raced down the back roads and onto the highway.

I hoped Josephine was okay, that she didn't owe her existence to that house. Frankie had told me once that a ghost could be emotionally tied to an actual physical structure. If those four walls were the only things keeping Josephine with us, I could lose her for good. So could Matthew.

It felt like it took forever to reach the lights and the crowd at the midnight Cannonball in the Wall event. The whole town was there and possibly a good part of the citizens from outlying counties. Cars packed the field below Cannonball Hill.

I felt dizzy and more than a little strung out. I'd be dead right now if Matthew hadn't intervened. Now I was about to expose the secret that would not only bring down the Wydells, but also Matthew's long-dead brother, Lieutenant Colonel Eli Jackson, who had been the one to duel with Colonel Vincent Wydell. But it had to be done. We'd identified our killer. Now we just needed to expose him.

Montgomery Silas stood on the platform overlooking the crowd. A band played "Dixie" as he waved and smiled. To his credit, he appeared twitchy and he was sweating heavily. His hair stuck out in a few places where it

shouldn't, and he had the overall look of a guilty man. I
liked to think that was because he believed he killed us.

Ellis parked haphazardly near another squad car and
flagged down the officer, who was out of his car directing
the crowd. "We have a situation. My radio's dead, so use
yours. I need all officers to approach the stage and wait for
my command." Then he used the officer's cell phone to call
and request a warrant to search Montgomery's house. "I'm
pretty sure we have probable cause," he said, turning to me,
"but I'm not about to let him get off on a technicality."

I nodded. "Okay, so they're gathering evidence while we
confront him." Only this was a man who had hidden his
true colors from us and from the whole town. He wasn't
going to come quietly now.

"The search warrants for his home and office should
come through within the hour. If he still has that secretary,
we'll find it. In the meantime, we're walking, talking proof
of attempted murder," Ellis said, helping me up the hill.
"And we need to get that Bible back before he destroys it."

"Easier said than done," I said as we crested the hill.

People stared as we made our way through the crowd.
Avery, the cute blonde psychic, turned around directly in
front of me, her eyes wide. She gave me a slight nod as I
passed. "Good luck."

I'd take it.

I saw my friend Lauralee several yards away, with her
husband. It seems they'd hired a babysitter and made a
night of it. She didn't see me and I kept walking. We
needed to lie low if we wanted to try to confront
Montgomery. Virginia stood on the stage next to him,
waving like the queen of England.

The band finished the song to the cheers of the crowd.

I purposely looked away as I ducked past my fifth-grade
teacher and my favorite clerk from the dollar store.

"The documentary crew is filming everything," Ellis muttered, his eyes on the stage. "This could be really good or really bad."

The microphone gave a hollow ring as Montgomery took the lectern. Close up, it was clear that soot streaked the collar of his white shirt. His neck and face appeared ruddy, and sweat slicked his temples. He also had a noticeable bulge in his tailored tweed jacket. It could be the Bible. It could be a gun.

He glanced to Virginia, who nodded for him to speak. "My fellow citizens," he greeted the crowd. They cheered and he benevolently waited for a break in the applause. "Tonight marks the one hundred and fifty-second anniversary of the Battle of Sugarland!" He grinned at the documentary cameras as the crowd went even wilder. "This is going to take all night," he said, clearly enjoying it as laughter filtered up toward the stage. "I'd like to give special thanks to Virginia Wydell and the Wydell Foundation for making sure this inspiring, compelling story is told to the world." Just then, he spotted me in the crowd and his eyes went wide.

He thought he'd killed me, and now I was coming for him.

Montgomery lost his train of thought and had to scramble to continue his speech. "We...we have always come together each year to commemorate our ancestors for their fortitude and courage," he said, distracted, his eyes following Ellis and me as we advanced on him.

My gunshot wound throbbed and my head swam. It was almost enough to make me forget the nervous churning in my gut. If Montgomery didn't have that Bible, this was all for nothing. And I was about to make a royal fool out of myself in front of the entire town. Again. But you know what? I didn't even care about that. I wanted justice.

The crowd burst into applause for our town killer. We pressed forward.

"The history of Sugarland is a celebration of honor and family." Montgomery bit his lip as the emotion of it hit him hard. "In a time of great desperation and darkness, the people of Sugarland came together in spite of their differences to protect their home. We all know the story—"

"And it's not the right one," I said, stepping out onto the stage. Montgomery froze. Virginia didn't. It took a second or two for the crowd to even notice me, but they sure paid attention when she stormed past Montgomery's lectern and grabbed me by the arm, the one attached to my injured shoulder. It hurt like nothing I'd ever felt before and I cried out.

"My, my, dear," she said, dragging me close to the microphones so everyone could hear. "You appear as if you're having *another* mental breakdown."

"Hardly," I gritted out.

She pressured me toward the front of the stage. "Help her get off before she embarrasses herself," she said to the people below.

"Stop it." I forced her to unhand me. Virginia would make sure I didn't have another shot at the microphones, so I had to speak now. "The movie, the story," I announced, all eyes on me. The microphones broadcast my voice; the lights from the documentary cameras made me squint. "It's all based on a lie. Ellis and I have proof."

Meanwhile Ellis moved in behind Montgomery and yanked the Bible from his inside coat pocket. "He tried to kill us tonight in order to hide this."

Virginia's hold on me slackened. "Kill them?" she gasped. She whispered the next part, but the microphones caught it anyway. "You said you just burned the house down."

Montgomery paled and covered the microphone in front of him with his hand. Too bad Virginia had paid for about six other ones. "It's not like I planned for them to be in it!" he hissed, his voice echoing over the crowd with amazing sound quality. "Now calm down. The old Hatcher place is gone." The crowd gasped, and he realized he'd been heard. No doubt Virginia had ordered the best microphones. "It doesn't matter," he announced quickly. "That building had absolutely no historical significance."

"This is a disaster," Virginia murmured as the crowd began to boo.

"I'm all right, Mom," Ellis said drily, "thanks for asking."

"Obviously," she said, dismissing him, even though he was clearly bloodied. "You need to stop this nonsense right now," she ordered. "Whatever you think you're doing. Stop."

The cameras came in for a close-up and she waved them away. "Stop!"

We were only getting started. I closed in on Montgomery. "You shot up Maisie's house so you could search it for this." I held up Pa's Bible. "You tried to frame my sister."

Virginia gasped. "*That's* why you took her keys?"

"Then you shot us, took the Bible, and left us in the burning house to die." I had the crowd's full attention now.

Montgomery stumbled backward, looking for an escape, but he ran straight into another cameraman.

"Darla Grace learned about the Bible, didn't she?" I pressed.

"You killed Darla Grace!" Virginia squeaked, completely losing her careful veneer.

Montgomery turned and ran, straight into the police.

Virginia stood shaking and staring at Montgomery. "Darla called me the night she died and said I might want to hold off on funding. That you both would talk to me in the morning." She drew a hand to her mouth. "You made sure she never did. I gave hundreds of thousands of dollars to support a man who would murder my son." She turned to Ellis, clutching for his hand. "What's in that Bible?"

He gave a quick nod to me as I took to the lectern. There, I stood in front of the documentary cameras, in front of the town of Sugarland, and read Lieutenant Colonel Hatcher's final confession.

Chapter Twenty-Seven

THE HISTORY CHANNEL still wanted to air the documentary. Only instead of focusing on Sugarland during the war, they talked about the history of small-town politics and how one family can distort the truth for generations. Virginia refused to give any more interviews, but it didn't matter. They used footage of her gushing about the Wydell legacy and backed it up against the proof that it hadn't happened that way.

The film production company shut down. Beau's movie-star dreams were dashed. And the town tried to return to normal.

As normal as it could be for a small town embroiled in a murder investigation.

Ellis's search warrant proved quite fruitful. The police found the secretary under Montgomery's bed. Frankie had been right. People did hide important things in their bedrooms. He'd preserved the secretary as he'd found it. The letter pointing to the Bible, as well as the document proving Maisie's parentage, were still tucked inside. Turned out Montgomery had no problem destroying lives, but he did draw the line when it came to protecting historical artifacts.

Melody's car keys bore his fingerprints, and the bullet casings Josephine found for me on the hill matched the rifle he owned, a very modern gun with an excellent scope. He could have killed us at Maisie's kitchen window if he'd wanted to.

Maisie's inheritance letter hadn't gone over well with the Sugarland elite, but it appeared to be legal. Virginia would still fight her in court. Her most prized possessions—her empire and her reputation—lay in tatters, but she held strong to her husband's money and her 1980s-era plantation home. We'd see how that turned out.

Beau had returned to being furious with me, which I considered a blessing.

Maisie hadn't been so cordial after she learned she'd slept through Melody's arrest, the burning of the old house on the hill, and Montgomery's exposure as a liar, murderer, and thief. Not to mention being outed as an heiress. She dealt with it by fishing in my backyard lake with her shotgun. Who knew you could catch carp that way?

I let her stay while we got her house cleaned up, and Ellis installed new windows. Heiress or not, she didn't cotton to staying in a hotel and I wouldn't have suggested it anyway.

She made fast friends with Lucy, cooked me real meals, and helped water the rosebush in the trash can. I nestled Frankie's urn in the dirt underneath, to try to give him an extra boost. But so far, he remained stuck at my place. His lamentations grew even more intense after Josephine's hound dog, Fritz, showed up at my back door, looking for love. I took it as a reason to hope that she'd survived the burning of her home with her spirit intact. Frankie looked at it as one more creature who could wander free while he watched his undead life pass him by.

I told him we'd keep trying. And we would, as soon as the gunshot wound in my shoulder healed a bit. It hurt. Ellis had an ugly injury as well. Montgomery's bullet had struck his right side, just above the hip.

I was left with the uncomfortable notion that Montgomery could have easily finished us off—shot us each in the head—if he'd wanted to. But I don't think he'd ever planned to be a killer, so he'd taken the coward's way out. Thank heaven.

At least we'd found justice for Darla, who hadn't been so lucky.

All said, it was a week before I felt strong enough to sneak back into the library.

I parked out front this time, on a crisp October morning. Melody was expecting me. She'd been sent home after Virginia's humiliation and Montgomery's subsequent arrest for murder, and now she was picking up extra shifts while Sheila Ward, our library director, tried to put everything back to rights.

Melody and I did our best as well. My sister had found a new place for the boxes and coatrack that had occupied the storage closet off the lobby, and requested that it be locked until further notice. I had a few things to do as well.

Melody greeted me at the door. "Best hurry," she said, eyeing my bag with Frankie's urn inside. "The library opens at nine o'clock on the dot. And I wouldn't put it past Sheila to show up early."

"You know I'm not a morning person," I said, breathing in the familiar scent of old books. I made my way toward the back, and as I did, I pulled a copy of *The Vampire Lestat* from my bag.

"Is that ours?" Melody asked.

"It is now," I told her as we skirted the desk and made our way to the back hallway. "I need to leave this for a friend."

Melody crossed her arms over her chest as we reached the door to the stacks. "If you don't mind, I'll stay up here."

"No problem." I smiled. The air belowground felt chilly, but the heavy dread had disappeared, at least for me. I didn't see Matthew around, so I left the book on his chair. I had no doubt he'd find it soon enough.

Melody waited for me at the top of the steps. "It's done?"

"Yes," I said, noticing her relief when we returned to the main reading room. "Now I just need a private moment."

She nodded. "Come get me when you finish," she said, treating me to a wink. "I'll be in my office." I watched her go, her shoulders square and her manner confident.

I was glad to see how well she handled herself after Darla's death, the allegations against her, and her boss's arrest. She'd had a few nightmares about her arrest, but had assured me she'd be fine. I hoped that was true. Melody had a great head on her shoulders, and she was one of the strongest people I knew.

Frankie held his own as well, considering he'd had his hopes for freedom dashed. Still, we'd find a way to unground him somehow. I'd promised him.

"Frankie, I'm ready," I said. This time, I didn't demand. I didn't rub at his urn or try to be smart. I took a deep breath as my skin prickled and I felt the air around me shift. A dull light settled over me and I stood in another world.

Silvery light bathed the space around me.

The poker players were back. Stoutmeyer dealt cards while Gregson and Owens studied their hands and ribbed each other. I saw the field hospital in the reading room and quietly made my way to the third bed on the right.

"Private Baker?" I crouched down next to the military cot. A small flame flickered over the indentation in the pillow. "I heard you'd like me to take down a letter."

I waited patiently as the flame stilled. "I know she's gone." His voice was like a whisper in the air. "But I need you to write it down. I need it to be real before I go."

"I have a pen and paper right here," I said, producing them from my pocket. "I'm ready."

"My dearest mother," he said slowly, practiced, as if he'd thought about this a good long while. "I forgive you." I nodded, writing his words. "Now sign my name at the bottom. Don't say private. Just say 'Johnny.'"

I did. And with the final stroke of my pen, Johnny Baker's flame flickered out. He was gone.

I stood, not quite sure what to make of it, or where I'd even deliver the note, when Frankie materialized next to me.

"Sometimes, you just need somebody to listen," he said.

True enough. "Thank you for this," I said, "and for everything, really." Yes, he complained sometimes, but he'd always been there for me when he could. "We make a good team."

He raised a brow. "The last 'team' I was on earned me this," he said, lifting the brim of his hat, revealing his death wound. He shoved the fedora back into place.

"Well, this team is going to focus on less dangerous projects from now on. I'm not doing this for a living," I reminded him.

He nodded, as if he'd expected that. "I'll stick around and see how that works out. It's not like I have a choice."

The library doors creaked open, but it wasn't the injured Confederates this time. It was Ellis. He glanced around, surprised to see me alone. "Are you...working?" he asked, hesitating before he approached.

"Frankie and I were just finishing up," I told him. The gangster had already wandered over to join the poker game. "How's your mom?" I asked when he drew near.

He shrugged. "Let's just say you're not coming over for Thanksgiving dinner anytime soon."

I hadn't been out for revenge, just the truth. "At least she can look at my wedding reception tape if she wants to cheer up."

"I hear she's baking up some rhubarb pies," Ellis said drily.

I shouldn't have smiled, but I did. A pair of ghosts had caught my attention. It seemed Josephine didn't need her house in order to be herself. She was currently mashed up against the circulation desk, kissing Matthew Jackson for all she was worth.

She caught me watching and blushed.

"No need to be embarrassed," I said as they materialized next to me. "It's a new millennium with new rules. I'm glad you're expanding your horizons."

She'd let her hair down, and it flowed out in ghostly tendrils behind her. "Now that our secret is out in the open, Ma moved on. I suppose she needs the rest. And I think she was holding Pa down, because he's back. Although he just putters around the forest and lets me go where I choose."

"Good," I said. Maybe Jeremiah Hatcher could find some peace as well. "I just wish I could help Frankie."

At Matthew's questioning gaze, I explained how Frankie was trapped on my property.

"The solution is quite simple," he explained. "I've seen it done before."

"Really?" I asked. I wished Frankie hadn't been off goofing. He'd want to hear this.

"With his ashes mostly gone, you need to find the one thing he treasures above all else. Place that with his urn, inside if possible. That will give him the strength he needs to leave you."

Wow. That was it?

"Thanks," I said. "We'll work on it from that angle." Presuming Frankie was in tune with his needs and emotions enough to understand what he truly considered valuable above all else.

Still, I wanted Frankie to be happy, even if that meant his leaving me. So we'd try.

Josephine chewed at her lip. "Verity, maybe it's not my place to give advice of this nature, but...you should kiss your man more often," she said, as if she were scandalized by her own suggestion.

I glanced at Ellis and couldn't help but smile.

"What?" he asked, aware that he was missing out on the joke.

I reached up and slid my hands over his shoulders, and then I kissed him. If it shocked him, he didn't show it. In fact, he kissed me back with so much enthusiasm I wondered if I'd be the one putting on a show for Josephine for a change.

"That's enough," I said, drawing back with a grin. "We have an audience."

Ellis mirrored my mirth. "I figured." He leaned down and brushed his lips once more against mine. "Can't fault a guy for seizing the moment."

I played with his uniform collar. "You realize we just broke the curse."

He cocked his head and waited for me to explain.

I couldn't help but blush a little. "We kissed, and we didn't have to be buried alive, shot at, or set on fire to do it."

He tightened his grip on me. "Let's break the curse again, just to make sure," he said, getting saucy. "We certainly don't want to take any chances."

~THE END~

Author's Note:

Thank you so much for dropping in on Verity, Frankie, and the rest of Sugarland. I'm truly grateful for the wonderful response this series has received. I'm also excited to report that I'll be continuing the series for at least three more books. The next book, *The Haunted Heist*, will release in early 2016. In the meantime, you can sign up at www.angiefox.com to receive an email when the next book comes out.

And because it's fun, I give out ten free advanced reading copies of my next book in each email. Be sure to check for your name on the winner's list!

Happy reading,

Angie

Available now!
A LITTLE NIGHT MAGIC
A fabulously fun collection of short stories by Angie Fox. Includes two new Southern Ghost Hunter shorts.

Excerpt from
GHOST OF A CHANCE
Available in the A LITTLE NIGHT MAGIC anthology

Chapter One

The smell of fresh-baked sugar cookies filled my kitchen, and the tinny sound of Frank Sinatra singing "White Christmas" echoed from my outdated iPhone. Behind me, the ghost of a 1920s gangster hovered while I pulled the last hot tray from the oven.

"Move. I don't want to burn you," I said automatically, realizing only afterward how ridiculous it sounded. Any object—hot or otherwise—would pass straight through the specter.

Frankie appeared in black and white, his image transparent enough that I could just make out the cooling trays on the kitchen island behind him. He wore a pin-striped suit coat with matching cuffed trousers and a fat tie.

He inhaled as if he could smell the crisp, warm cookies. "That's a killer batch, right there," he observed while I jockeyed around him, "but I gotta tell you, most of the gun barrels are crooked."

I winked, surprising him. "Everybody's a critic."

I'd given in to holiday cheer and let him tell me how to shape the last of the dough, and he'd chosen the things he loved most. Which meant I had a baking sheet full of revolvers, cigarettes, and booze bottles—all oddly shaped because, truly, who has cookie cutters for that sort of thing?

I placed the tray on a rack to start cooling, glad I'd included the surly gangster in my holiday festivities. He was technically a houseguest until I could find a way to free him. Although I had no clue what I was going to do with his contraband cookies.

I couldn't eat them all or explain them away to guests.

"What's next?" he asked before I'd even transferred one cookie off the baking tray, never mind the dough-flecked countertops or the dishes. The man obviously hadn't spent much time in the kitchen before.

"Why don't you go outside and look at the holiday lights?" I suggested. Perhaps that would get him into the spirit of the season.

My sister, Melody, had lent me a few strands of white ones in the shape of magnolia flowers. I'd foraged some lovely greenery from the woods and done up the front and back porches with pine garlands and homemade balsam wreaths. I'd been too broke to buy ready-made decorations, but these looked nicer anyway.

He snarled at the suggestion that he might be entertained by pretty decorations. "I'm Frankie the German," he clipped out, as if his words themselves should command respect. "Men fear me. Women want me."

"I'm very happy for you," I said, trying to straighten out a revolver barrel as I gently transferred the cookies to the cooling rack. "But this is the holiday season. It's the perfect time to take a break from inspiring fear. Try to live a little," I suggested, ignoring his scowl. "How about I finish cleaning the kitchen, and afterward you can challenge me to a game of chess."

Otherwise, he'd get bored and start making cold spots all over my kitchen. It felt nice in the summer, but right now, it would ruin the yeast bread I had rising.

He clenched and unclenched his hands a few times. "All right," he said, eyeing me as he glided through the stove and out to the back porch. His voice lingered in the air behind him. "You know I won't go far."

"Do I ever," I murmured. It was my fault he couldn't leave.

I'd tied him to my land when I accidentally emptied his funeral urn out onto my rosebushes. At the time, I'd believed my ex-fiancé had given me a dirty old vase in need of a good scrubbing or at least a rinse with the hose. But as it turns out, there's a reason why ashes are customarily scattered to the wind or at least spread out a bit. When I poured the entirety of Frankie's remains in one spot and then hosed him into the ground, the poor gangster had become my unwilling permanent housemate—at least until I could figure out how to set him free.

Only two people knew I had a ghost for a houseguest: my sister, Melody, and my sweet, strong almost-boyfriend, Ellis. I planned to keep it that way.

I transferred a cookie shaped like a bundle of dynamite that could have almost passed for a nice grouping of holiday candles, except for the "TnT" Frankie had made me etch into the side.

Frankie had opened up a whole new ghostly world to me, and let's just say things had gotten a little crazy after that.

I left the tray on the stove to cool and brushed off the well-worn green and white checked gingham apron that had belonged to my grandmother. I tried not to sigh. I missed having a house full of people for the holidays. Of course, Melody had stopped by just this morning, and my mom was coming in town next week.

I began sudsing up the sink and placing my mixing bowls into the warm, soapy water.

If I were honest with myself, I missed Ellis. We'd become close enough that I felt his absence when we couldn't spend time together. He'd been booked solid with family events, and it's not like I could have joined him. Not after I'd broken my engagement to his brother and barely defended my livelihood and home from his vengeful mother.

He'd come by when he could.

And as if I'd summoned him out of thin air, I heard a knock at the door. It couldn't be. I dried my hands on my apron. Melody liked to knock and immediately walk inside. My friend Lauralee, too. I had an open-door policy at the cozy antebellum home I'd inherited from my grandmother. But when no one sauntered in, it made my heart skip a beat.

"Ellis?" I called, making sure I'd turned the oven off. And that my messy ponytail wasn't completely covered in flour. Oh, who cared if it was?

I hurried down the hallway to the foyer and dragged open my heavy front door.

"Matthew," I said, surprised.

The ghost of Major Matthew Jackson of the Union Army stood on my front porch, with his hands clasped in front of him, appearing almost shy. His image wavered and came into sharper focus. I could see the crisp lines of his uniform jacket, along with his high forehead and prominent cheekbones.

I'd met Matthew on my last adventure. Most of the time, I could only see ghosts when Frankie showed me the other side. But Matthew was one of the most powerful spirits I'd ever met, and he could appear to me on his own. He was also one of the more shy ones.

"Is everything all right?" I asked.

Major Jackson didn't get out much and I couldn't imagine what would bring him to my home.

He dipped his chin and glided straight through the glass storm door I'd neglected to open, his mind clearly elsewhere. I stepped back as he entered the foyer.

He stopped when he'd made it barely a few feet inside. "My sincerest apologies for intruding on your afternoon." He gave a formal bow, appearing somewhat awkward in his social skills, but clearly trying his best.

"It's quite all right," I assured him, gesturing him further inside as I closed the door. "My friends are always welcome. What can I do for you?" I didn't know the formalities involved in a late-nineteenth-century house call, and it's not like I could offer him a sherry, so we might as well cut to the chase. Still, I couldn't quite help myself from asking, "Would you like to sit in the back parlor?" just as my mother would have, and my grandmother before her.

Perhaps it was genetic.

He nodded and seemed more at ease with my formal response. I led him through my empty front room to the once-elegant sitting area in the back. The pink-papered walls and polished wood accents appeared so strange without the heirloom rugs and furniture the room had once held. Unfortunately, there wasn't much left besides a second-hand chessboard, a lopsided futon, and a purple couch I'd brought home after solving a ghost-related issue for a local merchant.

Matthew opted for a place on the couch while I tried to sit elegantly on the edge of the futon.

"I've come to ask a favor," he began earnestly.

Oh my. I crossed my legs at the ankles and sincerely hoped his favor didn't involve me opening myself to the spirit world. Yes, I'd been able to do a lot of good in the few times I'd ventured forth, but it had been scary and dangerous. Besides, I was a graphic designer, not a ghost whisperer.

As much as it pained me, I had to learn to start saying no.

Matthew cleared his throat. "I would like to locate a Christmas gift for Josephine."

"How sweet of you." I felt my shoulders relax. That didn't sound frightening or dangerous, and I was glad to see a relationship developing between the two ghosts. They'd reconnected during my last adventure. He'd been hurt and so very alone. She'd been shy and had suffered terrible luck with men—until that fateful night in the haunted woods. It had been rather romantic. "I'm sure Josephine would love anything you decide to give her, as long as it's from the heart."

Josephine cared about him for who he was, which was a rarity in Matthew's life. His own family had disowned him for joining the Union Army, and the local ghosts hadn't made him feel welcome in the afterlife for the same reason.

He glanced away before his gaze found mine. "She means everything to me," he said, with an urgency most women only dreamed about. "That's why I want to give her my mother's opal necklace. Before the war—" he cleared his throat "—my mother said I could have the necklace when I found the girl I wish to marry."

"Oh, Matthew." I drew a hand to my chest. "You're going to propose?"

"At Christmas," he said simply.

I felt myself go a little teary eyed for them, for that perfect connection where you *just knew*. How wonderful for Josephine. She'd waited a hundred and fifty years to be loved like that.

"I just need you to get me the necklace," Matthew said.

I blinked back my tears. "What?"

He leaned forward, resting his elbows on his knees. "It's at my family estate, now occupied by the seventh generation of Jacksons."

Oh, I was familiar with the Jackson compound on the edge of the county, with its twenty sprawling acres and huge main house, occupied by his real, live descendants, none of whom would be pleased if I showed up and explained that the spirit of their great-great-great-uncle needed a family heirloom, a jeweled necklace for that matter, and I'd just be taking it...

"Why don't you go get it?" I suggested perkily. Most spirits couldn't interact with the living world, but Matthew's unusual strength made him an exception.

Like he hadn't thought of that.

Matthew's gaze dropped. "I can't," he said simply. "My mother told me I could never go home. Not after I signed my enlistment papers."

I wished I could hug him. "Oh, sweetie," I began. "Are you sure that's not all in your mind?" It had to be. I knew it was. But if he hadn't been able to get over it for more than one hundred and fifty years, I didn't see how I could make it happen tonight in my parlor.

He stood abruptly. "I'm not part of the family anymore." His shoulders heaved. "She said so." He took two paces away from me, as if he couldn't even face me as he added, "She'd never let me in the front door and I don't think I could handle even trying."

"I understand," I said, coming to my feet. I wanted to help. I did. But, "I don't know what I can do."

"We could steal it," Frankie said from above my left shoulder. I jumped as the ghost shimmered into view next to me. Sometimes I think he did it for fun. "I can have us in and out of there in two minutes," he reasoned. "Five if they try to foil us with a cannonball safe."

"I can't steal an antique necklace," I balked.

"Don't worry," Frankie said, opening his hands, as if this were old hat. "I'll teach you how."

Learning how was *not* the issue. "You don't even know why we're doing this," I pointed out.

"Fun?" the gangster guessed.

Matthew turned to face us, clearly vexed by Frankie's questionable morals.

He'd better get used to it.

"There's no need for stealing," the late soldier insisted. "The necklace is rightfully mine. And it's on the ghostly plane, so none of my living relatives would even know."

That meant someone had died with it. "Does your mother have it?" I asked, taking a wild guess.

Matthew gave a slow, sad nod.

Frankie crossed his arms over his chest, frowning. "That's a lot less fun," he said, eyeing the other ghost, as if he'd let Frankie down. "I see where this is going."

So did I. Matthew wanted me to borrow Frankie's powers to see the other side, something I'd promised I wouldn't do again.

It wasn't only that I put myself in danger every time I opened myself to the ghostly plane, but I had to use Frankie's spirit energy to do it. The unnatural energy flow temporarily weakened him to the point of making parts of him disappear. Plus I used the opportunity to do nice things for other people.

Let's just say Frankie wasn't a fan.

"I don't believe my mother is a vengeful ghost," Matthew assured me. "Although I haven't spoken to her since I left to enlist. Even though she's angry with me, I don't think she'd go back on her word," he added hopefully.

Frankie eyed him up and down. "Anything else in her stash? Something to make it worth our while?"

"Frankie!" I protested. "We don't blackmail our guests."

"Technically," he said, holding up a finger, "it's extortion."

Hmm. "What if Matthew lends me *his* powers?" I asked. Then Frankie would be off the hook.

My guest drew back. "Oh, I most definitely could not," he said, as if I'd shocked him. "Josephine would be so very jealous."

Frankie huffed. "So this guy gets to have both a girlfriend and his powers."

He needed our help. I turned to Matthew. "How can we be sure your mother is still in her home?" She might have concluded her earthly business and gone to the light. And if that happened, she would have taken everything she'd died wearing with her, including the necklace.

Matthew strode to the old marble fireplace and rested a hand on the mantel next to Frankie's urn. "I still go home every Sunday. I watch my family from the yard. My mother still lives in that house."

Today was Sunday. "Did you check today?" Frankie pressed. He and I both knew ghosts weren't great at marking time.

Matthew turned to us. "I saw her through the window right before I came to you. She was upset. There were loud people pulling up in cars and vans. A party supply truck ran straight through me."

"That's right," I murmured. This was the last Sunday before Christmas. The Jackson family had been hosting their annual Christmas party on that same day every year for seven generations. "It's the day of the big party."

"It is." He lowered his eyes. "She was so busy with everyone else she didn't see me. She never sees me."

"I'll talk to her," I said quickly, and over Frankie's most inappropriate cursing. "Maybe I can get her to speak with you."

"No," Matthew said, clenching his hands at his sides, "I did the right thing. I'm not going to pretend otherwise or beg for her forgiveness. But I won't let her go back on her word about the necklace, either. Ask her for that. Please," he added, softening. "I have a new life now. That's all I want."

"Okay," I assured him. "I'll slip in tonight, during the party." Lord knew how, but I would.

"You think about asking me?" Frankie frowned.

"Yes, I did." I planted a hand on my hip. "Frankie, would you like to go to a legendary holiday party?" I could take him out of my house if I had his urn with me.

The gangster frowned. "It'll probably be full of stuffy society types."

"And ghostly ladies," I added cheerily. "I hear they love gangsters."

"I would be hard for them to resist," he agreed grudgingly.

"Then it's settled," I told him. We'd figure out a way into the Jackson's holiday party. We'd speak with the spirit of Matthew's mother.

I'd get the necklace for him and more. Somehow, I'd find a way to give the soldier an even better Christmas than he could imagine.

GHOST OF A CHANCE
Part of the A LITTLE NIGHT MAGIC anthology
by Angie Fox
Available Now!

About the Author

New York Times bestselling author Angie Fox writes sweet, fun, action-packed mysteries. Her characters are clever and fearless, but in real life, Angie is afraid of basements, bees and going up stairs when it's all dark behind her.

Angie earned a Journalism degree from the University of Missouri. During that time, she also skipped class for an entire week so she could read Anne Rice's vampire series straight through. Angie has always loved books and is shocked, honored and tickled pink that she now gets to write books for a living. Although, she did skip writing for a week this past fall so she could read Victoria Laurie's Abby Cooper psychic eye mysteries straight through.

Angie makes her home in St. Louis, Missouri with a football-addicted husband, two kids, and Moxie the dog.

If you are interested in receiving an email each time Angie releases a new book, please sign up for new release updates at www.angiefox.com.

Also be sure to join Angie's online Facebook community where you will find contests, quizzes and special sneak peeks of new books.